BLUE MURDER

BLUE MURDER

Vivien Armstrong

This first world edition published in Great Britain 2006 by
SEVERN HOUSE PUBLISHERS LTD of
9–15 High Street, Sutton, Surrey SM1 1DF.
This first world edition published in the USA 2006 by
SEVERN HOUSE PUBLISHERS INC of
595 Madison Avenue, New York, N.Y. 10022.

Copyright © 2006 by Vivien Armstrong.

British Library Cataloguing in Publication Data

Armstrong, Vivien
  Blue murder. - (A Detective Chief Inspector Roger Hayes mystery)
  1.   Hayes, Roger (Fictitious character) - Fiction
  2.   Police - Isle of Man - Fiction
  3.   Isle of Man - Fiction
  4.   Detective and mystery stories
  I.   Title
  823.9'14 [F]

ISBN-13: 978-0-7278-6367-6
ISBN-10: 0-7278-6367-3

Typeset by Palimpsest Book Production Ltd.,
Polmont, Stirlingshire, Scotland.
Printed and bound in Great Britain by
MPG Books Ltd., Bodmin, Cornwall.

One

Hayes slowly opened his eyes. It was dark apart from a battery of winking green lights dancing across TV screens behind a counter where a girl with blonde hair was haloed by a lamp. His temples began to throb and he shut his eyes rather too abruptly, transferring the dancing green lights behind his closed eyelids.

After some heroic reconsideration, he experimented with the eyeball trick again and squinted at the woman behind the bar. If this was a dream the place was like no other pub he could conjure up and certainly a place with a shy clientele. Was he drunk? Had he passed out after closing time, unnoticed by the barmaid? As if sensing his irritation she looked up and, after glancing at the screens behind her, rose and crossed the room, hips shimmying inside a very severe outfit buttoned to the neck.

'You might have turned off the TV,' Hayes croaked, the vision with the Marilyn Monroe wiggle fading in and out of focus.

'You're awake,' she said, touching his wrist, which seemed to be caught up in a mess of cables.

'What time is it?'

She laughed. 'Past your bedtime, Roger! I'll get you a drink, shall I?'

Without waiting for his order she sashayed back to the bar counter, returning with a mini-glass of cloudy liquid.

'Absinthe?' he murmured, downing the tot with a grimace. She giggled, and, in all fairness, Hayes had to admit she was decent enough to serve him after hours, though Scotch on the rocks would have been friendlier. His mind seemed to ebb away on this puzzling thought and he slept again, waking in strong sunlight to find his dream dissolving, and with it the girl with the yellow hair.

Two

The sunlight and the smell of disinfectant made it all too clear. Hospital. A single room, the winking monitors still doing their stuff, but his wrist was unhitched from the drip. Everything was tidied away including the blonde behind the counter. Or had he dreamed her? He tried to sit up but winced as an iron band clamped his chest, the sheer effort of movement bringing him out in a sweat.

How had he got here? Traffic accident? Heart attack? Tussle with a grizzly? He had no idea, a worrisome consideration for a detective chief inspector. That much he *did* remember. And Roger? Hadn't she called him 'Roger'? The struggle to complete this most basic identification threw his brain into overdrive just as the door burst open to admit a dapper guy in a lightweight suit leading a retinue of one senior-looking matron type and two anxious acolytes. Hayes wryly congratulated himself on being the focus of this medical posse and hoped his diminished mental faculties would sharpen up before the inevitable quiz to follow.

'Ah, our hero awakes!' boomed the bigwig leading the party. Although of less than average height the man carried himself royally, his sparse grey hair contrasting with a ruddy complexion, plump cheeks bursting with bonhomie. 'Excellent. My name's Harrison, and I am open to fulsome gratitude for cobbling up the damage, Mr Hayes, though hitting your head on the kerb as you went down was overdoing it.'

Hayes. Well, that was one clear fact in the swirling mist fogging his brain. Hayes? Roger Hayes? Detective Chief Inspector Roger Hayes? That sounded OK. But 'hero'?

The starched apron constraining the big bosom moved in,

3

passing case notes to the surgeon who, ignoring Hayes' garbled reply, preceded to put the student types through the third degree. Their stumbled responses ticked more boxes for Hayes, who gathered that the stitchwork on which Harrison prided himself was necessitated by stab wounds penetrating the ribcage and slicing a lung. Ouch.

'You're a lucky man, Mr Hayes. Just missed your heart, massive loss of blood. How much do you remember of the incident?'

'Not a lot,' Hayes croaked, finding his voice inexplicably hoarse. 'Whatever it is I've been dosed with seems to have short-circuited total recall.'

Harrison laughed. 'Don't worry. It will come back all too soon.' He turned to his unsmiling assistant. 'No reason to keep the investigators out in the cold any longer, Sister, but we shall continue medication as before. Until tomorrow. Fit young man like Mr Hayes here should be up and about in no time.'

Harrison sketched a half salute before turning on his heel and harrying his retinue into a brisk departure.

Hayes closed his eyes, hoping a believable sequence of events would slide into place. He explored the painful area behind his ear and found it uncomfortably taped over. A new nurse hurried in and threw him an anxious grin before taking his pulse and checking the chart clipped to a board at the foot of the bed. An injection returned him to a blissful nirvana and it was another twenty-four hours before he was almost, as his all too cheerful surgeon had promised, 'up and about'. Sitting up and stumbling about with a stick, at least.

He searched the bedside table and discovered his iPod, neatly stowed with his watch and a wallet containing fifty-six quid, keys, credit cards, a car-parking receipt and a match folder from somewhere called the Rose Room. The only interesting item was the torn half of a ticket to the Wigmore Hall on Saturday, June 19th, seat B14, for a 7.30 performance. Pictures gradually emerged. A floodlit stage, Grieg's piano concerto. Champagne? He sifted through the wallet hoping for more clues. No warrant card, though. He confronted the ward sister on her next round.

'My ID card's missing, Sister.'

'Your boss took it. Signed for it.'

'Who was that?'

'Er, let me think. Big red-faced man. Superintendent Walker? Ring a bell? I can look it up if you like. He said it was normal security procedure.'

'Walker?' Light dawned. 'You mean Waller! Superintendent Waller's been here?'

'Mr Harrison wouldn't allow visitors at the time. But he's coming back. Would you like to give him a ring? I'll fetch the contact number, shall I?'

She brought in a portable phone and plugged it in, leaving it on the bedside table. Hayes got through straight away, recognizing Waller's gruff response with relief.

'Hear you're on the mend, Hayes. The local CID need to talk to you about the incident as soon as your medic gives the all-clear.'

'Listen, sir, I'm a bit confused. Any chance of you coming in before the Met get hold of me?'

'That bang on the head did you no good, did it, Hayes? More trouble than the slashes to the ribs, I bet. You should have been quicker on your feet, mate, getting stuck by a mugger's hardly going to look good on your CV, despite the headlines you got yourself in the press.' The terse response gave way to a cackle of laughter.

'I'm serious, sir,' Hayes insisted. 'Do me a favour, fill me in. It's like being banged up in here: no TV, no newspapers and apart from a saucy remark from one of the porters I'm all at sea.'

'They're keeping you on ice till they get a statement.'

Hayes gripped the phone. 'You could wangle your way in, sir. Grapes? Bunch of daisies? I feel like a frigging leper, not even allowed into the day room. Did I kill someone?'

'No such luck. The villains legged it with the lady's sparklers still attached to her finger. Nasty business.'

Waller abruptly rang off, leaving Hayes with nothing but the dialling tone.

Three

A mugging? A lady with diamonds sparkly enough to attract a street attack? Hayes battered his sluggish brain with a fusillade of unanswered questions. Her rings were a problem. Did he know any woman like that? The single ticket to the Wigmore Hall could be relevant but was Roger Hayes the sort of bloke to pick up a woman at a conservative venue famed for string quartets and soloists on the way up or on the way out? Not exactly a singles bar, though the match folder from the Rose Room sounded suspicious.

He fitted his iPod and began to doze to the balm of a slow movement only to jerk awake on the alarming recollection of Waller's parting shot: the poor bloody woman had lost a finger! Christ Almighty. No wonder the Met were anxious to hear his version of the attack. Hayes gave a rueful grin. Trouble was, his version was as full of holes as a Swiss cheese.

He called over to a cleaner mopping the floor on the far side of the room. 'Excuse me, miss—'

The startlingly beautiful black girl with the Nefertiti profile turned towards him. 'Yes, sir?'

'Could you tell me what day it is?'

She gave a grin which lit up the whole room. 'Why, it's my birthday, sir! How did you guess that?'

Hayes raised both hands in mock dismay. 'Magic. But really, give me the date.'

'Tuesday June 22nd,' she proudly announced.

'Well, happy birthday. How many candles on the cake?'

'Candles? Oh, you mean how old? Twenty-two today. My man's takin' me out tonight. Dancin'.'

6

'Congratulations.'

The door swung open and the ward sister swept in and abruptly told the girl to finish up in the corridor. She grabbed her bucket and mop and flew out.

'As you're feeling so chatty, Mr Hayes, you won't mind receiving visitors.'

Hayes shrugged, giving Nursie no satisfaction from his response. During his brief stay he had already picked his favourites: the regular nurses were OK and his surgeon seemed a decent sort, but for boosting your spirits the porters won hands down. A cheery bunch, unabashed by any bawling out from the staff and clearly amused to have a policeman laid out by what he had gathered from their constant banter had been a run-in with a couple of teenage muggers.

He replaced the iPod on the bedside table as a pair of burly strangers was ushered in. The sister closed the door and could be loudly instructing all within earshot, 'Mr Hayes is not to be disturbed.'

The older man of the two pulled up a chair, leaving his sidekick to stand apart, leaning against the nurses' counter and gazing round the bare room, with not so much as a pot plant to soften the clinical effect.

The senior bloke introduced himself but kept his distance as if Hayes had something infectious about him.

'Superintendent Bill Jameson, local nick, and my sergeant. Glad to see you looking better. Last time we met you were laid out on a trolley. Not a pretty sight. Treating you well are they, Chief Inspector?'

'Excellently. Not that I can't wait to get out of here and back to work.'

'Oh, they won't let you out in a hurry. A period of convalescence at the very least, I'd say. Nasty work, internal bleeding's no joke and a slice off a lung will keep you off active service for a good while yet.'

Hayes bristled, irritated by Jameson's curt dismissal of any workable recovery. Was his medical history to be passed round like the week's astrology forecast?

'Let's get this over with, Superintendent.' Jameson's tone hardened. 'A statement, Hayes. We have an account from Mrs Paget but corroboration by what we would call a professional witness would be helpful.'

'You have the advantage of me on that, Superintendent. My recollection of the incident is sketchy. As you seem to have a full report on my medical condition, you are no doubt aware that apart from the stabbing I apparently hit my head on the kerb, the consequence of which being that I have only the haziest idea of the entire evening of, I assume, last Saturday?'

The detective sergeant lounging in the background perked up, taking a notebook from his pocket and exchanging knowing looks with his boss.

'Shall we start with your attendance at the concert on Saturday night, Hayes? You drove up from Renham, we assume. Your car has been located parked in a multi-storey facility behind George Street. It's quite safe,' he assured him.

'The piano recital was given by a gentleman called Franz Bulgari, a friend of yours I understand. The manager confirmed that you were invited backstage after the performance, and the two of you later took a taxi to share a late supper at a restaurant called the Rose Room. OK so far?'

'You have spoken to Mr Bulgari? He confirms all this?'

'He flew back to Paris on Sunday morning before news of the attack broke but we spoke on the telephone. He agrees that you were alone and parted about a quarter to midnight, Mr Bulgari taking a cab back to his hotel and you yourself setting off back to the car park on foot.'

'Right. And I *was* alone?'

'You remember none of this?' Jameson barked.

'Well, Bulgari and I go back a long way, we were students together at the Royal School, and I vaguely remember the concert and champagne afterwards backstage, but the lady involved is a total blank.'

'That figures, Inspector. According to Mrs Paget you were accidentally involved. She says she had been spending the evening with a friend and was making her way through Manchester Square in the hope of picking up a taxi. It was raining quite heavily and she had forgotten her umbrella so was focused on looking out for a free taxi and taking little notice of her surroundings. It was quiet, nobody about, and as she turned the corner two young men wearing hoodies jumped her. She screamed and you steamed to the rescue. Out of the blue, she says. Mrs Paget had no idea you were walking behind and obviously neither did the muggers. A dark-coloured estate was idling nearby and after the attack the two assailants jumped in and the car took off at speed. The lady had the sense to make a mental note of the registration number and it was later found abandoned in Southwark.'

'Stolen?'

'Of course.'

'And after slashing this poor woman to get at her rings, they've gone to ground.'

'''Fraid so. Mrs Paget was very brave and, despite her injuries, phoned for help – probably saved your life, Hayes. There was a lot of blood.'

'Pity she didn't hand over the rings without arguing about it. Would have saved both of us all this,' Hayes glumly remarked, waving a hand towards the battery of screens set above the nursing station.

'A feisty woman. Lost her handbag too. Funny thing, Hayes, the way women go on about their bloody handbags. A nice enough lady, but raised hell about losing her address book and stuff – made more of a hullabaloo about it than losing her pinkie. Made all the headlines in the Sunday papers, though. A good-looking woman like that scarred for life.'

'Did I land any punches on the thugs before the knife came into play?'

Jameson shrugged. 'No idea. But as the two of 'em got clear away it looks as if you came off worst. Sorry about that, Hayes. Off duty too,' he added with a chuckle.

After further questioning the sergeant drew up a handwritten statement, such as it was, and Hayes signed it, hoping that would be the last of it until the muggers were arrested. If ever.

When Jameson had gone, he sipped the tea the orderly set down and rechecked the drawer of the bedside table. No cigarettes, thought as much. But his mobile? Presumably the cheerful ring tone of a mobile phone was as unwelcome in here as his cigarettes.

Four

Later that afternoon he tried to phone his boss. Jenny Robbins answered.

'Superintendent's out, sir. Can I give a message?'

'Er, no. I'll ring later.'

'Sorry to hear about the attack. How are you feeling?'

Jenny Robbins was, Hayes had to admit, the brightest constable attached to Renham's CID, and an attractive redhead to boot.

'Pretty lousy, since you ask. It looks as if I'm going to be stuck here for a while. I was hoping Superintendent Waller would be about, I'm worried about who's leading the team on that suspicious death we were investigating before this happened.'

'A new guy's been transferred from Aylesbury, sir. Chief Inspector Morton. Bit of a Teletubby,' she added in an under-tone. 'Preston calls him Tweedledee.'

Hayes snorted. 'Cut it out, Robbins, it's too painful to laugh. Who's Tweedledum? No, let me guess.'

'Well, the guv'nor gets on with him like they were joined at the hip.'

Hayes was not amused. Having someone take over the Newbold poisoning case, the most interesting enquiry to land on his desk for months, was like pulling the rug from under his feet.

'I'll tell the Super you rang, then.'

He could hear the fuzzy background noise of office backchat interposed with telephones ringing and doors slam-ming. He felt trapped like a dog in quarantine.

'Can I do anything for you?' she whispered, sensing his extraordinary mood, so unlike the chief inspector who cracked the whip around the station.

Hayes paused, then admitted to himself that beggars can't be choosers. 'Well, since you ask, you could do me a personal favour, Jenny. I'm kitted out with some hospital gear but I'd prefer to have my own as it looks as if I'm being kept here for a while yet. Could you pop over to my digs, the flat over the butcher's? You've been there. My landlord, the butcher in the shop, will hand over a key, he knows you. I need my tennis shoes from the sports bag in the hall cupboard, toiletries, some jeans and a sweater for when I'm able to go outside in the garden here . . . and anything else you think might be useful. Sergeant Preston's got contacts at the youth club. Ask him to get one of his lads to bring it in for me, will you please?'

'What about pyjamas?'

'Haven't any. It doesn't matter.'

'Excuse me for asking, sir, but what happened between you and Pippa? You remember I lodged with her when I first got transferred to Renham nick and I thought you two were close. The cottage is on the market, I noticed the board as I was driving in this morning.'

Hayes swallowed a terse retort. 'We split. Pippa got a PR job with the new opera house in Wales.'

Jenny took the hint and dropped the subject. The on-off relationship between the DCI and his lively girlfriend had been a matter of ribald speculation in the canteen for months. Wales, eh? Well, he probably asked for it.

It was Wednesday night before Waller put in an appearance and Hayes was surprised to discover how pleased he was to see him breeze in, bringing a robust tang to the sterile atmosphere of his lonely room. Waller dropped a weekend case by the bed and drew up a chair. Hayes carefully pulled himself up and gripped his boss's hand.

'Well, how are you, lad? Feeling OK?' Waller plumped

himself down, the flimsy plastic chair creaking ominously. 'The missus sends her regards. Been badgering me to come up to check you over, but,' he said, opening his ham-like fists in a helpless gesture, 'you know how it is, especially now we've got this poisoning lark on our plate.'

'Any progress?'

'Not much – it all hinges on the housekeeper's alibi holding up. She's got a dodgy history as it turns out, left an old folks' home in Didsbury in suspicious circumstances. Poor old Newbold never knew what he'd taken on. He'd have been better off booking himself into a nursing home if he needed to be looked after instead of trusting himself to a woman he met in the pub. Not as if he couldn't afford it.'

'I gather you've got some help from Aylesbury.'

Waller stiffened. 'Who've you been gabbing to, Hayes?'

'I asked Jenny Robbins to fill me in.'

'Ah, yes, well, we've struck lucky there. DCI Morton's a crack detective. Dealt with a similar scam last year. These silly old farts are soft targets when women like Pat Lockyer are on the lookout for a cushy number. Anyway, don't you worry about all that, chum, you just concentrate on getting fit.'

Hayes tried to speak but Waller raised a hand and ploughed on. 'Robbins sorted out some kit for you and said to pass on good wishes from the butcher, forget his name, that landlord of yours. She packed it up in a bag,' he said, giving the weekend case a kick. 'Oh, and Mrs Waller sent this for you, thought I should do the right thing being as you're not allowed grapes according to that bossy cow in charge here.'

Waller looked uncomfortable, a bedside manner not his forte. He handed over a paperback thriller containing kind words neatly penned in a flowery get-well card from Joyce Waller.

Hayes was touched and muttered his thanks, which Waller gruffly cut short.

'No sweat. Now, listen up, I've got some good news. The assistant chief called me in yesterday to discuss re-manning.

The government's pushing for more uniforms on the beat, a bigger ethnic intake, all the usual malarkey. He put it to me that as a bloke with an excellent track record you would be the best man for a new unit that is being set up at Scotland Yard. More of a security job, something to get your teeth into, and—'

'A desk job.'

'Well, a promotion goes with it, Hayes. Make you up to superintendent, give you a chance to pick your own team.'

'But a desk job?'

'Basically, yes. I suppose so . . .'

'I'm no bloody cripple, sir. This stabbing's nothing long term, I've not lost a leg, for Christ's sake.'

'No, no, of course not, matey. But face facts. A damaged lung's hardly useful on active service. CID's a young man's game, intelligent blokes like you are more useful in set-ups like this one the assistant chief's talking about.'

'I'm not ready for the knacker's yard yet!'

Waller became heated. 'No need to shout, lad. You're going to be here for at least a couple of weeks and after that a spell at the police convalescent place at the seaside. Renham's not exactly a key posting, is it? Look on this new unit as a step-ping stone. Could end up with gold braid all over you, and promotion as a result of a street brawl must be a first.'

'I thought you just said the top brass picked me out for this new job because of my CID experience, not because I'd been knifed by a pair of urban thugs.'

'But you got your name splashed all over the papers, see? High profile. They liked the fallout: "Off Duty Policeman Risks His Life to Save a Lady".'

'Balls. They've been looking for an excuse to shunt me off the Thames Valley Force ever since that Oxford busi-ness, and—'

Waller rose, his mouth hardening. 'Now, now, don't get excited, Hayes, no need to drag out all that old history. Think it over, there's no rush. When you've got the all clear from here and done a stint of convalescence, the ACC wants to see you, wants to explain the ins and outs of the new unit personally. Blimey, Hayes, you should be over the moon, getting a chance like this. When you've calmed down you'll see the sense in it. Look on the bright side: moving to London you'll have all the time in the world to ponce along to all those highbrow concerts that got you into this mess in the first place.'

H ayes slept badly for the next few days despite the magic potions doled out at regular intervals. He allowed himself the wry conjecture that the knockout drops would prove addictive. Nothing like a regular copper with few vices apart from casual sex and smoking ending up with a taste for pethidine or whatever it was so freely dispensed courtesy of the NHS.

June had turned out to be a sizzler, the temperature soaring, heat bouncing off the walls of his monk's cell, as he had grown to regard it, like a hammer blow. He was often forced to draw the blinds, shutting out the light and increasing the feeling of claustrophobia. The crack to his skull was causing a persistent headache and proving more troublesome than the knife wounds, which were, as the dour ward sister uncharacteristically confirmed with a smile, 'healing splendidly'. Hayes guessed she would be glad to see the back of him, the journalists cluttering her ward in an attempt to interview the 'have-a-go inspector' fiercely denied access.

By the weekend Hayes had extended his horizons, hobbling to the day room to watch the cricket on TV or limping outside, where a little-frequented courtyard garden offered welcome shade.

Jenny Robbins had done a brilliant job packing the weekend case Waller had brought in. Apart from the kit he had asked for, the darling girl had poked around his flat and added T-shirts, underpants and a pair of Bermuda shorts in mind-blowing shades of orange and maroon. He had never worn the bloody things before, a sarcastic throw from his ex-wife on her return from her honeymoon in Hawaii with her new trophy spouse. The divorce had been bitter but, on reflection, he now admitted the poor kid had deserved better than living hand-to-mouth on a policeman's pay. Her mantra had grown monotonous: 'With your CV you could get a decent living in the music business, where all the real money is . . .', et cetera, et cetera.

Truth was, being tipped out of college with only the mediocre prospect of any sort of career as a pianist was never going to be good enough for Roger Hayes. The years of study and hours of piano practice had left him with only failure and falling blindly into marriage, and joining the police force, as seemingly the only job on offer at the time, had made him feel like a racehorse turned out to offer donkey rides on the beach. As it happened, police work had proved a surprising success, but the marriage was never going to work.

On Sunday afternoon Hayes had settled in the deserted courtyard to escape the stream of hospital visitors pounding past his door, trapping him in his overheated box of a room, when the nice Irish nurse brought a surprise visitor. Hayes stood hurriedly, the Sunday papers strewing onto the grass.

'A visitor for you, Rog. Mrs Paget.'

The woman approached, holding out her hand and looking decidedly nervous. It took a moment for the penny to drop. 'Er, Mrs Paget?' he murmured. 'You must be the lady who—'

She smiled. 'That's right. Not exactly your damsel in distress, Inspector, more like your auntie out too late at night who deserved a drubbing.'

Hayes shook his head and cleared a space for her on the garden bench. 'No, no, of course not. It wasn't all that late, the street was well lit and we were in the centre of a city, for Heaven's sake. No, Mrs Paget, don't blame yourself – just bad luck.'

She seemed a nice enough woman, as Jameson had said. Fiftyish at a guess, carefully made up, and wearing a flowery button-through dress which she held in place with a band-aged hand as she sat down. Hayes bent to gather up the scattered newspapers, and as he turned to face her he caught a ripple of laughter struggling under her polite smile.

He grinned, opening his arms wide. 'It's these damned Bermuda shorts, isn't it? A jibe from my ex-wife. She thought it would shame me out of my boring holiday gear. Been shoved to the back of my knickers drawer for years but since I've been here these shorts have been brilliant, and give the porters no end of amusement. If you like, I'll go and find a dressing gown – I'm not used to visitors here.'

'Oh, sit down, do. I came to thank you. I would have been before but I was in rather a tizzy after the attack and my brother insisted I stay with him to pull myself together. I only came back on Friday to see my doctor about the amputation. You heard about that, I suppose . . .?' Her voiced trembled and Hayes hoped she wasn't going to go into details.

'Ah, yes. My boss outlined the damage. I am so sorry, Mrs Paget.'

She brushed this aside. 'My fault entirely. As my brother quite sensibly said, "Why argue about stuff like that? I'll buy you new rings if you want." But that wasn't the point, was it, Roger? You don't mind if I call you Roger, do you? I was just so mad. How dare those ruffians jump out on me like that, push me around, threaten me with a knife? How dare they!'

Hayes nodded, having heard this sort of response before. No good arguing with the lady, no good at all. He patiently heard her out, feeling a headache starting to kick in, wishing the poor woman would work off her guilt trip and leave him in peace.

At last she dried up and gripped his knee. 'Sorry about that, Roger, I just had to let it spill out. My brother urges me to put it behind me, just forget it. But it's difficult. I still feel bloody furious, to tell you the truth. Not so much about losing my rings, or even losing my finger, but because my confidence is all shot to pieces. I'm not sure I want to live in the city any more . . .'

Hayes rallied. 'Oh, it's early days, Mrs Paget. Let it simmer. Go back to your brother's place for a while and let the police get on with tracking down these boys. Did you get a good look at them?'

'Sadly, no. I could not in all honesty pick out either of them on an identity parade. Superintendent Jameson is hoping they will try to sell the rings or use my mobile: that would trap them.'

She bent down and fished about in her handbag, rising triumphantly with a cellphone in her damaged hand. 'Here, take it, it's yours. When they had driven off and you were knocked out and bleeding everywhere, I knelt down and went through your pockets. Felt sure a young man like yourself would have a mobile on him somewhere. Why is it, whenever you need a passer-by or even a cruising taxi, there's never anyone about even in London on a Saturday night?'

Hayes pocketed the phone with a smile. 'I thought it had been confiscated along with my cigarettes.'

'When the police arrived we were bundled off in separate ambulances, they wanted to get you to hospital without delay, and I stayed to explain what had happened. They assumed the phone was mine but all my things had gone with my handbag, blast them. I'm sorry I've been so long returning it, Roger. But, tell me, as an inspector who must get callouts on mugging cases all the time, what do you think? Will they catch those boys? You must feel as frustrated as I, especially as you had no cause to help me and then end up so badly hurt. How are you?'

'Great. I'm hoping to get out of here before long, and if I promise to take some time off they'll probably have me back in harness in a month or so. Problem is they have issues about my returning to Renham. It's a bit like being on leave,' he quipped. 'While I'm forced to take time off someone else gets my job and it looks as if they'd like the new guy to stick around. I've been offered a desk job but it doesn't appeal.'

'Like you said to me, my dear, it's early days. But I've got a proposition for you. No, don't look like that, hear me out.'

She fixed him with a determined eye and Hayes knew he'd better pipe down and listen.

'As I was telling you, Roger, I've been staying with my brother, Bill Caxton, used to be a champion TT rider years ago, you may have heard of him? He lives on the Isle of Man. It's a remarkable place, a sort of Ruritania,' she said with a chuckle. 'Stands between the north-west coast and Ireland, a self-governing dependency and attractive taxwise. It is also a lovely summer destination and Bill runs a delightful spa and sports club plus a few holiday lets.'

'Sounds impressive.'

'Well, I was talking things over and Bill said he wants to thank you for saving me as you did.'

Hayes feebly protested, sensing that Mrs Paget was likely to turn embarrassingly grateful.

'No, it's true, Roger. If you hadn't been there God knows what would have happened to me. Now, don't interrupt. Bill and I have a suggestion. How about a month or two's leave on the island? All expenses paid? You're a single man I understand, no ties?'

Hayes shrugged.

'Well, then. The Caxton Spa has a resident medical staff and the highest recommendation. Here, I've brought some brochures. You don't have to decide right away, perhaps you have plans to convalesce elsewhere?'

'It has been suggested,' he retorted drily.

'The island's busy high season but Bill feels sure a bit of a break in a luxury hotel spa would set you up no end.'

Hayes shook his head as he leafed through the brightly coloured brochure illustrating suntanned couples lounging by the pool, and individual log cabins dotted round a huge lake fronting a house looking for all the world like a French château.

'Very generous of Mr Caxton, very kind indeed. But I

can't see myself in a smart set-up like this. My Bermudas would lower the tone!' He attempted to return the brochures but Mrs Paget was having none of it.

'Believe me, you can enjoy all the privacy you wish, Roger – it's no holiday camp, very quiet in fact, exclusive to residents who like to relax with people they own know. But if you'd feel more comfortable doing your own thing, Bill has a self-catering place he lets out in the summer. An old house right on the beach, converted into flats.'

He was tempted. The prospect of being shunted to a convalescent home for ailing retired policeman haunted him.

Mrs Paget continued to rattle on. 'All expenses paid, Roger. Stay as long as you like. Here, Bill's sent this return air ticket for you to use whenever you feel well enough to leave hospital. When you've thought it over, give him a ring – I've stapled his business card to the brochure. It would ease my mind if you accepted, my dear. It's the least Bill and I could do for you after what you've been through.'

'Mrs Paget. I'm quite overcome.'

'Georgina. Call me Georgie – we could almost be blood kin after what you risked coming to my aid as you did.'

She quickly rose and brushed his cheek with a kiss, waving her bandaged hand in a tremulous farewell as she swiftly left him before he had a chance to disentangle himself from the newspapers draped over the Bermudas.

Six

That night the weather broke with a vengeance, a thunderstorm of Wagnerian drama lighting up the sky, rain overflowing the gutters and sluicing down the window of his room. But next morning, the sky lay over the dirty roofscape like watered silk and the temperature had dropped to a bearable level.

After breakfast, seated at a table in the day room with two heart patients recovering from by-passes who were anxious to catch the overnight Test match score, Hayes obediently swallowed his medication and took Bill Caxton's brochure out to the courtyard, spreading a towel on the wet bench and settling down to consider Georgina Paget's proposal.

The spa hotel was much as he expected, the juice bar and yoga classes making him wince, but the place was definitely top class and the gym and pool would certainly help to strengthen his muscles.

At two o'clock he presented himself for a physio session and afterwards showed the brochure to the therapist, a nice young thing called Gemma, whose slight frame disguised the power of an orang-utan.

'What do you think of this?' he asked, passing over the Caxton Spa bumf while he got dressed.

She perched on the desk and quickly leafed through the coloured pages to check the list of personnel at the back.

'Oh, Jeremy Baines is on the staff. Lucky blighter. Trust Jammy Baines to land a job in clover.'

'You know him?'

'We trained together in Edinburgh. He's listed here as a

22

specialist in sports injuries, which might help in your case. And consultant medic to the TT race teams? Fancy that! I suppose motorbike spills would soon pile up the paying customers.'

'Is he any good?'

'Brilliant. Surprised he settled for the Isle of Man, though. The Mayo Clinic in the States was his goal when we were students. Ambitious chap.'

'According to my contact, the island has special status taxwise, attracts rich residents. Something like Guernsey, I imagine.'

She passed back the brochure and smiled. 'Wouldn't have put you in the luxury-spa bracket, if you don't mind me saying so, Inspector.'

Hayes demurred and pulled the belt of his dressing gown tighter. 'Well, thanks for the pummelling, Gemma. Same time tomorrow?'

Back in his room he made a quick phone call to his sergeant, Roy Bellamy.

'Afternoon, sir. Heard from the guv'nor you're making good progress.'

'Yeah, slow work though. How are you managing with the new DCI? Any leads on that poisoning case?'

'Flat as a pancake, sir, but your stand-in's a hot shot with the computers, I'll give him that. Tracked the suspect's history back to base despite two changes of name. Seems she was working with diabetic patients before, so saying she was unfamiliar with insulin injections is a load of bollocks.'

Bellamy abruptly broke off and Hayes could hear an unmistakable growl in the background. 'Can't stop now, sir, the Super's just come back. Anything I can do for you?'

'I'm worried about my car. It's stuck in this multi-storey car park and it looks as if I shall have to leave it there for far too long – I'm thinking of going abroad for a bit of leave when I get out of here. Is there any chance you could send someone to pick it up and leave it at my digs? My landlord will tuck it away at the back of the shop.'

'Leave it with me, sir. We're a bit pushed with this Newbold case, but I can send Robbins. She's got to check out the suspect's records in London, driving back in your motor would be no problem at all.'

'I'll send a cheque, shall I?'

'No need, sir. I'll ask Jenny to call in on her way through. She can collect the keys and you can pay her in cash if that's convenient.'

'Brilliant.'

Bellamy lowered his voice. 'Any idea when you'll be back, sir?'

'That's up to the Superintendent,' Hayes curtly retorted before breaking off as the door opened to admit a motherly soul trundling the library trolley.

'How about a nice detective story, dear?'

Later that evening, after several hours weighing his options, Hayes put through a call on his mobile to Bill Caxton's home number. He answered right away, a firm tone of voice which encouraged Hayes to get straight to the point.

'It's Hayes here. Roger Hayes. Mrs Paget kindly passed on a very generous offer which I thought I'd better check out with you, Mr Caxton.' He roughly outlined the proposal that seemed to be on the table. 'Now, have I got it right? Or was Mrs Paget disguising her extraordinary offer as a thank-you from yourself?'

'Absolutely not! My idea entirely, Mr Hayes. If it doesn't appeal perhaps you would prefer a cheque? Georgie is a determined woman and feels badly about the way things turned out for you.'

'Good God, no cheque, *please!* But . . .' he paused, 'as a friend? As your guest? Is that really what you had in mind?'

Bill Caxton launched into a fulsome appreciation of Hayes' defence of his sister and described the advantages of a period of convalescence at the Caxton Spa Hotel and Sports Club. 'But if you prefer, there is a self-catering apartment free at Finch House. Only a small studio flat, but it might suit you better. The other holiday lets on the premises have been rented out till mid-October, a regular booking from a band which entertains at various venues on the island all summer. A nice bunch, good friends of mine who've been playing here each season for years. No kids, no animals, so it would be nice and quiet, and, of course, the facilities at the spa would be at your disposal at any time. You would need transport, though, Finch House is on the coast at Port St Agnes, several miles from Douglas. Will you be fit to drive?'

'Oh yes. And thank you for the air tickets. I am entirely bowled over, Mr Caxton. Your generosity leaves me lost for words.'

'You'll come, then?'

'How could I refuse?'

'Good. Look, there is one thing I must get off my chest before you commit yourself. Georgie was adamant that we *owed* you, but I have to admit I have need of your professional advice. There've been a number of serious attacks on club members, seasonal muggings which the local police seem to have set aside as the crimes of visiting villains attracted by the wealthy people who are resident here. But I suspect that my organization is being specifically targeted, and I fear these deliberate attacks will get worse, end in another victim getting killed. So you see, my offer is not entirely altruistic, Mr Hayes. An experienced detective on the spot would be a huge relief to me, your presence unremarked, of course. No one need to know your background, and if you could do no more than keep an eye on the situation and perhaps make a few suggestions regarding security, I would be the one in your debt, Chief Inspector.'

Seven

The next ten days showed a swift improvement in Hayes' recovery and the all-clear from his consultant came none too soon, the boredom of his incarceration as irritating as a heat rash.

He packed his bag with alacrity, shoving his warrant card back into his wallet with the exhilarating confirmation that his identity had been returned to him at last.

The weeks in hospital had been something of a watershed; it was the first total break since he had joined the force and a bleak demand to take serious stock of his future. Was a return to the old slog in Renham really what he wanted? Would work with the new unit at Scotland Yard, desk job or not, be more interesting? And a leg-up to superintendent wasn't to be sniffed at, was it?

Waller had hinted that a request for early retirement on health grounds would be given sympathetic consideration but Hayes felt this to be a cop-out. And even with a fat pension to cushion any new start, what the bloody hell was he supposed to do? Start a security firm? Set himself up as a concert agent, as Franz Bulgari had suggested? Bulgari had been a buddy throughout their college years despite Franz's starry technique and sexy performance on stage, which had left Hayes way behind even before the death knell of 'mediocre talent' had been sounded by his tutor. But they had kept in touch, and sailing into the blue on the tail of his comet was tempting.

'I could recommend a dozen promising young soloists who'd jump at the chance of being represented by a bright

26

spark like you, Roger. Might even dump my current manager, a useless bugger who insists his deaf aid is of absolutely no consequence. We would make a brilliant team, pal,' Franz insisted. 'Why not spend some time with me on tour while you're still officially on sick leave? See how the life suits you? You've no wife to tie you down and we're both in need of fresh impetus – I've got stuck on a plateau of opportunity and, forgive me, but I get the impression that your own career's gone flat.'

The suit which he had worn on the night of the stabbing had been tidied away on his arrival but had survived the attack astonishingly well. Only a button ripped off, a slashed pocket and smears of blood on the collar, which one of the orderlies had scrubbed out in a kindly attempt to see their headline-grabbing Good Samaritan off the premises in good order. Not that they need have worried: the news story had finally ceased to feature, the assailants remaining at liberty, and only a bleating reference to 'crime on the streets' by a vote-seeking Tory MP linking Hayes to Georgina Paget and her cruelly injured hand.

He ordered a taxi to take him to the airport and, having withdrawn a scandalous amount of cash from his account, relaxed for the first time in weeks with a cigarette. As they boarded the plane he glanced around at his fellow passengers. They were a sun-kissed bunch, and he was the only one who, pasty-faced, had missed out on the best summer for years. He settled into a window seat and watched the runway peel away as the plane climbed into the clouds.

Bill Caxton had insisted on meeting him at Arrivals and Hayes felt his spirits lift. The heavyset bloke wearing a T-shirt with Caxton Spa spelt out across his chest was easy to spot and Hayes took a shine to him immediately. He seemed a no-nonsense type of guy with a refreshingly direct approach and perhaps less of the city polish of his sister. They sauntered out to his car, Caxton matching his pace to Hayes', the scar crisscrossing his chest still tender.

'I'll take you straight to Finch House, shall I? And if you

like what you see, we can drop off your bag and lunch at the Spa? OK by you, Roger?'

'Sounds terrific.'

The day had clouded over but glimpses of the sea glistening in the distance were entrancing. They covered several miles at speed, passing wooded hills and quaint villages, recalling Georgina's reference to the island as being a little Ruritania. As the Jaguar slowed down at a bridge Caxton raised his baseball cap and shouted, 'Good morning, Little Folk.'

Hayes chuckled. 'What was all that about?'

'We're a superstitious lot on the island. Whenever you cross the Fairy Bridge you must wish them good day. Worth keeping in their good books, and as an ex-motorbike competitor I've always believed in luck.'

They pulled off the road onto a lane, single track and winding, the approach to Finch House more like a private drive. The building dominated a cliff below which cottages clustered around a harbour.

'Port St Agnes used to be a flourishing fishing village but tourism's taken over and the only boats left are those hired out to visitors.'

'The island relies on tourism?'

'Partly. But it has its own government, Tynwald, an ancient concession which allows certain taxation exemptions plus grants which support a finance industry. The place also attracts a number of wealthy residents who enjoy certain advantages from living away from the mainland. It's too complicated to put into a nutshell, but, believe me, Roger, this island's no impoverished outpost stuck out in the Irish Sea.'

He slowed down a hundred yards from the front entrance to allow Hayes to appreciate the imposing pile of Victorian Gothic architecture calling itself Finch House. Hayes was certainly impressed, though probably not in the way Bill Caxton assumed. The place was huge. Narrow windows were shadowed under overhanging eaves, rugged pinnacles breaking the roofline like a series of stalagmites, the gloomy facade dominated by a tower topped by a lightning conductor. Hayes' immediate impression was its similarity to the mansion in *Psycho*.

'Like it?' Caxton enthused.

'A real knock-out, Bill. Takes my breath away.'

Caxton pulled over to the main entrance and grabbed Hayes' case from the boot. 'You OK with stairs, chum? The flat's on the second floor at the back. No lift.'

Hayes stiffly hauled himself out of the low-slung sports car and smiled. 'No problem. Lead on, Macduff.'

Eight

Bill Caxton gave him a five-star tour of the spa before they settled to lunch in the hotel restaurant. Hayes had to admit that the place had class, though the clientele seemed a bit glum. The restaurant was only half full, most of the customers having already passed through to the lounge for green tea or the poison of their choice.

'The low-calorie option's not everyone's choice,' Caxton said with a grin, passing Hayes a menu which rivalled any gastronomic oasis he might have encountered and was certainly an improvement on hospital fare. 'You look as though you need feeding up. Make the most of it while you're here, the chef needs all the encouragement he can get, these picky diet freaks make him depressed. When we've finished here I'll sort out your membership card. Charge everything to the account, and I mean everything. Feel free. Georgie insists we've got to send you back home in fine fettle. Think of it as a small appreciation of your courage – the commissioner's not going to give you a medal, is he?'

'As a matter of fact, I think he's offered me the boot. Disguised as promotion but nevertheless a desk job.'

Caxton sobered. 'Really? How come?'

'My current boss has been looking for a polite way of elbowing me off his patch, our methods never synchronized. But enough about me, how's your sister? Did they manage to sew back the finger?'

Caxton shook his head. 'Never found it. They did a thorough search of the crime scene but it was, as you know, a wet night and the bloody digit must have got kicked into the gutter and flushed down the drain. The press got it all wrong: that mugger didn't chop off her finger and make off with it with her rings.' He sighed. 'All hype. It was Georgie's fault for putting up a fight like she did. As she struggled, she clashed with the guy wielding the knife and that's how it happened. An accident. But a clean cut, it's healed well and my sister's no moaner. No matter what I say it wasn't in her nature to give up her stuff without a fight. You got the worst of it, I reckon.'

Hayes shrugged. 'Yeah, but your sister's maimed for life. My troubles will be over as soon as I've got myself fit.'

They were the final stragglers in the restaurant and Caxton suggested they took coffee in his office. Hayes guessed that this might be the moment for his benefactor to spell out the worries he had touched upon, his anxiety that the Spa had been targeted. He couldn't blame the bloke for having a hidden agenda; shelling out on a free vacation at this expensive bolthole was going to cost big-time and this, ostensibly a generous no-strings gesture at the behest of Georgina Paget to whom Hayes was a perfect stranger, was hard to believe.

Caxton's room overlooked tennis courts at the back, his office walls plastered with dramatic shots of former Manx TT races in which he featured in sexy black leathers. It was a younger, slighter version but the man had certainly not gone to seed, and, as a motorbike champion, racing must have paid off handsomely to set him up with a luxurious spa hotel plus God knows how many other properties on the island.

They settled on a sofa and waited until the waiter had left them alone before Hayes introduced the question which had been troubling him ever since their original telephone conversation.

'You mentioned serious attacks on your members here. Another victim killed, you said?'

Caxton tensed. 'That's right. The police are not convinced but I think my organization is being targeted. Membership has dipped since last summer when the muggings started. Here,' he said, taking a folder from a briefcase at his feet, 'we've kept all the press cuttings plus my own personal notes of each incident.'

'The attacks were on the premises?'

'No. The locations varied, the man who died last month was attacked in a side street off the promenade here in Douglas. He had been bludgeoned and probably kicked to death. The previous victim, who died last summer, was a friend of mine, a man called Derek Fields, a businessman. He lived in Ramsay but he also was attacked in an alley not far from here. A member of this sports club of course, a keen squash player.'

Hayes leafed through the cuttings. 'Says here Mr Fields died from a heart attack. He was sixty-six years old, perhaps squash was not such a good idea.'

'That's right. The cause of death was a heart attack but was probably brought about by the trauma of being mugged. He died the day after – the muggers took his cash but they must have been disturbed. No valuables were stolen, not even his Rolex, and his injuries were no more than a dusting over – he didn't even report the incident to the police.'

Hayes stiffened. 'Really? Why was that, do you think?'

'Didn't want the hassle, I presume. Derek was a rich man, losing cash would be preferable to going through a useless procedure with the police. Forgive me, but frankly people like Derek Fields have little regard to the plods here, and in the season the place attracts the usual percentage of baddies. The other victims, six in all, were all men, all members here, three who joined at the start twenty years ago when a spa hotel like this was unique. I have commercial competitors now, and I've been warned that an American consortium is taking an interest in buying up property on the island.'

'You have received offers to sell up?'

'Not as yet. But there have been four attacks already this season, all reasonably fit men and all stripped of their money by two hoodlums who seemed to know what they were after.'

'All men, you say? Single men, out on their own late at night? Apprehended in backstreets? Let's not beat about the bush, Bill, do you have a problem with queer-bashing on the island? Are you suggesting these men were simply mugged, or was there an anti-gay element?'

Caxton flushed. 'Well, to be frank, I've had my doubts about one or two of them, but Derek Fields was a married man with grandchildren, for God's sake, and this hotel is no pink palace, if that's what you're thinking!'

'No, no, of course not, but, at first glance, it strikes me as odd that these blokes were attacked in the early hours in insalubrious areas of town. You must admit it sounds fishy.'

'The police have been discreet, but my business is suffering, Roger, and one more season like this with membership numbers falling like autumn leaves and I shall have to rationalize my investment. The staff are jittery and it doesn't take much for the members to jump ship. There are plenty of other fancy sports clubs here.'

Hayes replaced the cuttings in the folder and stirred his coffee. 'What do you want me to do, Bill?'

'I'm not asking you to interfere with the police investigation, of course not. But it would ease my mind if you were receptive to the problem here. Is security OK? Is there something going on I should know about? Nobody here or at Finch House need know about our little private arrangement and news of poor Georgie's mugging isn't current gossip, so if you prefer to keep a low profile about your own involvement in the incident, I'm certain no one will put two and two together. We are very insular here, troubles on the mainland, especially in London, don't interest us, and the headline grabbers are almost exclusively local. The editor of the newspaper here is a sensible chap. Marty Lewis knows that downplaying any violence, especially during the season, is best for tourism. The holidaymakers are mostly families, no one associates the island with the sort of thuggery that happens on city streets.'

Hayes rose to go and tucked the folder under his arm. 'I'll

think it over, Bill. No promises, but sometimes a fresh approach is helpful. Now, I'd better get my skates on. May I order a taxi at the desk? I need to go back to the airport and hire a car.'

Caxton leapt to his feet. 'I'll drive you back to Finch House, if you like. There's a garage in Port St Agnes I can recommend, a friend of mine runs it, he can let you have a set of wheels no problem.'

Hayes stood his ground. 'No thanks, Bill, you've done enough. I'll get out from under your feet and sort myself out at the flat. The other tenants? A band, you said.'

'Yeah. Phil Bailey and the Blues. Great guys, you'll have a wonderful time with them. They're out working every night, of course, but not what you'd call a loud bunch so you can enjoy your privacy. Drop in to see me here in the morning – let me know if you need anything.'

Caxton accompanied him to reception, where a girl in a yellow tracksuit held the fort. She exchanged cheeky banter with Bill, passing a locker key and a membership card to Hayes while she telephoned for his taxi.

When he emerged from the foyer the sun had slipped well below high noon but the warmth still beat down strongly, percolating his thin suiting with the benison of cloudless skies.

Phil Bailey and the Blues, eh? Sounded like the sort of band you'd book for the Policemen's Ball.

Nine

Hayes hired a nifty little runabout, a small red Mercedes which reputedly went like the wind, and did a swift recce of Douglas, the main town and thriving tourist centre with its wine bars, a Victorian theatre, a promenade thronged with holidaymakers and an impressive complex called the Villa Marina. All very nice. He had never contemplated a trip to the Isle of Man but it certainly had a good feel about it.

He had picked up some maps from the car-hire place and found a park bench in the sun to check his whereabouts. Port St Agnes was about five miles along the coast and it seemed there was scope for exploring the less publicized pony tracks inland.

His disquiet about accepting Caxton's largesse gradually dispelled as the prospects the island offered became clear. In addition, there was a pleasant break from his usual haunts to look forward to, even if Caxton thought that a real live detective on the premises was going to throw up any solution to the attacks on his members. Hayes could appreciate the man's anxiety but in all probability the victims' connections with the spa were coincidental, and any advice he, a man with no local knowledge, could offer during a short convalescent stay would surely have been covered by the police, wouldn't it? But there was no escaping the fact that at least one seemingly random mugging had ended in a brutal murder, and, in all fairness, he owed it to Bill Caxton to take a fresh look at this extraordinary spate of attacks.

He walked stiffly back to the main street, concerned at

the loss of fitness after lolling about on his hospital bed. The sooner he got back into shape the better. He found a sports shop and kitted himself out with a dark blue tracksuit and trainers, and a snazzy pair of swimming trunks. Hopefully, once he got a bit of a tan the jagged scar above his belly would disappear. A mini-supermarket dealt with the rest of his shopping list, and he drove back to Port St Agnes feeling in control of his life for the first time since the accident.

By the time he reached the lane leading to Finch House, the sun was setting, the avenue of cypresses overhanging the approach giving the impression of a dark tunnel. But suddenly the lane opened out and the extraordinary edifice was silhouetted like a craggy outcrop, the row of dark lancet windows as intimidating as arrow slits. He grinned at the prospect of settling in what amounted to a film set, a bizarre monument to its long-departed creator.

He parked the car in a yard at the back under what he decided must be the windows of his flat. There were no other vehicles apart from a scruffy minivan and a motorbike, the atmosphere eerily silent for a large house rented out, according to Caxton, to an entire band.

He trudged to a rear door beyond which a passageway lead to a flight of stairs. Tradesmen's entrance? As he was passing, a door off the passage abruptly opened and a ferret-faced man carrying a bucket stepped out.

'Oi! What's your game, mister?'

Hayes spun round, his shopping bags bouncing against the wall.

'I'm moving in. The name's Hayes. Who are you?'

'Oh, sorry, Mr Hayes. Mr Caxton warned me you was on your way but we have to be careful see, Mr Caxton's very particular. You taking number seven?'

'Er, yes, the small flat at the back. Mr Caxton brought me in through the main door this morning, but I suppose,' he said, nodding towards the Mercedes, 'it's OK to leave my car in the yard?'

The scrawny caretaker, if that was who he was, nodded.

'Yeah, sure. The rest of 'em's rehearsing down at the Paradiso. Be back shortly. Park anywhere you like, mate. My name's Kevin, by the way. I'm the odd-job man here. Mr Caxton lets me live in, I keep an eye on the place and everythin' . . . Old house like this is always on the blink one way and anuver but Mr Caxton's done a smashing job renovating the flats, money no object, like.'

Kevin wore oil-stained denims and a sleeveless T-shirt, his clothes hanging loosely over a scraggy frame, his face dark as a Gipsy's. His arms were tattooed to the wrist but the sinewy muscles were not those of any sort of weakling.

'Help you up with your bags, Mr Hayes?'

'No thanks, I can manage. Isn't the back door normally locked?'

'Supposed to be but wiv everyone in and out all hours it's fuckin' impossible. I keep telling Mr Caxton but short of giving each bloke an extra key, I'd spend all bloody day and half the night playing doorman. And even if we gave the girls spare keys they'd bleedin' lose 'em an' all. Lock themselves out once a week as it is, come wheedling round me to sort them out.'

'Girls? I thought it was just a band renting here?'

'Yeah, well, Phil has girls an' all, course he does. There's that singer, DeeDee, she's the worst, and the married couple's s'posed to share their keys but don't seem to be on the same planet half the time.'

Hayes shuffled towards the stairs, sensing that given half a chance Kevin the handyman was an ever-flowing stream.

'Right, Kev, see you around.'

He bolted upstairs and, breathless, unlocked the door to number seven. The windows faced west and a blood-red sun was setting on the horizon in a blaze of glory. Unfortunately, there was no sea view, merely a bird's eye panorama of the backyard which, if Kevin's hint that the area was used as a parking lot was true, might prove a noisy backdrop to any early nights Hayes planned as part of his recovery.

The flat was small but immaculately appointed. It

comprised a sitting room with a kitchen alcove, a shower room and loo, all newly fitted out, and a double bedroom with a garden aspect. Hayes' hasty drop by with Caxton before lunch had been a lightning glimpse of the set of tiny rooms that, on second sight, struck him as just what he was looking for, not too much space and clean as a whistle. The kitchenette was decently equipped, a Formica-topped dining table set up under the window, and a wide sofa fronting a television set. Hayes dropped his shopping in the kitchen and opened a bottle of merlot, retreating to the bedroom to test the springs and get a feel for this island he had washed up upon like a castaway.

He had bought a couple of guidebooks and added a local paper to catch up on forthcoming events. No TT trials until August: a pity. He had been looking forward to the motor-bike races. But the rest of the press coverage was interesting, not least because the sunny overview spared no column inches on any bad vibes about violence on the streets. He hoped the phantom muggers would not add his own name to the list of vulnerable spa members who were worth turning over. Been there, done that.

Perhaps the unlucky victims had offended the island's fabled Little People, forgotten to pay their respects when crossing the Fairy Bridge?

Ten

He woke with a start, the cacophony of vehicles playing bumper cars to squeeze into the yard below as rackety as a motocross. He groped for his watch: one fifteen, by God. What had he let himself in for? Voices drifted up through his open windows, the build-up of heat in his top-floor room causing him to throw off even the cotton sheet.

The noise continued, Phil Bailey's band clearly still revved up after a Friday night gig. He tried to settle back to sleep but when raucous laughter was augmented by the undeniable explosion of what sounded like a full milk crate crashing down the stairs onto the landing right outside his room, he lost his rag completely and, throwing on his Bermudas, flung open the door to bawl out his new neighbours.

The figure on the dimly lit landing spun round. Hayes stopped short. It was a frizzy-haired blonde wearing a midnight-blue beaded mini, both hands pressed to her cheeks in mock consternation.

'Oh, bugger. Sorry. Didn't know the top floor was let. We've been using the attic as a wine store and I've just sent a whole stack of booze crashing down the stairs. Phil'll kill me. Give me a hand – please!'

Hayes' eyes swivelled between the vision on the landing and the broken glass of several bottles, the contents already streaming down the uncarpeted stairs.

'I'll get something on my feet,' he muttered. 'Don't move!'

He threw on a T-shirt and tennis shoes and reappeared with a dustpan and brush and a roll of kitchen paper. She stood immobile, the sounds of a party already in full throttle issuing from downstairs, the heady scent of her perfume mingling with the aroma of a four-ale bar. The breakages appeared to include bottled beer and red wine, the vodka and whisky surprisingly intact.

Hayes' temper had evaporated under the charms of this girl who had destroyed his first night of the 'peace and quiet' Bill Caxton had promised. Between them they mopped up the worst of it and shunted the broken glass into a fire bucket full of sand conveniently to hand at the bend of the stairs.

'Blimey, I bet you're a dab hand with the spring cleaning,' she giggled, her own contribution to the salvage operation now reduced to stroking Hayes' head as he bent to shuffle the last fragments into the pail.

'Leave the rest, sweetie, I'll get Kev to tidy up. But you'll have to come down with me, save me from Phil's rage when he finds out I've chucked most of tonight's jungle juice down the stairs.'

'Three of the bottles are OK. Here, stack them back in the box. It wasn't your fault, the handle's busted, might have happened to anyone.' Hayes heard his voice taking on a soothing tone and mentally rued the rush of blood which had propelled him out of bed and straight into this debacle: hardly a great start to the introduction to his fellow lodgers.

She grabbed his arm. 'You've *got* to come down now, no excuses. It's much too early to go to bed, for Heaven's sake. Come down and meet the others, it's Friday night!'

Hayes was not at all sure what difference Friday night made but he backed off, suddenly aware of his Bermudas.

'Is it a party?'

'No, nothing special. We generally take a while to wind down after four ghastly hours at the Paradiso. It's their weekly dinner-dance and Phil trots out all his old arrangements, sixties stuff, terrible rock-and-roll favourites. Even the Twist, for Pete's sake. Come on,' she wheedled, 'you look fine. Phil's probably already changed into his joggers, likes to think he's a swinger, poor old sod.'

She propelled him down to the ground floor, cradling the

cardboard wine box in her arms, and shoved him forward, no argument, straight into the fug of a knees-up already in full swing. 'What's your name, by the way? I'm DeeDee.'

Hayes slept late and rose accompanied by a real headbanger. He crept out of bed to make coffee and sat at the table by the window, staring out at the deserted car-parking area, trying to recall details of the previous night's shenanigans.

The party had erupted in the former drawing room of Finch House, a panelled salon lit by a single chandelier which did little to break through the smoke-laden atmosphere. At one end of the room a low dais supported a grand piano and a bloke operating what looked like a full-size play deck which belted out a heavy disco beat. The sofas and chairs had been pushed to the wall leaving a small dance floor heaving with the energetic spasms of a dozen or so oddly dressed people. Two men wore identical gear comprising a strange combination of a spangled electric-blue blazer and frilly shirt, all very 'last century', the women sporting the sorts of frock Hayes imagined were sold in provincial department stores as 'cocktail wear'.

DeeDee dumped the remaining bottles on a makeshift bar and attempted to make herself heard above the din to a red-faced swinger with a nicotine-stained comb-over. 'Phil, this is Roger, our new lodger, Bill's friend he told you about. He helped me clean up the broken glass.'

His eyes widened. 'You lost your key again, DeeDee? You broke in, smashed a window?'

'No!' She laughed. 'I was fetching the booze from the attic and the bloody carrier broke and the whole lot crashed down the stairs. I told you it needed two pairs of hands to lug it down here, Phil, and you know what a clumsy cow I am at the best of times. We saved most of it,' she added. It was the sort of witness statement Hayes would have rubbished in any interview room but he now reluctantly regarded himself a collaborator, DeeDee's wide-eyed innocence clearly a well-practised escape mechanism.

'We saved three,' Hayes quickly put in, holding out his hand. 'You must be Phil Bailey, and these other folk,' he said, nodding towards the dance floor, 'are presumably the Blues.'

Hayes sipped his morning coffee, recalling the mad jamboree with no little embarrassment. It all seemed to dissolve into a bit of a nightmare after that, the intake of too much vodka after weeks of involuntary abstention going straight to his head. He must have met most of the band during the course of the night but only retained a clear recollection of DeeDee and the bandleader, Phil.

He forced himself into the bathroom to survey the damage. The bleary-eyed figure confronting him in the mirror did nothing to enhance his self-esteem. Ashen features reflected brutally in the glass, his black hair erect as quills, the pale body marked, as if by a mischievous graffiti scribbler, with a jagged scar below the chest, the raw damage accompanied by evidence of a series of minor jabs. He appreciated the full grisly effect in the unforgiving morning light for the very first time. 'No doubt about it, chum. A serious dose of spa treatment is unavoidable.'

He slipped out of the silent house like an intruder, and drove off at speed back to Douglas.

The girl on reception at Caxton Spa greeted him nervously, her formerly perky manner muted. 'Oh, Mr Hayes, you're here! Mr Caxton's been waiting for you. He's in his office and—'

'OK. I know the way.' Hayes hurried off down the carpeted corridor and knocked at the door.

Bill Caxton was already on his feet as Hayes stepped inside, his face creased with anxiety. Hayes irritably wondered if he was expected to dance attendance on cue each morning but smothered this dyspeptic response as his 'golden hand-shake', as it were, pulled him through and shut the door.

'Roger! Thank God you've come. There's been another attack. Last night! A poor devil I've known for years, Charlie Lyons, in hospital with a cracked skull.'

Eleven

Hayes slumped into a leather sofa and tried to concentrate on Caxton's anxious spiel.

'Slow down, Bill, I'm losing the plot. Charlie Lyons, you say? Caught in this back lane called the Cut, a regular haunt of hookers? How old was the poor guy?'

'Sixtyish, I suppose.'

'Single?'

'Divorced, but currently living alone I believe. I'd have to check it out. I knew his ex but can't say I liked the kid, too young for Charlie, and anyone else but a silly old fart like Charlie would have recognized that she was never going to be a stayer. Former showgirl he picked up at the Villa Marina, tall girl, all legs.'

'His first wife?'

'Yes. Kept his head until Belinda came on the scene. Charlie was no fool in other ways, a very astute businessman, import—export, built himself a great big place near the west coast, indoor swimming pool, the lot.'

'But he used the Spa?'

'Socially. Played tennis with a scratch team we put together to play other sports clubs on the island.'

'Did you know he frequented the Cut?'

Caxton sadly shook his head. 'Dangerous game. Surprised me when I heard, but maybe he needed the excitement after Belinda pushed off and, as rumour has it, took him to the cleaners with a big divorce settlement. Poor old Charlie probably thought an anonymous bang with a working girl would be less expensive.'

'Did you know him well?'

Caxton shrugged. 'Not really. A nice enough guy but a bit of a workaholic. Ran his business round the clock but when he did give himself playtime he really got stuck in.'

Hayes sighed. 'What do you want me to do?'

'Just nose around. Keep off the police investigation but take a look at the big picture. I'm too close to the action to take a broad view, I admit it, but there's some sort of pattern there, Roger, and for the life of me I can't make it out.'

'Have there been other muggings this summer? Holidaymakers beaten up and robbed?'

'Not that I've heard. But the tourists are generally family types. The people I'm worried about are all residents, wealthy men known to splash their money about. Charlie liked the horses, made a decent profit from the bookmakers so he said, so I wouldn't be surprised if he carried too much in the way of readies in his wallet.'

'Would he have fought back?'

'I guess so. Luckily, he survived with only a cracked skull. Why don't you visit him? He's at a private clinic at Port Erin, the Marlborough. No need to wear your policeman's hat, just call in as a sympathetic fellow-victim sent on my behalf. I could phone through and introduce you if you like. Would that be asking too much, Rog?'

Bill Caxton slumped at his desk, weary resignation sitting on his shoulders like an incubus. Hayes reluctantly felt obliged to take up the challenge but his heart wasn't in it. Rich men bundled in dark alleys and relieved of their cash? Perhaps on a nice sunny island such attacks were rare enough to promote the sort of paranoia Bill Caxton exhibited, but his fear that the muggings were some sort of exclusive threat to his members, a coordinated scheme to ruin his business, was pure crap. However, in the circumstances, the least he must do, he admitted, was to make an unbiased review of the attacks and set Caxton's mind at rest.

'Look, Bill, I'm a stranger here and that's probably a good thing, but before I go calling on your friend Mr Lyons, I

44

need to get some background here, get the feel of the overall problem. You mentioned that a chum of yours is the editor of the local paper. Would he play ball if you asked him? Give me an hour or two of his time so I'm more in touch with the full set-up?'

'Marty Lewis. I'll give him a buzz, shall I? You are OK about this, aren't you, Roger? I don't want to embarrass you on any professional grounds.'

'I'm on sick leave and have a personal interest in muggings, don't I? Perhaps I'm trying to widen the scope of my experience to write a feature for the *Police Gazette?* No harm in that, is there? I would prefer it if my stay at Finch House and your generous subsidy of my convalescence here be kept under wraps. We don't want to allow any suspicion to surface that I'm your agent, do we?'

Caxton heaved a sigh of relief. 'Anything you can find out will be a relief to me, you know that. But let's change the subject. How do you plan to use this sick leave of yours? The facilities here are entirely at your disposal and the personal trainers and medical staff are first class.'

Hayes produced a pack of cigarettes and smiled. 'Fags are not welcome here, I presume?'

'Definitely not.' Caxton laughed. 'Give yourself a chance, Roger, you're not long out of hospital.'

'Right. What do you suggest?'

'First off a check-up with our lady doctor. Cheryl's a sweetie but will ask you a lot of questions, make an assessment and recommend an exercise programme. OK? I'll call her now, shall I? Then you're free to play it how you like. As you're self-catering at Finch House I suggest you eat here, Cheryl will devise a diet sheet with our nutritionist, but in your case it'd be more a case of eat well, drink less and smoke not at all. Charge everything up on your club card and brace yourself for a huge interest from our lady members – a new bloke on the scene, especially a loner, goes down a treat with the rich divorcees. We are the most up-market sports venue on the island, so far, and attract big spenders.'

'Cuts me out, then,' Hayes chirped.

Caxton frowned. 'It's the way things are shaping up, I'm afraid. Regular flights from Liverpool and London, and once the casinos catch on, the type of tourist we've been used to will inevitably change. Until now, we've had only one casino but gambling in glamorous surroundings attracts growing interest. So far it's been enjoyed mostly by local residents, but once the market opens up the atmosphere of the island will inevitably alter, and possibly not for the better. That's why foreign investors are showing interest. The island could turn into a little Monte Carlo once the big boys muscle in.'

'Mafia?'

'Don't ask me. I just about keep my head above water and hope our little enterprise here doesn't begin to look too tempting.'

'Ever thought of expanding into the casino game yourself? This place would be perfect. You've got plenty of land to extend on the hotel side and its vicinity to the airport is a big attraction, punters from Ireland for a start.'

Caxton bit his lip. 'Too chancy. I'm not big enough to swim in those financial piranha waters and joining a syndicate would take away my independence. No, Rog, if I'm doomed to go under, at least I'll go down fighting my own corner.'

There was a knock at the door. It was the girl from reception.

'Sorry to interrupt, sir, but there's a man from health and safety who needs to speak with you.'

'About what?'

'Something to do with people swimming in the lake, he said.'

Caxton nodded. 'I'll be right out, I'll walk down to the lake with him.' He turned to Hayes. 'Would you like to see Cheryl about your assessment?'

Hayes nodded, hoping this lady doctor of Caxton's wasn't going to put him through any sort of hoops; his hangover was persisting like a black dog at his heels. Caxton made a

46

brief call to his medic and arranged an immediate appointment for Hayes, who allowed himself to be quick-marched to the surgery where Dr Cheryl Maine did, in fact, prove to be a 'sweetie'.

'Do sit down, Mr Hayes. I've been looking forward to seeing how well you're recovering. Bill tells me you were stabbed.'

She was a horribly healthy-looking girl with muscles to prove it. Hayes held up his hands in mock surrender. 'Be gentle with me,' he pleaded.

Twelve

Being Saturday, the gym was busy. Hayes glanced at the heaving bodies fighting with Caxton's torture equipment and decided to follow Dr Cheryl's advice and take it slowly. A bronzed Travolta lookalike in a Spa T-shirt and Lycra shorts hurried over, all smiles.

'Hey, you're new here. I'm Lenny – would you like me to show you around? Sort out a programme for you?'

'Er, well, thanks, Lenny, but perhaps we could do that next week?'

He handed over his assessment card and Lenny glanced at Cheryl's recommendations with interest. 'Sure. Quietens down after the weekend. Would you like an appointment? How about Monday? Say nine o'clock?'

Hayes grinned. 'Make it later, I'm sleeping in if I can swing it.'

Lenny returned to the desk and consulted his book. He looked up, smiling encouragement, and scribbled details from the assessment form on to an exercise sheet. 'Eleven suit you, Mr Hayes?'

'Fine. The doctor's recommended cycling and swimming. Said I could hire a bike at the tennis pro's hut. Where's that?'

Following directions, Hayes located the hut and rented a mountain bike for a month. The sun shone, the day stretched out ahead blissfully unscheduled, and his hangover had miraculously lifted like morning mist.

He wobbled off towards the lake, quickly discovering the pleasure of spinning along the winding tracks between trees where the sunlight alternately shafted down or was obscured by the canopy overhead.

He tuned his iPod to a bouncy number and did a circuit of the hotel grounds to get his bearings. Several sun-worshippers were already staked out by the pool and the sound of tennis balls bouncing on the hard courts was as rhythmic as the solid beat of the music in his ears.

Bill Caxton's spa was impressive. The original building with its mansard roof and long windows had converted to a Frenchified hotel with ease. There was a wide terrace on the south side set about with garden chairs and tables where elegant couples took in the view with their aperitifs, and the house overlooked a deep lake, the surface mostly obscured by a mat of water lilies. The estate was surrounded by a crumbling brick wall broken down in several places.

Hayes rode to the far side of the lake, following a cycle track which led to a dozen cabins discreetly hidden beyond a copse. His chest muscles had started to ache, the tautness of his barely healed scars causing him to gasp. He braked suddenly and almost fell off as he collided into an inoffensive sapling which sprang back, uncomplaining. He decided to give himself a rest and dropped onto a mossy bank, leaning against the tree and adjusting the iPod, which had slipped down to his neck.

He wished he had thought to bring a bottle of water; the heat of midday was bringing him out in a sweat even in the shade of the woodland. After getting his breath back, he pushed the bike through to a clearing in front of one of the cabins where an unoccupied sun-lounger tempted him into the sunshine. He lay back, mopped his forehead and readjusted the personal stereo to a soothing string quartet before closing his eyes. Perfect. But his reverie was short lived as he felt a sharp jab in his ribs.

'Hey, Roger! You stalking me?'

The chirrup of her voice as she snatched off his earpiece brought Hayes awake with a start. He shot up, whipping off his sunglasses and glowering.

'What?'

She stood over him like a skinny wood sprite, all brown skin and frizzy blonde hair. 'Don't say you've forgotten me already. And after all we've been to each other!'

'Christ, DeeDee! You gave me a bloody fright. What are you doing here?'

She laughed. 'Same as you. Escaping. Would you like a beer?'

Hayes shook his head. 'No thanks, last night's party did my head in. But some water would be great.' He nodded towards the cabin. 'Yours?'

'Phil's. He rents it for the season and we take turns. Roz and Roma get the lion's share but they're buttoned up in the office checking the bookings.'

'Roz? Phil's wife?'

'Yeah. You missed her last night – she and Roma bunked off into Ramsay after the gig.'

'Roma?'

'She's a harpist.'

Hayes smirked. 'Not part of the Blues, then?'

'Roma lives at the house with us but Roz books her dates, two afternoons at the Palm Court in Port Erin, and she does a lot of private do's, weddings, cocktail parties and stuff.'

They moved into the cool interior of the cabin and DeeDee pulled a robe over her bikini. Hayes eyed her furtively as she bobbed about in the kitchen fixing sandwiches and fetching two small bottles of sparkling water from the fridge. He gazed around the cabin with interest, its interior decorated in a folksy style, unvarnished wooden furniture blending with polished floorboards cosied up with rag rugs.

'This is nice,' he said as she passed him a plate of ham sandwiches and a bottle of Evian. 'Phil's a decent sort of employer, laying on a bolthole like this for the band.'

'The men don't use it much but I sometimes stay overnight just to get a bit of peace.' She nodded towards a put-you-up settee against the wall. 'The crowd at the house is pretty friendly but Roz can get on your tits. Bloody woman's always trying to push us into extra bookings. I already do a regular stint at the casino as well as fitting in with Phil's idea of "strictly ballroom".'

'Roz takes a commission on the bookings?'

'You bet she does. Makes a mint out of Roma for a start, but at least she's kept Phil's show on tour. Without Roz – as she never ceases to remind us – Bailey and the Blues would have been off the road years ago. Tell me, Rog, what's a guy like you doing here? Not exactly your sort of place, I'd say.' She lit a cigarette and momentarily disappeared behind a haze of smoke.

'I had an accident,' he brusquely retorted.

'Thought you looked a bit peaky. What happened?'

'A mugging. Let's talk about it later.' He rose and brushed off the crumbs. 'I'd better push off. Thanks for the break, DeeDee – perhaps we could have dinner one evening? Does Phil give you a night off occasionally?'

'Sundays. But on Sunday nights I'm booked in at the casino for a double session, which only leaves time for an early supper between shows. Say, seven o'clock?'

'Great. Tomorrow night, then. I'll pick you up there. Want to dine in or is there somewhere nearby you like?'

'I'd better stay put, my get-up would look freaky in daylight. There's a cafe on the ground floor which serves good food round the clock.'

'Formal?'

'Black tie only on Saturday nights or gala evenings but a suit's OK. I'll look forward to it,' she said, her eyes starry. Hayes guessed that young DeeDee Miller got pretty bored with back-to-back gigs with Phil's outfit, which seemed to leave little space for a girl like her to have any fun.

He cycled back to the tennis courts, locked his bike in the shed and made his way to the locker room for a shower and a change of clothes. Saturday afternoon was probably the worst time to try to track down the editor of the local paper but with yet another mugging putting out one of Bill Caxton's club members, any lively newsman would still have his nose to the grindstone, surely?

He was in luck. The newspaper office operated seven days a week and his insistence on seeing Marty Lewis at the behest of Bill Caxton did the trick.

The girl on the reception desk took his card through to a back office and made a discreet phone call. When it came to reporters, it was helpful to have a warrant card as a backup; impressing on Mr Lewis the necessity to keep Hayes' professional identity secret would have to come later.

Thirteen

Hayes followed the girl upstairs to the newsroom, which was deserted apart from a cleaner working her way between the desks. Marty Lewis stood at the open door of his office, holding out his hand in greeting.

'Ah, Mr Hayes. Welcome. Your first visit to the Isle of Man?' He ushered in his visitor and, closing the door behind them, offered Hayes a seat at a circular meetings table set apart in the narrow leg of the L-shaped room.

Marty Lewis was a far cry from the scruffy reporters Hayes had encountered in the course of his investigations in rural Buckinghamshire: the man had the strong build of a rugby forward, his bull-like neck thrust forward in a gesture Hayes imagined could easily turn belligerent. But on this occasion Lewis was Mr Affability himself and Hayes decided to play it straight, or perhaps, more accurately, as straight as was minimally necessary.

Lewis wore the khaki linen trousers of a lightweight suit, the jacket draped over the back of his chair behind the desk. A dark brown shirt looked expensive and chimed with the gold cufflinks glittering at his cuffs.

'Sorry to bother you at the weekend, Mr Lewis, but Bill reckoned you might spare me some time to run over these muggings he's worried about.'

'No problem. We go to print Thursdays, so unless there's a big story only a small staff stays on duty at weekends. I'm only here myself because of the attack on Charlie Lyons. He's a friend of both Bill and myself so when I got Bill's call about your interest in these muggings I thought I'd better do some overtime and get the facts on paper. Didn't expect you this afternoon, though, Bill said you're on sick leave. A chief inspector no less – something of a busman's holiday for you, looking into our little local difficulty, isn't it?'

Hayes squared up to his informer, far from certain who was questioning whom. 'I was mugged myself, Mr Lewis. Stabbed. Lucky to survive a vicious attack. Naturally, the growing violence on the streets, even on an island like this, interests me.'

'You were on duty?'

'No. Returning to my car after an evening in London, the scenario identical to that of the victims on your list. Nothing was stolen in my case, the attack was interrupted, but from Bill's account he says the victims here were successfully robbed after possibly being lured into quiet backstreets. What's your take on this, Mr Lewis?'

'Marty. Please. Frankly I was not convinced by Bill's insistence that these men were targeted. There is a thread, probably coincidental, but perhaps, if I go over the list with you, matters will seem clearer. Your "interest" as you call it is not a professional one, I hope? I would not wish to be accused of interfering in a police investigation.'

'I have an understandable curiosity about the series of muggings which have happened here, of course. A new phenomenon, I imagine? Not the sort of robbery common during the season, tourists knocked over the head after dark?'

Lewis leaned back and regarded Hayes with an unblinking eye. 'Funnily enough, crime on the island is low key, bearing in mind we have a proportion of wealthy residents who, in any other context, would be regarded as rich pickings. Burglary figures are low, possibly because the more attractive properties are expertly alarmed, those with the most to lose often new residents who have retired here from abroad or from major cities in the UK and give home security priority. But Bill is right in one way, the poor devils who've been mugged this summer are all members of his sports club and, even with discreet reportage, we have had to print details which any discerning resident would instantly recognize.'

'But two deaths?'

'The first, Derek Fields, the bloke who died last year, is a doubtful one.'

'The heart-attack victim? The sixty-six-year-old squash player who died the following day?'

'Mm. I knew Derek, played golf with him, and I cannot discount that the stress factor must have played some part in his death, but from a dispassionate point of view he was barely slapped around, and as he refused to report the attack, the coroner took a generous decision about the cause of death. The names of the others are interesting, though.'

Lewis produced a typewritten sheet from a file on the table before him. He passed it over, keeping a copy for himself, and Hayes swiftly scanned the list of names.

'The one last year, Derek Fields, we've already put aside as questionable though he was undoubtedly attacked, and from what he mumbled when he was picked up, the thugs match descriptions quoted by this year's victims: a skinny teenager and a heavier accomplice wearing a balaclava. The muggings started again at Easter this year but there may have been others which were not reported.'

Hayes raised a hand. 'Sorry to interrupt, Marty, but what gives you that idea? Do you suspect an homophobic element here?'

'Not necessarily. Kerb-crawling or approaching prostitutes is professional dynamite whether they're rent boys or fluffy bunnies, and it gets doubly complicated if your wife learns about it from a police investigation. The situations were similar, all the attacks occurred late at night in backstreets frequented by hookers *and* transsexuals. It's a game which the authorities prefer to ignore but it happens even here.'

'Are you serious? I thought this island was the last place to support that sort of sex trade.'

'Don't you believe it. The summer season attracts all sorts and vice can be a popular diversion for tourists.'

'But these guys are residents according to the details on that list of yours. And the latest victim is a friend of yours.

Off the record, do you have any idea why he was mooching about the Cut?'

If Marty Lewis had an opinion about Charlie Lyons, the bloke in hospital with a sore head, he wasn't giving anything away. After a moment Hayes continued, 'Bill told me Mr Lyons had undergone an expensive divorce. Does his ex still live on the island? Perhaps she could enlighten us.'

Lewis let out a loud guffaw. 'Our Belinda? You bet she does – got herself a ranch-style place a couple of miles outside Peel. Marrying Charlie was as good as winning the lottery. Why would she move back to Liverpool? No, Belinda's settled in nicely, rumour has it she's starting up as a party planner. Plenty of scope here, a flourishing social life if that's what you like and Charlie introduced her to all the import-ant people. She's in the book if you're interested in a rags-to-riches story,' he said with a lift of the eyebrow, 'she may get there again,' he said with a lift of the eyebrow, 'she may get bored with the small circle of partygoers on the island and cast her net elsewhere when the novelty wears off.'

Hayes mentally put Charlie Lyons in his pending file and concentrated on the dead man on Marty's list.

'Francis Formby-Smith, age thirty-two, stockbroker and serious poker player according to your notes. Known locally?'

'A part-time resident, had a financial interest in the airline but inherited a bumper stake from his father and used it, quite successfully I understand, to play all the hot spots including Las Vegas.'

'No cash found on the body, it says here. And he died after putting up a fight. No one heard a thing?'

'Apparently not.'

'Also attacked in the Cut?'

'Yes.'

'But he could have got a girl into his car without the hassle of kerb-crawling, surely?'

Marty Lewis looked grave. 'He was on foot. And he was a cosmopolitan, fully aware of the risks of being bundled in a dark alley. In your experience, Mr Hayes, isn't the problem that these guys have is that compulsive risk-taking, gambling as a way of life becomes addictive, not only for money, which Formby-Smith had in shedloads, but also for sex? The frisson of living dangerously, picking up a girl on the street, risking God knows what health-wise and socially to get your rocks off must present higher and higher stakes.'

'You knew this guy?'

'By sight. I'd seen him at the casino on gala nights when the management lobbed hospitality my way, but I don't swim in the same waters as big hitters like that.'

'He was unmarried?'

'A professional bachelor. A brilliant match for one of our nubile young ladies, all the ambitious mothers practically wet themselves if he so much as glanced at their debutante daughters.'

Hayes sighed. 'What about these others? All rich? All advertising their availability on the dark streets?'

Marty ran through the list, encapsulating the relevant points, pointing out the characters most likely to open up to Hayes if he took an interest.

'The police seem to have written off these random attacks. Most didn't argue, handed over their wallets and suffered only minor injuries.'

'Sensible chaps!' Hayes murmured with feeling. 'I notice you've put telephone numbers by each name. Do you think they'd be willing to contribute to my little survey of mugging victims?'

'Most of them are suffering from dented pride, with hindsight wishing they'd been more heroic, so sharing the guilt with you will probably be cathartic.'

'You OK with me contacting them?'

'Providing you keep your source of information confidential. I'm as keen as anyone to put a stop to this spate of thuggery, especially since poor old Charlie got nobbled. I'd no great feeling for Formby-Smith but violence is bad for tourism and I love this island. We don't deserve to suffer

57

from the creeping criminality which people come here to escape.'

They spent a further forty minutes dissecting Lewis's notes and parted on more amicable terms than the initial sparring match.

Hayes drove back to Finch House in a thoughtful mood, and let himself into his snug little flat with a feeling of homecoming. At least Bailey and his bloody Blues would be out for the night and, if he kept his head down, he might escape further participation in their wind-down party games.

Fourteen

Hayes decided to stroll down to the village for a fish-and-chip supper, forcing himself to take the cliff walk and follow the flight of steps leading to the harbour. By the time he located the cafe he felt exhausted, confirming his suspicion that a full recovery would not be as swift as he had cheerfully imagined.

Seagulls wheeled overhead and their harsh cries echoed the ructions of tired children unwillingly dragged off the beach and back for tea and baths. The sky had paled to a washed-out indigo, one more perfect sunset moving relentlessly towards the horizon where a few dark clouds gathered like insolent harbingers of rain.

Port St Agnes was hemmed in between the cliffs and the sea, with a small sandy beach now all but swallowed up by the incoming tide. A row of cottages, mostly with No Vacancies cards in their windows, lined the main street, and, apart from a pub and a general store, whose proprietor was already moving the sand buckets and spades, lilos and postcard stands back inside, the commercialization of this outpost of the Manx tourist industry had remained undeveloped.

Brenda's Tea Rooms were enjoying an early evening rush, the tables crowded with sunburnt parents and kids noisily demanding Brenda's chips. Hayes hesitated at the door, quickly stepping aside to allow a middle-aged man with an aromatic packet of delights to emerge.

The man paused. 'You're Bill's friend Roger, aren't you? We met last night. Karl Brecht, the bass player – don't you remember?'

They moved out onto the pavement, Hayes ransacking his added wits. 'Er, well, forgive me, Karl, but I'm still a bit hazy about last night. I was going in here for a bite of supper but it looks busy. I'd better check out the pub menu instead. Pity. Your supper,' he said, tapping Karl's steaming parcel, 'is mouth-watering.'

'*Ja*. Brenda's a byword here. Look, Roger, I'm in a bit of a rush, Phil likes us to be on the road by seven, why don't I jump the queue and order a takeaway for you? Brenda's a mate, knows I work nights, and, as a regular, lets me cut through the passing trade and get served right away. We could eat back at my place, if you like.'

'You sure?'

'Cod and chips?'

'Great. I'll wait for you out here, shall I? But I walked down to the beach, you go ahead.'

'I've got my bike. If you're happy to ride pillion, we can be back in two shakes.'

Relieved of the prospect of a stiff climb back up to the cliff path, Hayes hopped on the back of Karl's Suzuki like a superannuated Hell's Angel and they were indeed settled in Karl's flat at Finch House in the promised two shakes.

His rooms were more spacious than Hayes' studio apartment, and overlooked the front drive, the walls pinned with amateur shots of birds in flight. Divested of his leathers Karl was showing his age, fiftysomething at a guess but wearing the indelible tide marks of a sixties swinger. His arms were closely tattooed, and although he was of below average height, the impression was of a remarkably fit individual with the saving grace of a full head of hair, a greying beard and startling blue eyes of undiminished sex appeal.

Karl cleared a table of notebooks, old CDs and a pair of powerful binoculars before Hayes could satisfy his curiosity, and they settled down to piled plates of fish and chips with a gut-wrenching selection of sauce bottles, mustard and pickles on the side. Karl set up some background music: gentle stuff, blues numbers and finally an interesting disc he insisted was a private recording of Woody Allen's jazz combo featuring a clarinet spot allegedly tootled by the old wizard himself.

'Over seventy now,' Karl remarked. 'I met him once, playing a club in New York. Impressive little guy but private, not like the normal Hollywood star at all.'

Hayes detected a faint accent. German? Swiss? Dutch? 'You play double bass with the Blues, you said. Been with Phil long?'

Karl laughed. 'For ever. Terrible arrangements, terrible old songs but a good man, something rare these days in the cut-and-thrust game we're in. If it wasn't for Roz, Phil and I would be retired by now, redundant as down-at-heel old brothel-creepers.'

'Roz is the live-wire agent, I hear. Second wife?'

'They got together after a New Year's Eve Millennium party at the Villa Marina. Poor old Phil didn't stand a chance. Like a beer, Rog? Or something stronger?'

Karl cleared the table and checked his watch. 'We've got plenty of time – coffee for me, I need the caffeine to keep me swinging for the rest of the night. Saturday's a bugger, fancy dress do every week at El Gringo's, a bloody awful venue full of boozers. No style at all but the manager's a pal of Roz's and tops up the fees with ciggies and gin.'

He rolled up a spliff and offered one to Hayes, who politely declined, po-faced, wishing Superintendent Waller could see him now, a sure-fire recommendation for a job as under-cover narcotics cop.

The air filled with a jungly haze, taking Hayes back in time to dim beer cellars and student digs where the circuit of weed seemed to elevate every banal conversation to a plane of Zen-like intelligence. He smiled, and, pointing to the photographs pinned to the wall, said, 'You a bird-fancier, Karl?'

'My hobby. I've got this fantastic camera, telephoto lens, the lot. Print my own negs in the laundry room in the base-ment. Once you get up in the hills here, the bird life is stupen-dous. I hit a snag last week, though.' He let out a hoot of laughter. 'You've been to the Spa hotel, I suppose. Seen the lake there? Brilliant. On a quiet evening you'd be amazed at the wildlife in the bulrushes, blow your mind it would. I borrow a little rowing boat hidden up there behind the cabins.'

'What happened? You fall in?'

'Hell, no. I rowed over to the far side and hid myself in the undergrowth hoping to get a shot of a barn owl and her brood who've hatched from a nest in the old boathouse. I'm just focusing on the bloody fledglings when who comes into the picture but two bints, starkers, having it off on the jetty.'

'Two women?'

Karl took a slow drag on his roll-up and eyed Hayes with the hypnotic stare of the ancient mariner.

'And?' Hayes persisted.

'Well, I wasn't going to let that go, was I? Let off six or seven shots with my zoom lens.'

Hayes began to wonder if accepting Karl's hospitality was such a good idea. Sharing voyeuristic fantasies with a middle-aged peeping Tom was not first choice for a fun evening. 'You said you hit a snag. Foul up the processing?'

'Not on your life! Like to see them?'

'Not a lot. I've seen naked ladies in the bushes before.'

'Not these two, you haven't. Who do you think it was? Here,' he said, extracting an envelope from under a pile of motorbike manuals and passing it over. 'What d'ya think, Rog?'

Hayes reluctantly accepted the prize and opened the envelope. The shots were, he had to admit, of professional standard and with a certain artistic merit in the circumstances. The pale bodies of two women lay entwined on the deck, the waist-length tresses of the dark one spreading peek-a-boo over the pubescent breasts of a young girl. The scene, though mildly erotic, was hardly in the porno class.

'Lucky you, Karl,' he said drily, passing the envelope back to his host.

Karl grew excited. 'But you've missed the bloody point, Roger. You didn't recognize them, did you?'

'Should I?'

'Well, maybe not. You're new here. But I was knocked right off my perch, believe me. The big brunette on top here,' he said, stabbing at the photograph, 'is Roz.'

'Phil's wife?'

'Yeah! And the kid is that harp-player friend of hers, Roma. They weren't at the party last night but you'll see Roma around – she links up with the drummer, Dean Driscoll, and his wife, Marie, at weekends. They're a young couple, and have taken her up like she needed rescuing from the oldies or something. Take her on picnics, to Sunday night discos, the lot. Joke is Roma's no kid – looks underage but I know for a fact she's twenty-four, I saw her Equity card when I was poking through Roz's desk in the office looking for my contract, checking up the small print in case Roz had slipped in some nasty little clause which sees me off at the end of the season. Not that I care. I've got this place in Chamonix I let out in the summer, which keeps me afloat. I use it myself all winter, skiing keeps me fit. But, hey, look at the time, I've got to get changed. Sorry to push you out, Rog, but it's been good having you over. P'raps we could do this again some time?'

'Yeah, sure. My treat.'

Hayes awkwardly extracted himself from Karl's sofa, feeling strangely light-headed.

Fifteen

Hayes woke early and got a weather forecast from the radio farming news. The threatened rain had slid off the chart and it looked like being another cloudless day.

The house was silent, Phil's band clearly having a sleep-in. In fact, after just one weekend at Finch House, he had already sussed out the routine: late start, afternoon dispersal to rehearsals or individual escape routes beyond Roz's control, followed by a noisy mass departure about seven and an even noisier return after midnight when they cooked a communal supper, smooched to late-night mood music and, if the alcohol was flowing freely, the decibels grew in volume until the early hours.

Hayes reckoned he could pick his way between this predictable programme but Sunday, their day off, was an unknown quantity. Presumably the girls caught up with their laundry and topped up their suntans and the guys just slept off yet another week on Phil's treadmill. Roz seemed to be the galvanizing factor, and even through the closed doors of his bolthole on the top floor her strident tones could be heard all over the building. He decided to make himself scarce for the day and packed up all the press cuttings and the notes pressed upon him by Bill Caxton and the editor, Marty Lewis, and sloped off down the back stairs to reclaim his car.

The open countryside beckoned beguilingly, misty hills and picturesque coves flashing past like pictures in a holiday brochure as he headed inland, a line of ponies trekking in the distance confirming his growing acceptance that sick leave was probably no bad thing. A stay here would never have occurred to him in the normal course of events, and he had to admit he could remember no recent vacation which had not involved passport, ski-wear and a frantic pursuit of 'leisure'. He ruefully acknowledged that 'leisure' was something he had, over the years, lost the hang of, but getting a knife in the ribs seemed a dramatic method of forcing him to take stock.

He pulled into a lay-by and studied the map. A by-road a mile further on led to an archaeological site which sounded interesting but, from the notes in his guide books, an ancient burial ground was probably not sufficiently riveting to attract too many visitors on a glorious day when the sandy beaches would surely exert priority appeal. He drove on and discovered the clearing, appropriately silent as the grave. He felt a frisson of disquiet as he laid out the car rug on the grass, as if the place had an haunted quality, a sensitivity he was reluctant to put a name to and ascribed to an overactive imagination fuelled by Caxton's superstitious tales of Manx trolls or whatever.

He cracked open a bottle of Budweiser and settled down to examine the mounds of reportage these unlucky victims had generated.

The ages of the unfortunates varied, the youngest being Francis Formby-Smith, thirty-two, the professional poker player who had paid with his life only a month before. The oldest, Derek Fields, sixty-six, was the man who had suffered a fatal coronary the previous year following an encounter with the muggers. The other four reported attacks occurred earlier this season, all men, all members of Caxton's sports complex, and all having lost only cash. Quite considerable sums, if they were to be believed, which only reinforced Hayes' conviction that the muggers were local tearaways buoyed up with the ease of relieving these rich bastards of their wallets.

But why carry so much cash? To pay off a hooker? Hardly credible. Even by Soho standards such large payoffs would be generous. One victim, a hairdresser called Terry Porlock, claimed to have lost over a grand. And why put yourself at risk in a dark alley? With a fistful of readies, Hayes imagined any up-market escort agency could provide suitable excitement within the discreet portals of a hotel.

The police seemed to have elicited no answers to these questions and persuading the victims to open up to a fellow-sufferer such as himself was unlikely to shake out any embarrassing secrets.

Hayes shuffled through the reports, growing ever more impatient with the sloppy police investigation. Pushing aside any bad publicity likely to harm the image of the island as a safe family holiday resort might work in the case of sporadic beatings, but here were at least seven men hit over the head and terrorized in apparently random hold-ups by kids or, if not teenagers, by amateur villains high on their unchallenged success. No guns were involved, no knives brandished, it all seemed a very odd style of robbery, the only men to suffer serious injury being those who had fought back, Formby-Smith paying the ultimate price.

Caxton's conviction that these attacks were some sort of scheme to give his members the frights and ultimately render his business vulnerable to a takeover was ludicrous. In all his years with the service Hayes had never come across such a convoluted plan to gain a commercial foothold – but then, what did he know? According to Caxton the island enjoyed special status, British but not in the UK, and the Manx finance industry attracted wealthy residents and a gold-plated advantage taxwise.

Hayes sighed, and tossed off the rest of the beer before shoving the papers back in the folder and, stretching out on the grass with his hands behind his head, gazed up at the limitless blue where a pair of swallows swooped overhead in a blurred circuit of avian aeronautics.

The best move would be to see the latest victim, Charlie Lyons, who was still hospitalized and who, with the mugging fresh in his mind, might open up to a stranger with a similar story to tell. But perhaps a word with the ex-wife would be more enlightening and, at least, give him an insight into the personality of this sixty-two-year-old chancer lured into the Cut after a bit of tail. Belinda Belville? Hayes rolled the syllables on his tongue, anticipating the sort of showgirl who had netted a silly old fellow in his sunset years. It was a familiar enough story but, human nature being what it was, Bill Caxton could have painted a rosy picture of his old friend. For all anyone knew, Charlie Lyons had been a wife-beater . . . .

He dozed off in the sunshine, waking to the excited arrival of a party of ramblers who loudly laid out picnics between the headstones and were clearly settling down to a well-earned break. Hayes scrambled up, responded amiably to their hearty greetings, grabbed his rug and scuttled back to the car.

He returned to Finch House in time to shower and smarten himself up for his date with DeeDee at the casino.

The place was hardly heaving, but a quiet elegance gave a pleasant first impression which encouraged Hayes to reconsider his preconceived idea of casinos gained solely from James Bond movies. He had abandoned his little runabout to the care of valet parking and strolled through to the cocktail lounge where DeeDee was performing.

The room was shaded by thick velvet drapes, DeeDee's piano spotlit against a background of potted hydrangeas, her silver lamé dress gleaming in the subdued lighting, her thin brown arms poised above the keyboard, her smile lighting up as she caught Hayes' eye.

She sang a toned-down version of an Edith Piaf number, her delicate fingering drawing out a tinkling accompaniment all but drowned by the chatter of the clientele. Hayes moved to a lamplit table nearer the piano, raising a hand in sincere appreciation at the end of the song. Dee-Dee grinned and vamped it up with a livelier rendering of 'C'est si Bon', which also sank without trace under the background murmur of the happy-hour crowd.

He ordered a whisky and water – 'No ice,' he muttered as he scribbled a note on the back of the wine-tariff card propped against the table light. 'For the pianist,' he said to the waiter, smiling across the room at DeeDee, her tiny figure almost obscured by the concert grand the casino felt appropriate for their cabaret star.

DeeDee paused and accepted his note.

'You're much too beautiful for this place. And *much* too talented. *A bientôt.*'

Sixteen

Over supper DeeDee suggested they spend the next afternoon at the cabin. 'Roz is off to Manchester for a couple of days to see her accountant and Roma works teatime at the Palm Court on Mondays so she won't be around either.'

'How about lunch at the spa? I've an appointment with the trainer at eleven to sort out my exercise plan but I could drop you at the cabin and meet you there later.'

'No can do. I'm at the rehearsal studio all morning with Jimmy O'Dell, the other vocalist. We're working up some new arrangements, a few thirties numbers and a couple of duets.'

'I haven't met Jimmy, have I?' Hayes said, his identification of individual band members based only on the hazy recollection of Saturday night's party and the distant view from his upper-floor window of musicians crowding into the minibus.

'Once seen never forgotten,' she replied with a wink. 'No, probably not. Jimmy's young, gay and very good-looking. Keeps his distance from Phil if he can. Phil can't stand gays, he's old-fashioned like that, calls Jim "Queenie" behind his back, but Jimmy's a great vocalist and plays the sax like a dream. One of Roz's finds, of course. She spotted him singing in some dive in London and, according to Karl Brecht, paid Jimmy big bucks to sign up for a season with the Blues.'

'But he's good, you say?'

'Flexible. Can croon like Sinatra or jazz up one of Karl's standards on his saxophone to inject some pizzazz into Phil's idea of the Blues style.'

'You like him.'

'Yeah, why not? I've got no problem with gays and Jimmy's a great musician, wasting his time with Phil's outfit but Roz upped the ante to rope him in and Jimmy's a real asset. I'm no fan of Roz's but, to give her her due, she's a brilliant agent and knows exactly what the hotels and clubs on the island are looking for.'

'Roz lives here?'

'Not really. The rehearsal studio in Douglas has its own bedsit, which I've heard she occasionally uses after a late-night session, but Phil has a house in Manchester where he goes for the winter while Roz buzzes round the country booking clients and sourcing talent.'

'Well, what do you think, DeeDee? How long will you be rehearsing?'

She shrugged. 'Can't say for sure. We're starting at ten but there's a lot to get through and Jimmy's a bit of a perfectionist. Why don't you drop by after your workout at the gym? The studio's tucked away in a backstreet behind the theatre, Petty's Yard, you can't miss it.'

Hayes brightened. 'I wouldn't be in the way? Perhaps I could help? Give me a music score and I'm in heaven.'

DeeDee shook her head in disbelief. 'You're kidding! You sight-read?'

'Listen, baby,' he answered in a hoarse whisper à la Bogart, 'given the tiniest bit of encouragement I'd even turn the pages for you.'

Hayes was not joking. This sudden fascination for the girl had hit him hard. And she wasn't even his type! Skinny arms and a scatty personality to boot, a crazy streak totally at odds with her astonishing talent. He wondered if the glancing blow to his head that he had sustained in the tussle with Georgina Paget's muggers had loosened a nut or two, left him vulnerable to her big brown eyes and fascinating insouciance?

He grew serious. 'What's your part with the Blues, DeeDee? When you're not doing your solo act at the casino?'

'Mostly just vocalist, but I can pump away at the electric organ when the rest take a break. We're not exactly *Top of the Pops* material but Roz knows what the punters want and it seems to pay off.'

'How long have you been with Phil?'

'Just this season. Roz caught my act on a cruise liner and I was tempted to jump ship. But I won't be signing up for another season. If I've made enough dosh I'm thinking of taking a job in Berlin with an outfit a mate of mine has set up.'

'Sounds exciting. Where's your family?'

'Glasgow, but I'm hardly ever at home. The Gipsy life suits me. And you? What do you do, Roger?'

'I'm between jobs just now. I'm thinking of settling in London when this break is over, but it's too early to say.'

A girl in a tuxedo signalled to DeeDee from the door and she rose to go.

'Can I wait for you after?' he said.

'Thanks, but it's OK, I've got my car. But you will come tomorrow, won't you, sweetie? Come to the rehearsal rooms whenever it suits you, Jimmy won't mind, he loves an audience. But no need to advertise it, though, those nosy buggers back at the house are always ready to put the boot in for me with Roz and I'm not her favourite bunny at the best of times.'

As soon as he'd paid the bill he followed her through to the cocktail lounge and soaked in DeeDee's soulful rendering of an old Billie Holiday number before quietly slipping away.

The lyrics echoed in his brain as he drove back to Port St Agnes. 'Strange fruit . . .' Yeah, DeeDee Miller was a strange fruit all right, a bittersweet exotic and strangely addictive. Hayes thrust this worrying notion aside and stepped on the accelerator, arriving back to find only Kevin, the odd-job man, in the courtyard, changing a wheel on Phil's Rover.

He sauntered over. 'Need any help, Kev?'

'Nah. Nearly done. Phil's paranoid about his bloody motor, convinced someone's spiking his tyres. Truth is his steering's all over the place, he's forever skidding off road, thinks he's driving a bleeding tractor.'

Hayes watched him finish the job and then bounded up the back stairs to enjoy an hour or two's quiet relaxation before Phil Bailey and the Blues crashed back into orbit for their late-night supper.

It was, he decided, a commune of sorts. Communal work, communal play and, for all he knew, communal love-ins.

Seventeen

Hayes' plan for an early night was rudely interrupted by a knock at the door just as he had sorted out his TV options. It was Karl Brecht bearing gifts.

'Hey, come on in. What have we here?' Hayes enthused, taking an unfragrant parcel from the hands of his unexpected guest. 'Fish?'

Karl followed him through. '*Ja*, mackerel. I took a boat out in the bay and got lucky. You fish?'

'Not for years. Sounds great.' Hayes moved to the kitchen counter, unwrapped the newspaper and revealed two silver mackerel, bright-eyed and so fresh that they looked all but ready to leap into the sink.

'We'll get together next time, *ja?*'

'Wonderful. Like a drink, Karl? Vodka? Wine? Beer? I'm all stocked up.'

'How about a night on the town? I was just leaving – Sunday night in Douglas is my only chance to sample the local talent.'

Hayes hesitated. Was Karl proposing a stag run?

'I'd better come clean, chum. I'm on sick leave, no sort of stamina for clubbing.'

'*Ach* no, just a pleasant excursion, introduce you to some decent entertainment, eh? We'll take the bike.'

There didn't seem any answer to that and, after thrusting Karl's catch in the fridge, Hayes followed him through the silent house to the front drive.

'It's very quiet, Karl. Everyone out?'

'Sunday's the only chance we get to break out. Roz

generally keeps an eye on us, doesn't want any trouble on the island, but when the cat's away . . .' he said with a wide grin.

Karl wheeled the Suzuki onto the drive, Hayes climbed aboard and they roared off in the gathering dusk towards the bright lights of Douglas. Karl wore what Hayes guessed must be his idea of funky leisure wear: a bomber jacket, cowboy boots, distressed jeans straining over a muscular rear end and a black T-shirt bearing Gothic lettering.

Hayes grinned. Funny to be taken under the wing of a middle-aged double-bass player who seemed to think that the new guy at Finch House was a potential soulmate. But perhaps Brecht had the right idea, they certainly presented like a couple of oddballs within the trad company of the Blues.

Karl stowed the bike well away from the designated parking spaces at the rear of the Griffin, a private club it would seem from the bouncer doing sentry duty at the door. Hayes transferred his wallet to an inside pocket and trusted that the burly presence of his host would preserve his barely mended stab wounds from fresh assault.

In fact, Hayes had got the wrong end of the stick entirely: as soon as they had negotiated the steps down to the basement fun area he realized that the Griffin was no seedy dive but an up-market club where Karl was a familiar face. The manager hurried over and greeted him with a manly hug and, after a spirited exchange in German, Karl introduced his guest, who was doing his best to acclimatize to the blinking disco lights flashing over the tiny dance floor and the surrounding gloom where individual tables were crowded with indistinguishable figures.

Karl snaked a path to a corner booth and greeted two pals who moved aside to make room for the newcomers. He thrust Hayes forward. 'Meet my friend Roger, he's staying at the house with the band.' Hayes shook hands all round, Karl's companions appearing, even in the dimness, as bright-eyed and surprisingly sober, sipping their wine like ladies at a tea dance. Hayes's anxieties about being dragged into a binge-drinking night out evaporated in the smoke-filled atmosphere and he plumped himself down and insisted on ordering a fresh bottle. 'Nice place this, you guys regulars?'

'Only decent club on the island. Best food for miles and bloody good entertainment.'

Hayes' eyes had gradually got used to the lighting and it became all too apparent that the place was a gay bar. Karl settled down with the menu and left Hayes to socialize. 'I'm afraid I didn't catch your name,' he said, addressing the older of the two seated at their table, a thin-faced guy with designer stubble, wearing an Arctic-white vest which emphasized his impressive tan.

'Terry Porlock,' he replied, 'and my friend here is Benny.' Benny sheepishly grinned but said nothing and Karl butted in to pass round the menu. 'Sausage and mash do you boys?'

Hayes hastened to excuse himself. 'Actually, I've already eaten, Karl, but you guys go ahead. What can I order in the way of drinks?'

After a brief discussion, the waiter took the order and the foursome settled down, the conversation level now made more accessible by the substitution of the DJ by a stand-up comic who struggled against a wall of indifferent back-ground chat to make himself heard.

'And what brings you to the island, Roger?'

'Believe it or not, convalescence. I'm on sick leave. A mugging. I was stabbed.'

His words fell like a stone, even Karl's china blue eyes widening. 'You don't say!'

The sun-worshipper – whose name Hayes had quickly realized was all too familiar from Marty Lewis's list of victims – eyed him with alarm. 'You're another victim of the Phantom Duo?'

'What? Oh, you mean the attacks here on the island? No, I was rolled in London and when I got out of hospital a friend recommended the Caxton Spa and I'm settling in for a few weeks to get fit.'

Terry turned on Karl. 'You told Roger about my run-in with our local villains?'

'No, of course not, Terry. In fact, I'm as surprised as you – I had no idea Roger had been mugged. It's the first I've heard about it, no one knew at the house, did they, Rog?'

Hayes shrugged. 'Nothing to be proud of. A couple of hoodies got the better of me – I was lucky to survive.'

Terry sipped his wine. 'Two teenagers? Were they caught?'

'Got clear away.'

'Happens everywhere,' Terry's sidekick put in. 'Lose all your cash, Roger?'

'They were interrupted.'

Terry's eyes narrowed. 'Lucky you. You may not have heard about our local tearaways but I got mugged only last week. My day's takings,' he said bitterly, 'I run a unisex hairdresser's, a cash business, and, stupidly, I had a roll of fifties on me that I hadn't got around to banking.'

'Bad luck. But you weren't hurt?'

'Caught me on the hop, but let's talk about something else. What's your line, Roger? Ever thought of settling on the island? It's a great place; lovely scenery, clean air and a standard income-tax rate of ten per cent with no capital-gains taxes and home to some of the UK's wealthiest tax exiles.'

The waiter returned with a tray of bangers and mash and the diners set to with relish. Hayes sipped his wine and debated how best to handle Terry Porlock. His story was full of holes. Why set out late at night with the day's takings in your back pocket, for God's sake? The man was obviously no fool but his account of the mugging was begging to be shot down in flames.

He decided to throw out a fresh line. 'Ever thought of extending your own investment, Terry? Going into the hotel business, say?'

'Mass tourism's taken a dive since cheap package tours to Spain came in. The island's more attractive to higher-spending visitors and wealthy residents these days, Roger. Folk come here for a break, like what they see and end up buying property. There are plans to introduce a zero rate of income tax for all businesses pretty soon and I wouldn't mind having a crack at the film industry starting up here. Local people have been renting out their properties for locations and several high-class productions have already been filmed here. You got capital stuck in a void, Roger?'

'Casinos are more my line. Any possibility of extending the trade here? There's only one casino and very nice too, but with cash burning a hole in rich residents' pockets maybe there's room for more. What do you think, Terry?'

He shook his head. 'No chance. One outlet is enough for the locals to stomach and we've already a stake in online gambling. Forget it, Roger. But this new film industry is interesting. Let's get together and talk numbers one night, eh?'

Benny had finished his meal and was eyeing the dance floor with interest, the stand-up routine now replaced by a cross-dressing vocalist with an overflowing bust and chandelier earrings. Aware of Benny's flagging attention to all the financial talk, Terry suddenly pulled the lad onto the dance floor and left Hayes and Karl to finish the wine.

Hayes glanced at his watch. 'Not wishing to spoil your evening, Karl, I think, if you don't mind, I'll go outside and get a cab.' He touched his chest. 'My ribs are playing up. OK by you?'

Karl frowned, all concern. '*Ja*, sure. You should have told me about the stabbing, man. I'd no idea. Can I run you back?'

They rose, Karl's face creased with anxiety.

'No, stay, it's your only night out all week. I'll see you in the morning. Thanks for a great time, I appreciate it.'

He weaved a path through the tables and went into the gents. The brightly lit interior was spotless, the tiled surfaces and sparkling mirrors a credit to a management patently aware of the money-spinning potential of the gay element even on an island famed for its reputation as a family holiday venue. A leather-clad guy was bending over the sink as he entered and turned a calm eye on Hayes as he locked himself in a cubicle. Hayes soundlessly climbed onto the toilet seat and, above the door, watched the bloke snort a line of cocaine. He waited until the man completed his routine, wiped the glazed surface and casually washed his hands before leaving. Hayes flushed the cistern and slipped away, finding himself back on the dark street, alone with the bouncer.

'Where's the best place to catch a cab?'

The muscle man grinned. 'Wait here, sir, we don't want you loose on your own around here. I'll be back.' He jogged to the corner and let out an ear-splitting whistle. With minutes he returned with a taxi and Hayes was bundled inside like precious cargo. Clearly, the management was in no hurry to expose their vulnerable members to yet more random assaults from the muggers Marty Lewis's local rag had headlined the Phantom Duo.

Hayes relaxed in the dark interior and wished he was more familiar with the scene. Bill Caxton had no idea how difficult it would be for a stranger to unravel local crime and almost impossible to link a series of muggings with any supposed plan to place the Spa at risk.

Eighteen

Hayes emerged next morning earlier than usual but found at least one of his fellow tenants had beaten him to it. A row was in full swing in the courtyard, an estate car clarted up to its axles in mud blocking the exit, and Kevin in a dangerous mood.

'I'm not doing it, Roma, and that's flat. Just look at it! You been on a motocross, kid? It'd take me all morning to scrape off all that bloody filth. Take it into Port Erin and get a power wash.'

The girl stood her ground, trembling with emotion. 'You *owe* me, Kevin! I've told you – I haven't time to hang about the car wash, I've got to be at a wedding at ten.'

Hayes ambled over. 'Can I help?' The girl spun round, her eyes bright with tears, confused by the appearance of the stranger. She wore a long chiffon dress and silver sandals, her short hair burnished like a golden cap. As he got closer he caught a strong whiff of her perfume: a musty exotic scent, not the sort of thing to associate with this English rose. Her eyes were teary and between bursts of anxiety she sniffed into a wad of damp tissues.

Kevin grinned. 'Hey, Mr Hayes, you're up early.' He nodded towards the car spattered with slurry. 'Our Roma here thinks I've got bugger all to do on a Monday morning.'

'What happened?' He turned to face her. 'I'm Roger Hayes by the way, we haven't met, I'm new here.'

'I'd booked to join a pony trek yesterday and the stables were down this ghastly farm track which was all bogged up with manure and cow pats. I can't arrive for a job at the

Buxton Heights with a vehicle looking like this. I'll have to get a taxi but they don't always want to take my harp – people are such shits! Anyone would think the harp was going to vomit on their nice clean seats.'

Hayes decided that this was an emergency that would be ungallant to sidestep. 'Tell you what, Roma, how about if you drive to the venue with the harp on board and I follow? We discreetly offload your instrument round the back and then I drive off and get yours cleaned up while you do your thing and I swap cars afterwards and leave the keys of a nice clean motor with the receptionist for you to pick up later.'

Kevin laughed. 'You a man of leisure, Rog?'

'Pretty much. I've no appointment till eleven and this poor girl is obviously short of time. How does it strike you, Roma?'

She flushed with relief and grasped his hand in both of hers. 'You're an absolute angel from heaven, Roger Hayes.'

They set off in convoy to the next town and Hayes followed Roma's estate car through a pair of wrought-iron gates that would have graced a stately home. The hotel was an ivy-covered manor house set in extensive grounds, the perfect setting for a summer wedding. Roma drove round the back and parked by the service entrance, leaping out with the alacrity of a gazelle to open the rear door and drag out a full-sized harp. Hayes parked in behind and hurried to assist, but, in fact, she had matters well in hand and swiftly man-oeuvred the harp onto a wheeled trolley.

'Can you manage?'

'Piece of cake. I generally leave the harp at my regular venues, the Palm Court or the Assembly Rooms, but, for special dates, I have to haul it round. You get used to it,' she said with a cheerful shrug.

'You seem to have a terrible cold, you sure you're up to this job?'

She blew her nose. 'It's nothing, just hay fever. Hits me like a hurricane at this time of year. I've got some Piraton in my bag, it'll dry up once I get inside.' She passed over her car keys and before Hayes could say more the thin figure in the fluttering silk dress had whisked inside and out of view.

She was, Hayes had to admit, the sort to trade on her vulnerability, could pull out the 'poor frail me' card at the drop of a hat. Roma was tall all right, but slight as a willow wand, and the elfin haircut completed a picture which belied her rumoured twenty-four years.

He shot off to Port Erin in the clarted-up estate car and, deciding to save his strength for his date with Lenny at the Spa gym, left it in the hands of a car-valet service, a painfully expensive option, and extracted a promise that the clean-up would be completed pronto. 'I've got a medical check-up in Douglas at eleven and I must get this mess dealt with immediately.' A hefty pre-service tip sealed the deal and Hayes wandered off to find a coffee shop.

In the normal course of events he'd charge up this job on expenses, he wryly admitted to himself, but, on balance, being in Roma's good books might well prove a useful intro to the island's smart set who Bill Caxton seemed to think were the targets of the muggers.

Worth a try, he reflected as he deposited Roma's car keys on the desk at the Buxton Heights Hotel. Sounds of laughter and loud conversation drifted from a reception room crowded with well-wishers, a pair of beribboned flower pedestals standing each side of the open doors. Hayes grinned: fat chance of the decorous strains of Roma's harp filtering through the pre-wedding champagne party.

His ordeal with Lenny, the personal trainer, went smoother than expected, Dr Cheryl's strictures on a suitable rehabilitation programme erring on the gentle side.

'You don't want to push yourself too quick,' Lenny insisted, 'and keep off the weights for a week or two.'

He emerged from the workout feeling surprisingly spry and was surprised to be accosted by a flabby-looking geezer in a white medical coat.

'Mr Hayes? I'm the physiotherapist, Jeremy Baines. Can

you spare a few minutes? I'd like to check a few details.'

For a physio Jeremy Baines hardly looked the part, a tubby little man with fleshy jowls, a man who seemed to have bypassed the exercise routine he was sworn to recommend.

'I've only just finished in the gym,' Hayes said. 'I'm a bit sweaty. Can we leave it until after I've showered?'

'No, I'd like to check you over now if you don't mind, Mr Caxton is anxious that we don't allow you to overdo it.' He smiled, displaying a terrific set of teeth, and Hayes allowed himself to be marched to his surgery.

'Your colleague, the Spa doctor Cheryl Maine, seemed quite happy,' he murmured, watching Baines scan Lenny's exercise sheet.

'Quite so. But you and I need to get acquainted straight away so we can measure your progress, eh?'

After a brief resumé of Hayes' hospital treatment, Baines proceeded to examine his blood pressure, heart rate and lung capacity. He then tested his muscular strength and, finally, let him go, though not without a warning about smoking and a po-faced ban on tantric sex.

Hayes retreated to the locker room in a state of mystification. What was Baines' game? The check-up had been an exact repetition of Cheryl's examination and even if Bill Caxton had put special emphasis on cotton-wool treatment for their new Spa member, it struck Hayes as being a suspicious attempt to cover all the exits. Did they think he was likely to sue if the convalescent routine proved disastrous?

As he got dressed Hayes wondered if Caxton had said more to his physio than was strictly necessary, had hinted that this new member was, in fact, a senior police officer whose curiosity about local crimes of violence was of special importance?

By the time he got to the rehearsal studio in Petty's Yard, DeeDee and Jimmy O'Dell were almost through. She beckoned him over and he sat quietly through their next number, a new arrangement of 'The Way We Were' which was subject to frequent stops while she scribbled corrections on the sheet music.

Jimmy was, as DeeDee had described, a handsome lad: dark hair smoothly parted, a pale complexion and easy manner. The two of them fussed with a final run-through and eventually, exasperated, DeeDee called over to Hayes. 'You said you could annotate, Roger. Could you be a sweet-heart and make a note of the changes with Jimmy while I take five? We've been working through these bloody songs all morning – an extra pair of hands would be wonderful.'

She disappeared into a side room before he could protest and, rising stiffly, Hayes climbed onto the low stage and introduced himself to DeeDee's partner.

Hayes settled at the piano and did a quick run-through with Jimmy hanging over his shoulder. Within minutes they were totally in accord and when DeeDee finally emerged her comic get-up didn't hit them for a full minute.

She had pinned up her hair under a man's wig, its light brown tresses waving almost to her shoulders. She struck a pose in the doorway and, grinning like a little brown monkey, snarled, 'Any offers, boys?'

Jimmy was not amused. 'Cut it out, DeeDee, we've got work to do. Roger's been terrific. If he'd been here from the start we'd have been finished by now.' He turned to Hayes. 'Could you take it from the top while DeeDee and I give it a final run?'

Dee pouted but reluctantly removed the wig and joined them at the piano, dumping the hairpiece beside Roger on the bench. 'I bet it's Phil's, don't you? His party gear.'

Roger picked up the wig and examined the label inside. 'It's not a pricey item,' he said. 'I've seen cheap stuff like this before – who does he think he's kidding? Where was it, DeeDee?'

'In the bathroom cabinet, in a box with shampoo and hair spray – I was looking for some aspirin.'

Jimmy grew impatient. 'Darling, for Heaven's sake! Let's get back to work. Put the damn thing back where you found it, it was probably left by one of Roz's clients after an audition.'

'She sees people here?' Roger mildly enquired, his fingers flicking through the sheet music on the stand.

'Yeah, sure. It's her office and this sound studio's perfect for trying out new acts.'

They worked through the next half-hour in harmony, Hayes delighted to find his lack of practice had not destroyed an ability to strum a reasonable accompaniment.

Later, over lunch, DeeDee gripped his arm in delight. 'You're a bloody godsend, Roger Hayes!'

'How about "an absolute angel from heaven"? I've already earned that one this morning from a lovely looking kid with tears in her eyes.'

Nineteen

They spent the afternoon lounging round the pool at the Spa, Roger reluctantly shedding his T-shirt to expose his pale torso to a bit of sunshine. It was very hot and the pool was noisy with a party of teenagers playing about in the deep end. But to cool off there was no alternative but to brave the larking about if he was to enjoy a few lazy lengths.

He climbed out to rejoin DeeDee, playfully splashing her brown midriff as he bent to kiss her.

'Good God, Roger! What happened to your chest? You look as if you've been attacked with a tin opener.'

He leaned across and whispered in her ear. 'A mugging. Does it look that bad? I was hoping a bit of a tan would help.'

She pulled him down and smoothed away his anxious frown. 'Actually, darling, it's quite a turn-on. Let's go back to the cabin, I'm cooked.' Dragging on a beach robe she waited while he collected up their stuff and they strolled down the woodland path towards the lake.

'Why didn't you go in the pool to cool off, juggins? The water's perfect.'

'Can't swim,' she admitted. 'Never learned, and I'm too embarrassed to start now – even little kids of five are like tiddlers in the water these days.'

'I'll teach you.'

'No thanks, I'm a terrible coward.'

'But you *would* really like to learn, wouldn't you?' he said, taking the keys from her and unlocking the cabin door.

'I suppose so, but not in that pool with everyone watching.'

'Trust me, we'll have you splashing about in a week, I promise. There's a quiet backwater beside the boathouse we can use, nobody ever goes that side of the lake.'

They closed the door and fell into each other's arms. Situated far from the swimming pool and the tennis courts, the lakeside was silent, a world away from Caxton's exclusive clientele enjoying a perfect summer in the sports complex.

They lay on the sofa bed and slept, exhausted by the heat. Later, growing restless as the afternoon drew to a close, DeeDee started to worry about getting back. 'I promised Phil I'd be on time, he's a terrible fusspot especially when Roz is not around to bully us.'

They arrived back at Finch House with a happy disregard of the likely comments of the band seeing them return together, and in a distinctly lovey-dovey mood. The Blues were, as they kept insisting, 'one big family', but the flip side of all this companionability was keen curiosity about any romance in the air. The only married couple, the Driscolls, took a protective interest in the singles, especially the girls, and particularly young Roma who, after even such a brief acquaintance, Hayes rather suspected was more than capable of looking after herself.

He wondered if the Driscolls knew of Roma's casual fling — if 'fling' it was — with Roz, which Karl had accidentally caught on camera. Very unlikely, Hayes decided. Roz's relationship with a girl who was not, strictly speaking, a member of the band might well have escaped general scrutiny, and from his own impression of Phil's dependence on his new wife, such secrets were best left undisturbed.

With an empty evening ahead Hayes decided it was time to get to grips with Caxton's list of victims.

The list was not long.

(i) Derek Fields, 66, dead from a heart attack the previous summer. Mugging later reported to the police by his widow, his wallet gone and the shock of the attack presumably contributing to his demise.

86

(ii) Francis Formby-Smith, 32, dead.

(iii) Pete de Verne, 71, reluctantly reported the attack in the Cut after a passer-by called an ambulance. Cash gone, amount unknown. Memory poor. Minor shoulder injury inflicted during fall.

(iv) Craig Durrant, 27, unemployed, living off compensation following industrial injury in which he lost a leg. Insurance claim on Rolex with diamond surround. Only twenty quid taken.

(v) Terry Porlock, hairdresser, 42. Over £1,000 missing.

Agreed, they were all members of Caxton Spa but the lame guy, Durrant, only used the indoor pool. The vicious attack ending in the murder of Formby-Smith was presumably the case the police were currently concentrating on, and for this reason Hayes decided to keep well clear. The best course would be to start with Caxton's friend Charlie Lyons, the latest victim and the one to whom Hayes had been introduced by Bill as being the object of a similar mugging. Also, the man's ordeal would be fresh in his mind which, from Hayes' experience of elderly informants, was vital.

He looked up the telephone number of the Marlborough Clinic and rang through to ask after poor old Charlie.

'You are a relative of Mr Lyons, sir?' the switchboard girl enquired.

'Er, not exactly. More of an acquaintance. My colleague, Mr Caxton, asked me to visit his friend on his behalf.'

'And your name again?'

'Roger Hayes,' he repeated, irritably aware that no such ring fence had kept his own uninvited visitors off the ward during his hospitalization. Clearly, the Marlborough was a very upmarket establishment.

'One moment, please.'

Muzak murmured in his ear like the sea, a plaintive folk tune unsuccessfully chosen to allay the impatience of waiting callers.

The music suddenly broke off and the gauleiter at the gate

informed him that, 'Mr Lyons discharged himself this afternoon, Mr Hayes.'

'Gone home? Already?' Hayes gasped. 'I thought he'd cracked his skull.'

'I really couldn't say. Good evening, Mr Hayes.'

Frustrated at the start of what he already deemed a lost cause, Hayes cooled down with a stiff vodka and tonic before deciding to pursue the ex-patient to his own doorstep if only as a sop to Bill Caxton's generosity.

A knock at the door interrupted his efforts to trace Charlie Lyons' number in the phone book and he rose to see who it was.

Karl Brecht stood outside all togged up in his Blues Band outfit, spangled lapels on a midnight velvet jacket. He looked sheepish.

Hayes grinned. 'Hey, get you! Come in, have a drink.'

'No time, man. Just off. Hadn't seen you all day, wondered if you were OK. You got back all right last night?'

'Yeah, sure. Sorry to break up the party but next time really is my treat.'

'You look a bit rough, if you don't mind me saying so, Rog. Feeling all right? Telling Terry about that stabbing of yours shocked me rigid. You should have said.'

'As a matter of fact I am feeling a bit down. Painkillers don't seem to work . . .' He pulled Karl through and closed the door. 'On the QT, Karl, I wonder if you could do me a favour?'

'Any time, chum.'

'Could I buy some grass off you? It dulls the pain.'

Karl looked anxious. 'Of course, Rog. No problem. Trouble is I've run out but if you need anything ask Kevin, tell him I sent you. We're just one big family here, and Kev supplies just about anything we need – E's, Viagra, you name it.'

'Snow?'

Karl stiffened. 'Don't know about any hard stuff but I'll ask around at the Griffin if you're pushed.'

'No, just party stuff, but thanks all the same, I'll cadge some smokes from Kev.'

He opened the door and Karl edged out, leaving Hayes with a nasty aftertaste, knowing he had probably blown his friendship with Karl Brecht. He'd overstepped the mark, but if he was to get even to the starting line with the local scene there was no alternative but to tap whatever vein he could.

Twenty

Getting no answer when he telephoned Charlie Lyons' home, Hayes decided to take a chance and make a cold call.

Sandy Lodge lay in a wooded valley about three miles from the coast and was surrounded by white railings which enclosed an expanse of lawn and a paddock where two donkeys raised their heads to observe his arrival. The house was newly built in the ranch style popularized by super-market designers. He parked on a circular drive behind an Aston Martin and rang the bell. After a moment he rang again, rehearsing his alleged interest in Charlie Lyons' unfortunate encounter with the muggers.

When he had almost given up, the door was flung open by a tall blonde wearing drainpipe denims and a flouncy gipsy-style blouse which disclosed an alluring glimpse of cleavage.

'Yes?' Her manner was cool.

'My name's Roger Hayes, I'm a friend of Bill Caxton's. He was anxious about Charlie and asked me to call on his behalf. I was surprised that Charlie had left hospital.'

She stepped back. 'Well, you'd better come in,' she grudgingly agreed and, after closing the door behind him, led them through to the lounge. The view from the bank of windows framed a glorious sunset above a wooded skyline.

She offered a cigarette box that Hayes declined, then lit up herself, hunching over the lighter with a worried frown. After a hungry puff, she dropped onto the sofa and invited him to take a seat. 'I'm Belinda, his ex. Charlie was anxious to get a specialist's opinion and so I fixed up an appointment with a neurosurgeon in London and Charlie flew out this afternoon.'

Hayes eyes widened. 'He was that badly hurt?'

She smiled grimly. 'I hardly think so. But Charlie was always a worrier about his health and decided he needed a second opinion. He uses a private helicopter service, of course, like many residents on the island, it's convenient for popping over to the mainland or to France or Ireland for the races. You're living here yourself?'

'No, a visitor. It was suggested I convalesce here at the Spa Hotel.'

'You've been ill?'

'Not exactly. I was mugged in almost the same circumstances as Charlie, which was why Bill thought he might appreciate a sympathetic ear.'

She paled, visibly shocked. 'You are another of those poor men who were attacked in Douglas?'

'No, in London, but Bill Caxton is very concerned about the series of muggings here. He thinks the people were targeted. Did Charlie think that?'

'Look, I've got to have a drink,' she said, and hurried across to a bar built into the corner of the room. 'What will you have, Roger?'

'Wine?'

'Yes, of course. Red? But I need something stronger. Charlie's little "do" has shaken me up. We're still pals, even after the divorce, and he has no one else. Tell me about your attack.'

Hayes sighed. 'Nothing unusual, a random hit when I was walking back to my car late at night. I was stabbed.'

'Crikey! You fought back?'

'Stupidly, yes.'

'That's exactly what I told Charlie. But he says he didn't argue but still got a fractured skull, nothing life-threatening but no joke for an old duffer like Charlie. I was always warning him about carrying so much cash around, as bad as his friend, Pete de Verne, another victim of that same gang it seems, seventy-one, silly old Pete. They think they're still cowboys, these stupid old men, and it's not as if they can't afford the loss. Nothing's worth being banged over the head for, in my view. I'm sorry you missed seeing Charlie, he would have felt better if he could talk to a fellow-sufferer. It's knocked the stuffing right out of the poor darling, feels his age, being rolled by a couple of thugs. I'm not sure he'll be the same after this.'

Hayes sipped his wine, eyeing Belinda with respect. She was not the gold-digging showgirl he had expected, she was genuinely concerned about her ex and it was a sad state of affairs that a bloke like Charlie Lyons had no one else to hold his hand at a time like this.

'Do you know what happened, Mrs Lyons?'

'Belinda. Call me Belinda. I've reverted to Belville now I'm staying on the island. I wasn't sure if Charlie might be embarrassed if I used his name when I set up my new business. Party planning,' she said in response to his glance. 'There's plenty of scope here, lots of rich folk who like someone to do all the organizing, someone to arrange things in style for them. It's a close community here, Roger, a bit incestuous if you take my meaning, but Charlie set me up nicely with a house on the coast and a generous settlement so I think I'll stick around for a while. Like I said, we parted amicably, and Charlie knows I'm nearby if there's a problem.'

'He confided in you about the attack in the Cut? Funny place to be in the early hours, wasn't it?'

She took a drag on her cigarette, staring into the glass of brandy in her shaking hand. 'He wouldn't talk to the police, too ashamed of himself, but, between you and me, Roger, I agree with Bill Caxton. I think he *was* targeted.'

'Why do you think that?'

'Well, he told the inspector he was just hanging about in the Cut on the off-chance of picking up a girl, but that wasn't the whole story. He had arranged to meet someone at one o'clock, someone who would take him on to a party.'

'Where?'

'The venue was a secret. He had been to these sex parties before. I found out about it after we were married, which pissed me off as you can imagine. But I wasn't really surprised. Poor old Charlie wasn't what you could call a stud even on our wedding night, but he thought marrying an experienced cow like me would eventually put it right. He used Viagra, of course, and between us we made a sort of a go of it but – you don't mind me confiding in you like this, do you, Roger? – strictly between ourselves he could only get his act together with strangers in an anonymous party atmosphere.'

'Group sex?'

'I suppose so. I don't go in for threesomes and it soon became apparent that with the best will in the world, Charlie's efforts to have a normal relationship with me were never going to work.'

'How did he hear about these parties? At the Spa?'

She looked surprised. 'At the Spa? Whatever made you think that? No, I'm not sure how it started but apparently he would get a text message and take it from there.'

'Expensive?'

'Oh yes, wildly expensive, and these orgies took place at a different place every time, but afterwards he couldn't remember where or how he got there, or so he says. He was told to arrive on foot and a car would take him to the venue and drop him home afterwards. Plenty of booze was on offer, of course, and I think his memory loss is genuine, I can always tell when Charlie's lying to me.'

'Did he know the other guests?'

She shook her head. 'He never said so but I warned him to be careful. Playing silly buggers on his home ground could be dangerous, leave him open to blackmail.'

'Did he get the Viagra on site?'

'Through the Internet, I think. He was anxious not to involve his doctor, silly man.'

'So what happened? He got a message, arrived at the rendezvous and, instead of being driven to a party, he got mugged?'

'That's about it.'

'Could he describe his attackers?'

'Not clearly. He approached his young boy in the Cut—'

'He recognized him?'

'Possibly — he was vague about that, knowing I was angry that he put himself in such a vulnerable position. But it may have been a coincidence, being there at the wrong time, and on the face of it looking for a working girl. He stood talking to this kid and then felt this terrible blow to the head. The doctor thinks it was probably a rubber truncheon, nothing sharp, like a hammer for instance.'

'But you said he approached this boy. Was Charlie gay?'

'Oh no! He loved women, he just couldn't get it up unless it was in an anonymous grapple with a load of faceless strangers. I suppose he thought this boy was going to take him to the car and drive him off on this mystery tour. I ask you!' She sighed. 'He confessed that he could never make love to a girl like normal, not even in his twenties. Poor lamb. But, there was no future for us. I did my best, and after a few months Charlie agreed that he should have warned me before we got married.'

'But he was generous?'

'An absolute diamond. I'm still very fond of Charlie and he relies on me. You won't mention all this to Bill Caxton or anyone else, will you? I just needed to share all this with a stranger. Charlie's been a bit of a worry to me lately and I can't talk to anyone we know, it'd be round the island in no time at all.'

'Do you think he flew off to London to escape further enquiries from the police?'

'Probably. But they won't catch these muggers, will they, Roger? Do *you* think the pair who robbed Charlie mugged these other men or just thought Charlie looked like a pushover?'

He shook his head. 'Hard to say. Did he take his mobile phone with him? The police could trace the sender of the text message and check any connection.'

'He destroyed it. Promised me he'd have nothing more to do with this fancy sex-party lot, but if that was his only source of satisfaction, who am I to say it's wrong?'

Hayes rose to go, feeling there was little more Belinda could contribute. 'I'll call you again, if I may? You'll be staying here till Charlie gets back?'

'No, I'll push off back to my own place as soon as I've secured the house here, and then I'll spend a few days in London to cheer up the silly old sod.' She delved in her handbag and scribbled a cellphone number on the back of a parking ticket. 'Ring me in a week or so, Roger, let me know if there are any developments at this end, would you mind?'

She followed him out into the darkness, and stood in the doorway until the tail lights of the little Mercedes had disappeared down the drive.

Twenty-One

Hayes' week settled into a routine of sorts dependent on DeeDee's free time away from the demands of the band. His fascination with such a skinny bird was something he tried not to think too much about. Probably something to do with being in a kind of limbo with no work and only a passing duty to get fit enough to return to real life, he persuaded himself.

Her sunny disposition was a huge turn-on after the turbulence of his relationship with Pippa, and her uncomplicated affection had no foreseeable future. The music was, of course, and Hayes had rediscovered an obsession which had, for years, been thrust into the background. When DeeDee was rehearsing or performing with the band, Hayes gravitated to the piano in the deserted drawing room at Finch House. At first he amused himself by running through the sheet music strewn around the small stage, a selection of thirties numbers and Beatles tunes. But, latterly, encouraged by the silence of the empty house, he had begun to struggle with classical pieces and had even purchased a selection of scores to test his confidence. He said nothing of this to DeeDee, who would have been amused by his earnest endeavours, and the only distraction was the occasional interruption of Kevin moving round the house with the vacuum cleaner. The two men struck an unspoken conspiracy about Hayes' fumblings at the keyboard, Kevin instinctively aware that the new lodger's little hobby was something best not mentioned to the rest of the crowd.

Roma's movements were less predictable but, occupying

the basement flat as she did, her scurrying between the gigs Roz had booked practically back to back left the poor girl no spare time to investigate the stumbling musical strains faintly issuing from the Bechstein in the drawing room.

Hayes' sessions at the gym had to be slotted in either early morning or during the evening when DeeDee was working. He did, however, insist on keeping up the swimming lessons that he bullied her into accepting in the early afternoons before a late lunch at the Spa Hotel. Their use of the cabin had been overtaken by Roz's return and they occasionally glimpsed Roma sunbathing with her by the water's edge.

The swimming lessons were conducted in a quiet leg of the lake beyond the ramshackle boathouse, which they found adequate for après-swim lovemaking. DeeDee gradually overcame her fear of the water and, ignoring a stern notice commanding, 'Deep Water. No Swimming. No Fishing', they splashed about between the lily pads like a couple of noisy frogs. Roz and Roma walked over one afternoon to see what all the fun was about and DeeDee determined on performing a doggy paddle without the lifebelt from the boathouse, which Hayes normally insisted she clung to while practising.

But Roz was not encouraging. 'You do realize you're not supposed to swim in the lake,' she said. 'The health and safety people have told Bill to watch it.'

'Oh, don't be such a wet blanket, Roz,' DeeDee snapped. 'I'll be good enough to join everyone in the pool next week. Roger's been brilliant – I'll get some proper coaching when he goes back to work.'

Roma brightened. 'When's that, Rog?'

'Soon, I hope.'

'You're from London?'

'No, but I'm thinking of moving there – a new career.'

'In what?'

He laughed. 'Top secret. Espionage, undercover stuff.'

The girls whooped with laughter and Hayes and DeeDee watched them stroll back to the cabin.

'Did you notice the jagged scar on her arm?' she said.

'Roma's? Well, I had, but only recently. It's well disguised. What happened?'

'Apparently she broke her wrist here last summer, fell off a breakwater or something. Poor kid couldn't work for weeks, could have ruined her career but she was OK after dozens of physiotherapy sessions from that bloke at the Spa, all paid for by Roz, of course.'

'You mean Jeremy Baines?'

'That's the one. According to Karl, who also had recourse to our favourite masseur after he badly tore a ligament, Roz got very jealous, thought Roma was getting too cosy with him, which is pretty paranoid considering Roma's obviously gay.'

Hayes feigned surprise. 'No, really?'

'Come on, Roger, it's bloody obvious.'

'Think so? She's very pretty.'

DeeDee aimed a blow at his head which he ducked, laughing, and rolled over on the decking dragging her into a firm armlock. The rest of the afternoon passed in an erotic wrestling match within the dark and cobwebbed interior of the boathouse.

'We've missed lunch,' he said at last. 'Fancy a takeaway back at the house?'

'Not really.' DeeDee pulled on a beach robe and frowned. 'Do you really think she's pretty?'

'Who?'

'Roma, of course! I bet you've been eyeing her up while I've been busting my lungs out all night with the band, fantasizing about her horny fingertips running up and down your spine, you dog.' She laughed, but a flicker of unease lurked at the corner of her mouth. 'Tell me, lover boy, what do you do when I'm working? All those hours with nothing to do.'

'Well, if I don't go to the gym I occasionally meet a friend in Douglas to talk man stuff, motorbikes, the TT races. And we've been target shooting at the local firing range once or twice.'

'What friend? I didn't know you had any friends on the island. You're a dark horse, Roger Hayes!'

'Marty Lewis. Bill introduced me. He runs the local newspaper. Nice chap. He's been intriguing me with stories about the mugging spree on the island.'

'It's not funny, Roger. One man's been murdered.'

'So I hear. Anyway, because I was duffed up myself, I'm naturally interested and he lent me a pile of press cuttings. There's a link somewhere but I can't put my finger on it. I tried to talk to an old guy called Pete de Verne who was one of the victims but he got quite tight-lipped about it, couldn't explain why he was hanging about in the dark streets late at night with a roll of fifties in his back pocket.'

'He was looking for a girl, silly. The Cut's kerb-crawlers' heaven, and I've heard even rent boys make a living there in the summer.'

'Mm. Well, it's a bit more tricky than that. Through a private source I've learned that there's a luxury sex circuit in operation on the island. Invitation-only and probably restricted to local men with a taste for high-class naughties.'

'I've seen that bloke at the casino.'

'De Verne?'

'Yeah. He gave me twenty quid to play "Blues in the Night". Big tipper. Made his money from property development – he's worth a packet.'

'Is he often at the casino? Perhaps that's where he won the money he lost in the mugging – won a windfall at the tables and decided to buy himself a little treat down the Cut.'

'If you're at the casino every week like me you get to know the regulars. Roz and Phil go there sometimes, though I don't think Phil enjoys throwing his money at a roulette wheel, but Roz likes dressing up and the food's good – better than the Spa, though they've stopped the free drinks for players – the licensing authority thought it put the punters at a disadvantage,' she added with a giggle. 'Can I see your cuttings? I never get round to reading the newspapers and only hear about local crime from gossip. But it's not a serious problem, is it?'

Hayes grinned and pulled her to him. 'Not for us, my sweet. The victims are all ageing porno addicts with money to burn.'

Twenty-Two

In fact when Hayes thought about it he had to admit that 'ageing porno addicts with money to burn' did not fit all the victims. The youngest featured in Monty Lewis's press cuttings was neither old nor rich. Craig Durrant was only twenty-seven and had been rolled over for petty cash and a watch.

He decided to give him a call and after unceremoniously dumping DeeDee back at the house drove back to Douglas to explore the suburbs. The press coverage quoted his address as Shelley Street, which was not much help without a number, the street comprising fifty or more terraced houses leading to a scruffy shopping arcade where several of the units were boarded up. Hayes phoned Marty's mobile number and caught him on the hop.

'I'm just off out, Rog, a civic reception – can't it wait?'

'Sorry, but just a quickie. The address of that boy Craig Durrant, the lad who claimed to be a victim of the muggers?'

'*Claimed* to be? You've got information?'

'Not yet, but I've been trawling through those cuttings and he's the odd one out. The others were all caked-up local bigwigs and Craig admits he only lost twenty quid.'

'Twenty quid *and* a Rolex, but I see your point. I'll have to call you back, check with the girl who covered the story. Won't take five minutes.'

Hayes sat in the car experimenting with the local radio stations and, good as his word, Marty rang back with the full address. 'What's your angle, Roger? Durrant's a surly devil according to my girl, Mary. She says she found him practically inarticulate about the mugging, spaced out on cannabis she reckoned, and he's got a big chip on his shoulder about the accident, which cost him half his leg.'

'An industrial accident, according to your report, but he was handsomely compensated, wasn't he?'

'Not enough, he says. Still existing on the payout and at a guess not bright enough for retraining.'

'OK, thanks for the tip, Marty. I owe you.'

'Oh, just one more thing. His partner pushed off after the mugging, a bloke called Tony who works behind the cocktail bar at the casino.'

'Durrant's gay?'

'Apparently so. You going round there now?'

'Seems a good time, too early for a night out – well, not if you're on the top table at a civic reception, of course.'

'Believe me, it's not a fun evening. Good luck with Durrant.'

Hayes parked the car at the end of the street and made his way to number fifty-two, well aware that several pairs of eyes tracked the progress of the tall, dark-haired stranger as he paused at Durrant's gate. The garden was untended and clumps of rye grass sprouted in the cracks of the concrete path. The windows were obscured by net curtains which had seen better days.

He rang the doorbell and heard the uneven scrape of what sounded like boots on bare floorboards. Durrant opened the door, instantly recognizable from the press pictures. Long hair to his shoulders and a sulky thin face. One leg of his jeans hung empty from the knee, and he supported himself on a metal crutch.

'Yeah? What d'ya want? You're not from the social, are you? Because I already told them I won't go to that rehab joint – it's not my scene.'

Hayes smiled, wishing he could flash his warrant card and give this moody blighter a reason to be more polite. 'No, I'm a colleague of the editor of the *Review*. He would like to do a follow-up feature on the muggings and hoped you would be interested.'

Durrant's eyes narrowed. 'What's the fee? I've got me pride, you know.'

'Fifty? May I come in?'

'S'pose so.' He leaned against the wall and widened the entry to let Hayes through. The place smelt bad, only a faint whiff of grass sweetening the small rooms. Durrant led him through to a back room, where his booted false limb lay on the hearthrug like a family pet.

Durrant grinned, his thin face breaking into a wicked smile. 'Gives me gyp so I take it off when I'm relaxin'.' Not used to it, see. I bet if I'd gone private I would have 'ad one made to measure, like.' He slumped into the only armchair, and after a moment, Hayes settled at the table, bringing out a sheaf of press cuttings and a notebook and trying to decide how best to bait the hook. The lad was obviously skint, any compensation won from the industrial injury claim long gone.

Hayes withdrew five crisp ten-pound notes from his wallet and fanned them out on the table beside his notes.

Durrant brightened. 'Well, what d'ya want to know?'

'My name's Hayes. I'm new here, I don't live on the island so I shall have to rely on your local knowledge, Craig. All right if I call you Craig?'

'Yeah, sure, but what sort of stuff you printing? I ain't keen on getting more photos in the paper, the kids round here started pelting me winders and calling out Peg Leg when I got in the news last time.'

'No pictures. Just a review. You heard about the poor guy who got beaten to death by the same two who knocked you out?'

Durrant shifted awkwardly in his seat, pulling at the pocket of his denims to extract a tobacco tin. 'You smoke, Mr Hayes?'

'I'm trying to give it up. You go ahead. Relaxes you, I expect. I know the feeling. The reason Mr Lewis asked me to take a fresh look at these muggings is because—'

'The Phantom Duo,' Durrant put in with relish.

'Yes, well, these two hoodlums got themselves a reputation

on the island, been at it since last summer so I hear. Between you and me, Craig, I was a victim of a mugging myself just like you and——'

'They got you in the Cut?'

'No, it happened in London a few weeks ago. A stabbing. Very nasty. But as I've been in the same spot as you and these other poor guys, Mr Lewis thought that between us we could get a fresh angle: you've got the local know-how, Craig, and I'm on the same wavelength as the victims, if you see what I mean.'

'You're not with the cops?'

'I'm freelance, between jobs like yourself, Craig. How are you managing?'

'Nothin' doin' but I get by,' he said, fingering the tobacco tin.

'Still in pain?'

'Nothin' like havin' a ton of bricks dropped on you to leave you gaspin','

'Terrible thing, constant pain. Nothing the medics give you does any good, does it? Turned to my own roll-ups in the end, only thing to work.'

'Yeah, me too.' He opened the tin and rolled a spliff, regarding Hayes with a defiant air.

'These thugs who robbed you. Did they threaten you with a knife, Craig?'

'Er, yeah, s'pose so, but it was dark, see, and quick, fuckin' quick. I was 'anging about for a mate of mine and when this geezer comes up and asks for a light, I thought nothing to it, like. Next thing I know I'm on the floor with a bloody great lump on me 'ead and me pockets turned out.'

'And they took your valuable watch? Insured, was it?'

'You bet it was, mister! Only bleedin' thing worth pinching, my treat after the payout, see. Oyster movement, diamond chips all round. Brilliant! No one round here'd ever seen anythin' like it. If my mum 'ad been alive she'd 'ave thought I'd won the lottery. This was my mum's 'ouse, rented it from Mr Bird and when she died he let me stay on.'

'You were working for a construction company, then?'
'Yeah, but we shared the rent, Tony and me, so no sweat.'
'But he left?'

Craig looked up, his head wreathed in smoke. 'You heard?'
'My girlfriend works in the cocktail lounge at the casino, she must have mentioned it. She's the singer, DeeDee – you know her?'

'Me? In the casino?' He snorted with bitter laughter. 'Never let me inside in a million years. Tony tried to get me a job as a messenger but they wouldn't wear it.'
'You've got form?'
'Me? A record? A bit of joyriding, shopbreaking, nothing serious. But since the accident nobody wants to know, do they?'

Hayes decided to tighten the screw. 'Now, between you and me, Craig, I wouldn't blame you for spinning a bit of a yarn here, mate. From my point of view, the Phantom Duo tossing you for twenty quid and a watch that's practically unsellable sounds unprofessional in criminal terms, and these two guys have hit the jackpot with every target apart from you, Craig.'

'Unsellable?' His eyes flared venomously. 'That watch was a bleeding masterpiece, worth five grand in the shop.'
'But it's not in a shop, is it, Craig? You well know that every one of those watches is numbered, traceable, no fence is going to shell out big bucks on a hot item like that. You claimed the insurance, didn't you? Got the police to verify you were the victim of a robbery and bob's your uncle.'

Hayes raised a warning hand to stem an outburst from his outraged informant. 'Can't say as I blame you, chum. Would have done the same myself if I'd had a pricy piece like that on my hands. Full insurance value instead of a measly resale price from a lousy pawnbroker. Did Tony put you up to it?'
'What's your game, Hayes? TV show? One of them investigative programmes?' Durrant sucked on his roll-up, his eyes flinty.
'Well, if you don't want to play ball it's no skin off my

nose, mate. Like I said, I'm doing an informal survey for Mr Lewis and if I can discreetly cross your name off his list it saves us both a lot of legwork. As a matter of interest, who's your dealer?' This last remark fell flat with the faint slap of a veiled threat.

Durrant struggled to retrieve his crutch, fighting a strong urge to beat his tormenter over the head with it.

Hayes slowly gathered up his notes and clippings, holding out the fifty quid with a sad smile. 'I'm not here to put your head on the block, Craig, you've got enough trouble without me stirring it. You could always deny anything that passed between a nosey runner for the local rag and a poor disabled sod with no means of making a decent living. A real sob story – who would believe me, an outsider?'

Durrant made no move to take the tenners and Hayes laid them back on the table. He paused, waiting for Durrant's greedy imagination to grapple with the situation.

Hayes closed in, and laid his wallet beside the cash. 'There's another fifty in it for you if you let me rub your name off this bloody list. You're muddying the waters saying you were targeted with these other rich bastards. Clever move, though, setting yourself up as a copycat victim, claiming the insurance and getting a load of sympathy into the bargain. If you tell me what really happened you're a hundred oncers in and, if you like, I'll ask Mr Lewis if he hasn't a job for you with the paper, eh? You'd have to start at the bottom mind, tea boy or something, but if you agreed to attend rehab and kept your nose clean, Mr Lewis would see you right. Think about it, lad, you're going nowhere dossing down here.'

Durrant subsided into his chair and finally allowed Hayes to take notes. At the end of his tearful confession, they adjourned into the shambolic backyard to share cans of lager and admire the amber glow of the street lamps now lighting up the rooftops with a false sunset.

He drove back via the Spa hoping to catch Caxton working late. The place was still humming with a determined hard

core of fitness freaks, and Lennie, his trainer, greeted him
with enthusiasm.

'Bit late for a workout, Mr Hayes. No problem, I hope?'

'No, I'm feeling great thanks to you, Lennie. Any idea
where Mr Caxton might be? He's not in his office.'

Lennie shrugged. 'Sorry,'

'No worries. I'll ring him on his mobile. Cheers, mate.'

Hayes managed to contact Bill Caxton at home, and gave
a brief rundown of the latest developments.

'And Durrant's willing to come clean with the police, you
say? Blimey! You'd better come over, Rog, and give me the
full story.' Caxton spelt out his home address, and within
ten minutes, Hayes was knocking on the door of a converted
farmhouse six miles outside town.

Caxton led him through to his study and they settled for
drinks by an unlit fire. The evening had closed in, and the
room, set on the north side of the old homestead, had a
dismal air.

Hayes went over the final arrangements with Durrant, and
Caxton leaned back wearing an expression of bemusement.

'Good God, Roger, you've got more than the police have
managed to wheedle out of that little shit in weeks. Fraudulent
insurance claim, eh? And you're sure there's no overall plan
targeting the Spa? Durrant's an exception, the other victims
were members of the club and wealthy men with influence
on the island.'

'Put your mind at rest, Bill. Frankly, I've never seriously
gone down that conspiracy route, but now one of the poor
devils has been killed in an attack, the police are going to
sit up and take notice. I have a few ideas of my own, and
if you're agreeable, I'd like to make more enquiries.'

'Hell, Roger! Having got so far you can't chuck it in now!
I'll back up any investigation you care to take up – you're
my private eye in all this, and you can leave the sensitivi-
ties of the local fuzz to me.'

'You'll find that the local CID won't welcome any interference. I shall have to play it by ear. You have contacts?'

Caxton bridled. 'I'm not without some clout here, you know. Leave it to me.'

'Sure?'

'Absolutely.' Caxton rose from behind the desk and clapped Hayes on the shoulder with enough enthusiasm to send vibrations thudding in his still-tender ribcage. 'Go to it, man! But keep me in touch,' he added, eyeing Hayes narrowly, like a man who was used to being in charge.

Hayes left with several unanswered questions banging about in the back of his mind. These islanders were a funny lot, and Caxton was no pushover.

Twenty-Three

He waited up that evening for the band to return from the Paradiso. Hayes limited his late nights with the Blues to two or three times a week, not entirely his choice but it pleased DeeDee if they could join the communal supper party as a couple and it cemented his standing as an accepted member of the gang.

Apart from himself and Roma, the band welcomed a few other outsiders and Kevin put in an appearance on a Saturday night. Supper was an ad-hoc affair, mostly organized by the Driscolls and consisting of fish and chips, pizza, burgers or curry with an occasional Chinese thrown in. Healthy eating wasn't in it but Phil encouraged this nightly bonding session and the Driscolls organized a system of sharing costs which seemed to suit everyone. After a hard night's work the prospect of an easy-going supper party afterwards smoothed the little frictions which were inevitable in any close community.

But after a few drinks, regular complaints would rise to the surface like scum, Karl aligning himself with Phil's stand on a 'trad' style while the younger element clubbed together behind the trumpeter, a natural troublemaker called Teddy Arnold, who had never recovered from his former engagement with a big band in Blackpool where he was allowed free rein with the arrangements. Jimmy O'Dell and DeeDee took a casual line with these factions, both regarding the Blues as a passing phase in a starry climb in the musical firmament.

But, on the whole, the late-night parties were good-natured,

Phil endeavouring, with a fair degree of success, to keep his motley crew on board, leaving Roz to crack the whip when necessary. Hayes was amused by the social contortions involved in what was a difficult juggling act, the disparate members of the band each with their own ambitions and one or two displaying artistic excesses on a par with an operatic ensemble.

Eventually, he and DeeDee slipped away upstairs to his flat and exchanged confidences of the 'How was your day, darling?' variety, just like an old married couple. DeeDee was a late riser, and after a performance her adrenalin still bubbled like champagne, leaving Hayes feeling distinctly jaded. He hoped it was the after-effect of his run-in with the muggers but privately suspected he was just a bit past all this late-night partying.

'Where've you been off to tonight?' she said, snuggling up on the sofa, entwined like a little brown monkey.

'I've been trawling the less affluent areas of downtown Douglas, visiting one of the mugging victims.'

'You still messing with that? You should leave it to the police, honey, you've been caught up in that sort of violence already. These thugs are dangerous.'

'I promised Bill Caxton I'd look into it. He thinks his members are being targeted.'

'Spa people? Why?'

He shrugged. 'There *is* a connection, every one of the victims is a member, but there are other links. Someone in the know is tipping off these attackers, and from my latest information, it seems likely that these blokes were being picked up from the Cut while waiting for a contact to take them to a party.' He recounted Belinda's slant on her ex-husband's dabbling with a sex ring.

'Now, don't you dare mention any of this to anyone, DeeDee, I was told in strict confidence, but it strikes me that the victims were more likely to be on the spot by arrangement than just hanging about hoping to pick up a hooker or, in one or two cases, a rent boy.'

Dee shot up, her eyes glinting with excitement. 'A sort of private club, you mean?'

'Invitation only, but expensive. The venues were changed each time and money was involved, which would explain the wads of cash these blokes carried.'

'But isn't that illegal?'

'A difficult area. No one's going to admit to belonging to such a sleazy circle, and unless underage kids were being exploited it's practically impossible to gather evidence without a formal complaint.'

'What about the bloke you saw tonight? Did he confess to being part of it?'

'Craig Durrant? No, he was a red herring, had nothing to do with the other incidents, got slotted onto the list by default.'

'Show me this list of yours, I may know some of these poor men if they're regulars at the casino.'

Hayes rose stiffly and fetched his folder from the bedroom.

DeeDee was pumped up by all of this, and snatching the file of press cuttings, she settled cross-legged on the floor to skim through Hayes' carefully handwritten notes, loose pages sent fluttering in her eagerness to explore the mystery. He patiently reassembled the strewn paper and waited while this extraordinary creature assessed his progress.

At last she looked up, her eyes sparking wickedly. 'Well, you haven't got far, have you, sweetheart? You'd never make it as a real detective, you know.'

He bit his lip in an effort not to grin. 'Well, I've been distracted, haven't I? All these bloody swimming lessons for a start.'

'Well, I'd say you've got to tie in the other guys to these exclusive orgies before you can eliminate the Spa. This hairdresser, Terry Porlock, I know him, I've been to his salon for highlights. It must be the priciest place on the island – maybe he's recruiting people on this party circuit.'

Hayes looked doubtful. 'Too dangerous, people would soon start to talk, a hairdresser's a hotbed of gossip. No, I've met him and he struck me as being too fly to involve himself in any sort of organizing capacity. Anyway, he was a victim, lost at least a grand in the scuffle.'

'OK. How about de Verne? I've seen him around.'

'Absolutely refused to discuss it. My guess he was just another oldie taking a final paddle in dangerous waters before he got too short-sighted to enjoy the show. He's over seventy.'

'Yeah, well, hope springs eternal, and with a dose of Viagra he could turn into a real swinger. Is he gay?'

'I don't think so, but if Terry Porlock was in on it, there must have been a bit of that on offer if only for viewing.'

'Threesomes? Girls putting on a lezzie show?'

'Good God, DeeDee, you've got a mind like a sewer!'

'Well, if big money's involved there has to be something a bit more exciting than a bob in the slot machine on the pier for a gawp at "What the Butler Saw".'

Hayes sighed. 'We may be barking up the wrong tree altogether, DeeDee. Belinda's story about her old man's partying may have been a one-off. Maybe these other blokes *were* selected from the Spa membership list, maybe they were hanging about the Cut to meet a dealer, cocaine *is* available on the island – that gay bar, the Griffin, is not entirely clean.'

'You've been to a gay bar!'

'Karl took me.'

DeeDee's mouth dropped. 'Karl's a cokehead?'

'No, of course not, just a bit of grass now and again. All I said was he took me there for a drink and, as a matter of fact, it was all good clean fun. That's where I was introduced to Terry Porlock.'

'Where does Karl get his stuff?'

'Well, if you must know we have a nice convenient source right on the doorstep.'

'You mean Kevin?'

'You know about Kevin?'

'Everyone knows about Kevin. He's a fixer, can get your anything, our Kev: smuggled cigarettes, cheap Russian vodka, you name it. How do you think Phil stocks up all that booze in the attic? Phil's never paid full price for anything in his life.'

Hayes wondered how far his policeman's hat had slipped that he could calmly accept all this information without so much as a blink, had smoothly accepted Craig's admission of fraud without demur, and was, if his criminal antennae had not entirely atrophied, now wading into a morass of drug-peddling, smuggling and the investigation of private sex parties which might, or might not, be connected with at least one murder.

DeeDee lit a cigarette, her face solemn. 'You know this list of yours could equally be of people who habituate the casino. Nearly all the wealthy residents join Caxton's, if only for tennis coaching or to consult that sport-injury physio bloke, I forget his name.'

'Jeremy Baines.'

'Mm. The Spa was the first of its kind here and the facilities are pretty exclusive, Caxton makes sure very few day tickets are issued because the members regard it as a neighbourly venue. Phil wormed his way in by renting a cabin for the whole season but Bill Caxton doesn't go in for holiday lets. This guy Craig who you reckon is off the list, what's all that about?'

'He's broke and was persuaded to get into a scam by, I suspect, his boyfriend, a chap you probably know, the barman in the cocktail lounge at the casino.'

'Tony? No, never! He's a very straight guy, wouldn't cheat even on staff tips left on the bar.'

'You sure? He left this partner of his high and dry. Craig's disabled, lost a leg in an accident and is smoking himself into the nuthouse on a cloud of cannabis. Craig's not in on this sex-party circuit but Tony would know about all the drug dealers in the area. I'll have to check it out. Perhaps one of these muggers – the Phantom Duo, as the locals call them – was posing as a supplier, meeting the victim in the Cut by arrangement, then, while the transaction was being made, the second guy beats him up and steals the cash. How does that strike you?'

'Utter crap!' She laughed, launching herself at him with

a flurry of blows. 'I told you, Roger,' she breathlessly insisted between wrestling holds, 'you'd make a bloody awful private eye. But,' she said as they slid to the floor, 'I'll speak to Tony myself – he'll never talk to you, but if there's anything fishy going on at the casino Tony will let me in on it. He trusts me. I'm a fellow slave on the casino treadmill, don't forget.'

Twenty-Four

Sunday evenings at the casino were DeeDee's chance to do her own thing. Unlike the Blues the management was not given to dictating the content of her performance, happy to let the pretty girl with the seductive style keep the punters happy with a variety of Continental numbers and sentimental 'standards'.

DeeDee enjoyed this chance to put on a quieter cabaret act and was unfussed if the clientele occasionally became noisily inattentive. For the most part, the couples enjoying a drink in the bar before dinner were quietly appreciative, the serious gambling element arriving much later to test their luck at the tables. The dress code was formal, and from her vantage point on the low dais Dee had a clear view of the passing trade.

When she broke off for an hour she slipped onto a stool at the bar and ordered her usual, a spritzer with plenty of ice. Tony served her with a smile, their regular stints on a Sunday night warming to something akin to conspiracy.

'Quiet tonight,' she said, regarding the sparsely filled tables in the mirror wall behind the bar.

'Yeah. Picks up later, though. Lucky you don't do the late turn, that bloke, Alonzo, who comes in from midnight, gets really pissed off with the lack of applause, vamps it up something rotten trying to get their attention.'

DeeDee laughed, flicking her hair off her face as she bent to trawl through the bowl of nuts Tony produced from under the counter.

'Where's that boyfriend of yours tonight?' he said. 'The guy who come in with you last weekend.'

'Roger? Well, I guess he hasn't got the stamina, eh, Tony?'

'Can't stick the pace?'

'To be fair, he's recovering from a mugging. Knifed. Still getting over it.'

'Blimey! Stabbing's no joke. You heard about my mate Craig getting mugged?'

'Mm. Roger went to see him. He's interested in these attacks on the island, but,' she said, leaning across the bar to draw Tony close, 'he reckoned it was all a scam, an insurance lark. You used to be Craig's lodger, didn't you?'

Tony drew back and began to mop the counter, eyeing the dwindling crowd which had started to drift towards the restaurant. 'I felt sorry for Craig at first, see, losing his leg an' all, but I soon found out he was a hundred per cent loser. That big compensation payout went to the poor bugger's head, got him into crack cocaine.'

'Expensive.'

'Nasty. These bloody pushers home in on a mug with money to burn, circle like sharks, offering everything from E's to the hard stuff.'

'He got addicted?'

'Never right once he got hooked. I'd get home from work and find him crashed out on the floor night after night.'

'But eventually the money ran out?'

'Course it did. And these dealers are not soft-hearted once they find out the cupboard is bare. But Craig was lucky in one way, his supplier was an old mate from school. The guy *had* to squeeze Craig to pay his boss so they cooked up this crazy idea between them: get Craig mugged like the others and claim the insurance on his fuckin' Rolex.'

'He told you all this?'

'Yeah. I walked out, left Craig to it. You can't do anythin' with someone whose brains are fried, even if, at the end, he was down to a spliff if he was lucky.'

'But the fraud went ahead?'

'I read about it in the paper, and when I faced Craig he

admitted it, said it was the only way out. He said Kev took the watch on account till he gets the payout from the insurance. You won't squeal to the police, will ya?'

'Kev? Kevin Webber?'

'You know him?'

'He's the caretaker at the house where I board, the band rent it for the summer.' She laughed. 'Kevin's into every rotten deal going. You think they'll get away with it?'

Tony frowned. 'Wouldn't be surprised. What did that boyfriend of yours think?'

DeeDee shrugged. 'We didn't talk about it much. I expect he thinks Craig's not worth pursuing.' She lowered her voice. 'There's bigger fish to fry, if you ask me. Have you heard about these sex parties that go on on the island? Ever been asked to come aboard yourself? Between you and me, Tony, someone at the Spa approached me and asked if I was interested. Said it was all good fun, no more than a night out with perks. But it sounded dodgy to me.'

Tony took a swift look around the bar and then confided, 'Me too. You keep right out of it, DeeDee. Heavy. But since that guy died after being mugged I hear the parties have been cancelled.'

'Tempting, though. I was offered a big bundle to tag along – it sounded OK, but nobody hosts a gig like that for square dancing, do they?'

They giggled, and speculated on the likely participants on the party circuit.

'You never saw a list, did you, Tony? I was told the guests were all respectable men with loads of dosh and this exclusive lark was by invitation only, the people on the list being contacted by the host himself.'

'Some parties were gays only,' he admitted. 'But I overheard a conversation at the bar and these A-list characters are apparently invited by text at the very last moment, so *someone's* got the key.'

The girl in the tuxedo signalled to DeeDee to resume her spot at the piano and she hastily downed her wine and strolled back to the dais, smiling sweetly as she settled at the keyboard and struck up a lively rendering of 'Let's Do It'.

Afterwards, back at Finch House, DeeDee found a few diehards settled round the dining table finishing off plates of pasta, Hayes standing behind a foursome sitting at a card table where Kevin was giving a master class in poker. He looked up as DeeDee joined them and gave her a hug. 'Would you like a drink? Or something to eat? There are some sandwiches going begging. The rest of the band have gone into Port Erin for a curry.'

She linked arms and drew him aside, passing on the bare facts Tony had been able to contribute on the Craig debacle.

'And Kev helped him stage the mugging?'

'Mm. And Kevin was Craig's supplier.'

'Kev hasn't the cash to run a drug ring on his own. Did Tony know who the big boss is?'

She shook her head.

'And Tony doesn't have a clue about the party list?'

'Only that the bloke who invited him to join in was running a gay evening.'

'He offered cash?'

'I suppose so but he only admitted that much because I strung him along saying I'd been propositioned too. But Tony's a familiar face, isn't he? Who would be on the party circuit who didn't recognize him? If the game's illegal, Tony could pose a threat, surely?'

'But he didn't play ball?'

'No. And he couldn't tell me any more about the drug ring. Kevin's the link, isn't he? Will you confront him?'

Hayes vehemently shook his head. 'No. Look, you stay here and keep an eye on Kevin while I have a dekko at his flat.'

'It'll be locked.'

'Breaking in's one of my special talents,' he quipped. 'I won't be ten minutes, if anyone asks, I've gone for a pee.'

Hayes reappeared like a shadow on the wall, the rest of the gang fascinated by Kevin's poker school. He pulled her to the door, waving a chummy farewell to the few remaining, and led DeeDee up to his room.

'Did you get in?'

He grinned. 'Next time you lose your keys, darling, just call on Uncle Rog.'

'Any luck?'

'Well, I found Craig's Rolex tucked under his shaving kit.'

'You stole it?' she gasped.

'No, of course not. Put it back like a good citizen, we don't want to give our Kevin the frights, do we? But I have to speak to Charlie Lyons. I'm supposed to have a check-up myself so I can kill two birds with one stone. I'll ring Belinda in the morning and make arrangements.'

'But you will come back?'

'Sure. Just spend a couple of days in London and fly back on Wednesday, OK?'

DeeDee looked doubtful, accepting this sudden change of plan with a wry grimace. But being the sparky girl she was, it took Hayes no more than ten minutes of dedicated charm to restore their cheerful bantering, and, in no time at all, the downy embrace of the big bed performed its magic.

Twenty-Five

'Hi, Belinda, Roger Hayes here. How's Charlie?'

'Good news, nice of you to call. The old guy's doing great, no serious problem with the bump on his head but he's staying on at the clinic for a week or so for a bit of R&R.'

'You staying on too?'

'Just to keep him company. Charlie's been good to me and the least I can do is stick around till he feels able to go home. I'm putting up at the Berkeley, so it's not all hospital visiting,' she added with a chuckle.

'Shopping?'

'You bet.'

'Actually, I shall be in town for a couple of days – any chance of a word with Charlie about the attack?'

'Unofficial?'

'Purely mutual interest. I have to see my own consultant for a check-up so it would be nice to have a chat.'

'Yeah, right. When are you likely to be around, Roger?'

'I'm flying in later this morning so would sixish tonight suit you both? Do you want to check with Charlie first? You've got my mobile number.'

'No, six will be fine, he'll be glad of a listening ear from someone who isn't bored rigid by his tale of woe.' She spelt out the address and ward details, and after a brief resumé of the latest news from the island, Hayes rang off and packed an overnight bag.

DeeDee had already departed for a band rehearsal at Roz's studio in Douglas but he managed to interrupt to bring her to the phone.

'I'm on a midday flight out of Ronaldsway, I'll ring you from the hotel but you can always reach me on my mobile. You take care now, kiddo, don't get involved with any snooping, these party people could be dangerous.'

'Yeah, yeah . . .' she drawled. 'Any chance of leaving me your room key while you're away? Your TV's better than the one in the lounge and I've taken a fancy to that big bed of yours. Mine's like a hospital cot and I can hear the Driscolls through the wall humping away every night – it makes me really miss you!'

'So you should. I'll push the key under your door before I leave. I'd better be off – give my best to Phil, tell him I said he works you too hard.'

DeeDee returned to the studio from Roz's office and picked up with a re-run of her duet with Jimmy O'Dell which, after a couple of false starts, earned muted applause.

'Roger helped us re-jig the score,' Jimmy said. 'You know what, Phil, he's a great pianist. Professionally trained.'

Roz perked up. 'A pro?'

DeeDee butted in with a curt denial. 'Don't get excited, Roz, he's not agency material.'

'What's his game, anyway?' Karl enquired.

DeeDee shrugged. 'Between jobs since his accident. He's gone back to London for a check-up – he was mugged you know.'

'Yes, I heard. Will he be back? We could do with a spare keyboard player if DeeDee concentrates on the vocals,' Jimmy suggested.

'Back Wednesday,' she assured him.

'Well, you'd better ask him, Phil. We sure do need a man who can actually read music,' Jimmy added with an acid glance at Teddy Arnold.

The rehearsal continued in fits and starts, Phil introducing some bouncy numbers for the tea dance programme at the Paradiso. DeeDee quietly slipped away to the bathroom when a fractious exchange started up between Phil and the Arnold guy. She closed the door on Roz's office and did a swift sweep of her desk. Nothing. A pile of unpaid bills. An almost illegible appointments diary with names scribbled in and violently embellished with exclamation marks and coded references presumably noting her clients' wage demands or doubtful abilities. She wondered what sort of score she herself merited in Roz's assessment but couldn't be bothered to rifle through the filing cabinet to find out.

After combing her hair in the bathroom mirror she idly wondered if the wig was still tucked away in the cabinet, and found it still in place. But she decided against an encore of her previous stunt by reappearing at rehearsal wearing the awful hairpiece. She heard footsteps approach and before she had a moment to think about it, the door swung open.

'You're wanted.' It was Roz looking decidedly miffed, clearly impatient to get Phil's gang off the premises so she could get back to work with her bookings. She stared at the wig in DeeDee's hand. 'What's that?'

'I found it on the shelf. Phil's?'

'No idea. Can't see him wearing a thing like that, must have been left by one of the Sunshine Boys after their audition.'

'Mind if I borrow it? Might make a change for my Sunday-night act at the casino. Didn't I see you there last night, Roz? With Roma?'

Roz moved to the mirror and touched up her lipstick. 'Phil and I were invited, but he can't stand the place so I took Roma along. I won fifty quid at the roulette table. Must have been my lucky night.'

DeeDee pushed the wig into her tote bag and they returned to the studio. Phil rushed through the rest of the programme, eager to get away to a round of golf at the Spa.

'Too bloody hot for me,' Karl murmured. 'Silly old sod'll have a heart attack swinging a club in this heat. You should watch him, Roz, not worth killing himself over a stupid game.'

'You're right. But does he listen to a word I say? Pays through the nose renting that cabin all summer and the girls and I are the only ones to use it. We ought to have a barbecue down by the lake one Sunday night and get our money's worth. How about it, guys?'

The band continued packing up their instruments, not exactly fired up by Roz's suggestion. The Driscolls responded politely but it was clear that no one was keen and Roz slammed off back to her office, closing the door firmly on the rest of them.

DeeDee drove back to Finch House with Jimmy and let herself into Hayes' superior apartment. It was certainly a better class of accommodation than her own single room. Kevin had dumped the weekly laundry delivery on the doorstep and after a long cool shower and making herself a sandwich DeeDee raised the window and stared down at the courtyard where Kevin was waxing Teddy Arnold's car.

Kevin's implication in the insurance scam did not surprise her but she was shocked by Tony's version of Kevin's role as a serious drug supplier. She had had him down as a petty fixer, a bloke who could lay his hands on cheap booze and, if you wanted, a few E's or amphetamines. But crack cocaine? And, according to Tony, Kev was working for a real hard man who, as he put it, needed to 'put the squeeze on' people like Craig who got in too deep and couldn't pay up.

Raised voices drifted up from below and, drawing back behind the curtain, DeeDee watched a bitter altercation unfold in the courtyard. Roma was attempting to push past Kevin to get to her car but he held her fast, his stringy suntanned arms pinning her against the bonnet.

'I've told you before, Roma, you *ask* before you borrow my motorbike.'

'You let me use it before,' she shrilled.

'Come off it, Roma! *Once*. I let you lend it *once* and you bloody *asked* first.'

'It was an emergency, Kev. My battery was flat and I had a date. Christ Almighty, what's got into you? I returned it safe and sound, didn't I? Anyway, who told you it was me? You were having a ball with that Driscoll woman, boozed to the eyeballs and not likely to want to take her out for a spin that late, were you?'

'And where were you going after midnight? Some date? Pull the other one, kid, you were off into Douglas, throwing your money at the one-arm bandits in the casino. You stupid cunt, don't you know you can never *win*? And anyway, I wouldn't be bawling my head off if you'd *asked*, would I? What pisses me off is that you pinched my leather jacket an' all.'

'I wouldn't touch your filthy jacket with a bargepole – stinks of grease like you, Kevin. It was in the unlocked pannier when I put my bag in there and was still there when I got back, so there. If you're so keen on keeping your stuff, why leave the key where everyone can see it hanging behind the back door with the garage keys? Anyone could have pinched the bike from here, dickhead!'

'You leave my bike outside the casino, Roma?'

'No!'

Kevin snorted. 'You're a bloody liar. I know all about your moonlighting jobs and if you don't find my stuff I'll bloody shop you to Roz, you see if I don't. Ask them mates of yours, them croupiers would spot designer gear like my biker jacket in a flash. It's worth a packet. Wouldn't put it past you to 'ave sold it to one of them bastards. That winner of last year's TT, the Irish guy, give it me. Collector's piece, signed his name on the back an' everythink. It's only 'cos it's been so fuckin' hot I ain't been wearing it or I'd've known it was gone straight off. Well, you was the last to lend the bike – you find it.'

'By the time I got back there was other things on my mind than checking the pannier for your stuff; getting locked out for one! You're getting like Old Mother Riley bolting up the main doors at bloody midnight. Lucky for me you were so busy sniffing round Driscoll's bum to remember to put up the shutters.'

'Mr Caxton tells me when to lock up, not you!'

DeeDee watched, fascinated, craning her neck to see the

final wrestling match before Roma managed to tear herself away and drive off. She poured herself a beer and considered the trouble poor old Phil had keeping his show on the road. Was it inevitable that this bunch of musicians and hangers-on would always end up at each other's throats, banged up as they were, week in, week out, far away from their homes and normal family life? It was a funny old Gipsy lifestyle, which wasn't helped by the heatwave, which was making everyone short-tempered.

She switched on the TV but there was nothing to grab her interest and so, with a sigh, she virtuously took it upon herself to make up the bed with the clean sheets and fold away Roger's laundry in the chest of drawers. She idly rifled through his papers, sifting the press cuttings he had tidied away. Underneath the files Hayes had stowed his camera, a pair of binoculars and a slim wallet. But it wasn't his wallet. With a sharp intake of breath DeeDee found herself with a police warrant card in her hands, Roger's photograph and details of identification all too clear. Detective Chief Inspector Hayes of Thames Valley Police. The lying bastard . . .

DeeDee sank to the floor, her hands shaking. Why had he never told her? And why was he here on the island?

Eventually, she recovered and returned the ID card to its hiding place, undecided whether she would confront Hayes with her discovery. She checked the time: one o'clock. He would still be in flight, no chance of reaching him for at least another hour. She decided to cool off, both mentally and physically, and went back to her room to change into shorts and a sun top. She'd show him! She'd take herself off to the Spa, sod Hayes, and, strictly against his rules, spend the afternoon perfecting her doggy paddle at the lake. Later, when she had had time to think, she would decide how to tackle this tricky devil who had kept her in the dark about his true reason for being on the island, whatever it was.

Twenty-Six

Hayes took the train from the airport and booked into a small hotel in Pimlico. He tried ringing DeeDee but her mobile was switched off so, after a snack at a coffee shop, he phoned Georgina Paget, his fellow victim in the mugging confrontation.

'Hello? Roger Hayes here. Remember me, Mrs Paget?'

'Yes, of course. How are you, dear?'

'Much better, thanks. That generous offer of Bill's to sponsor my recovery on the island certainly paid off. And you?'

'OK. Still too nervous to be out after dark but otherwise fine. Are you in London, Roger?'

'For a check-up, and also to follow up a line of enquiry about those muggings Bill was worried about.'

'Why don't you pop over for tea? I'd love to see you and you can fill me in with all the latest news from the island.'

'Sounds great. It's four o'clock now and I have an appointment at six. Would right away suit you?'

'Lovely.' She spelt out the address and rang off, leaving Hayes to pile into a taxi to find himself in Gloucester Square, north of the park, and unknown territory.

The sunshine was fitful, the temperature sultry as rain clouds massed in a determined assault on a shrinking expanse of blue. The atmosphere took on an eerie brightness, and a stillness hung in the air like a breathless pause before the storm.

Georgie Paget's town house occupied the central position in a terrace overlooking the square. He rang the bell and, after a few moments, during which he suspected the lady herself was peeping through the spy-hole in the door, was admitted.

After having been used to the sun-tanned features of his friends in the band, his hostess looked distinctly wan, and not a little confused. The effects of the attack seemed to have diminished her; Georgina Paget was a shadow of the woman who had dropped in on him in the hospital. Perhaps the trauma of the mugging was like a burn that, apparently only skin deep at first, continued to wound, the pain worsening with time.

She drew him quickly inside, smiling warmly and leading him upstairs to the lounge, an elegant room, cool and darkened by half-drawn blinds, the windows hermetically sealed against the traffic outside.

Georgie had prepared a Ritz-style tea with dainty cucumber sandwiches and a formidable gateau decorated with crystallized violets. Hayes' heart sank, hoping he could do justice to her efforts. He watched her pour the tea and tried to remember when he had last sat down to such a spread.

After an initial re-run of his stay at Finch House and an effusive appreciation of the Spa and her brother's generosity, he lowered his voice and asked, 'And your hand? Bill tells me there was no chance of putting you back together.'

Laughing at his odd turn of phrase, she relaxed at last. 'Putting me back together? Like Humpty Dumpty?' She held up her hand. 'Heavens, it's nothing, just means I can't crook my little finger when I take tea with the gentry. And you, Roger? You're mending well, I hope?'

'Absolutely fine. I shall have to think about getting back to work soon, but it has been a bit of a busman's holiday: I've been looking into those muggings on the island. One poor devil had died but I'm visiting another victim this evening who is convalescing in London, and I'm hoping to persuade him to be a little more frank than he has been with the Manx police. Before I reassure Bill about his fear that his members have been targeted, I'm hoping to tie up some loose ends with this man who, to put it bluntly, seemed to have been involved with a sex-party circuit which may be the link with the other victims, in which case the fact that they were all members of the Spa is coincidental.'

She nodded. 'It's a close social circle on the island. A lot of very rich people with offshore funds, and if they can let their hair down at a discreet private party, I can well understand how these events would be popular. Does Bill know about it?'

'Probably, but we haven't discussed it in any detail.'

'And one man had died you say?'

'Sadly, yes. It happens. But, like the incident we were involved in, violence can escalate if you retaliate.'

'Was this poor fellow stabbed?'

'Oh no. I suspect his injuries were caused by a beating-up that took a vicious turn. The difficulty for the police is that none of the victims wish to offer much information, and if they were members of this sex-party game, they must hope to escape notoriety; orgies involving important members of local society keen to stay out of the headlines make excellent copy and can do wonders for a local rag's circulation figures. But I'm all but certain the Spa's in the clear, so please don't worry about it. To change the subject, did you know that Bill's put me up in a house let all season to a dance band?'

Hayes attempted to lighten the tone by describing the unusual set-up, and Georgie was soon giggling at his caricatures of Phil Bailey's Blues men and their party nights.

'To keep my end up I've taken up an old hobby.'

'And what's that?'

'The piano. I used to play but work got in the way and I'm badly out of practice. Having time on my hands and a grand piano at my disposal every night, I rediscovered a dormant obsession much healthier than sex, but very humbling.'

Georgie perked up, jumping to her feet and pushing him

towards a Steinway half hidden by a potted palm. 'Would you? Please? It would make me so happy, Roger – it's the one regret about this beastly amputation: I can't really play any more.'

Hayes stiffened, suddenly aware of the permanent price Georgina Page had paid. She swept the photographs from the piano and raised the fall, pushing him to the stool.

'I'm dreadfully rusty, Georgie – you will be disappointed.'

'No, I won't! You can't imagine how I have missed making music in this room. Do you need sheet music? I've only classics I'm afraid, nothing at all trendy.'

'A little Beethoven? Would a battered section from a sonata do you?' he suggested with a grin.

She stood at his shoulder and after a brief pause Hayes launched into a piece he had been secretly practising at Finch House when the band had departed for the evening. He started hesitantly, his ears unfamiliar with the mellow tone of her beautifully tuned instrument, but after a few bars the music took over and he finished with a flourish of excited applause.

'Wonderful! Wonderful!'

'You won't mention this to Bill, will you? Our secret. My fellow lodgers are intensely curious about me, and I would be torn to ribbons if they found out I was really a classics fan. They're a nice bunch but "Strictly Ballroom".'

She placed a loud kiss on each cheek as he rose to go, and for a moment it felt as if they were once again conspirators in a strange plot.

When he got back to the hotel he tried to catch DeeDee before she departed for the show. Her response was cool.

'What's up, DeeDee? I tried to reach you earlier but your mobile was switched off.'

'I was at the Spa.'

'Good for you. I hope you haven't burnt that wicked little nose of yours?'

'Doing what?'

'Too much sun, of course. What else?'

'Poking my nose in your business?'

'Eh?'

'I found your warrant card, DCI Hayes.'

'Oh, shit!'

'Why did you lie to me?'

'I thought I'd take a break; you have no idea how defensive people get if they know there's a cop on the premises. I like being off duty . . .', he weakly added.

'Oh yeah? Then why are you poking about in the muggings? Doesn't sound like "off duty" to me, and after everyone's been free with the cheap booze and ciggies, not to mention Karl's weed. You going to cause trouble for them, Chief Inspector?'

It took Hayes all of fifteen minutes to calm her down but, eventually, too excited to keep the secret to herself, DeeDee blurted out her news. 'I've found out who's been mugging those old guys. All by myself', she crowed.

'What?'

DeeDee gave a blow-by-blow account of the overheard conversation between Kevin and Roma.

'I don't get it. She borrowed his bike? So what?'

'Not the bike, stupid! His jacket, his biker's jacket, was stolen from the pannier either from outside the casino or from the courtyard at Finch House. He's livid. Don't you understand? The jacket fits the description of the stuff the mugger wore, the bloke who approached the victims.'

'But hundreds of kids wear leather jackets, especially on the island – it's a craze since the TT riders started popularizing hot-rod style.'

'Just listen, will you? I went to the lake for a swim – no, don't interrupt, I know what you're going to say – well, I went there this afternoon and started prying into the old lockers and guess what I found? Kev's jacket.'

'And? Why should it be *his* jacket? They all look the same to me.'

'Just take my word for it, it's his all right. And it's stained!

And there was something horrible in the pocket, all smeared with *blood!*'

'Christ, DeeDee, you've been reading too many thrillers. Did you give it back to him?'

'No, of course I bloody didn't. I shoved it in my beach bag just as those two nosy tarts tied up to the jetty in a rowing boat and Roz asked me what I was doing at the boathouse. So I told them I was teaching myself to swim.

'"You're not allowed to swim here," Roz says, pointing to that notice that a blind beggar couldn't miss. "Yeah," says I, all nonchalant, "but next week I'm starting lessons at the Spa pool, so there!" But Roma didn't ask me about the leather jacket, which I'm sure she saw me stuffing into my bag, so I pushed off damn quick and I've locked it in your wardrobe at the house.'

He sighed. 'I wish you'd keep out of it, DeeDee. If you are right and we can nail Kev with forensic evidence from his jacket, you're putting yourself in danger – Roma could tell Kevin you've got his property and, before we know it, you'd be in it up to your neck. Have you said anything to anyone else about this?' he threw out with more vehemence than was wise in dealing with DeeDee in a dangerous mood.

She bridled. 'Well, no, not yet. But, if you don't come back and sort this out pronto I shall go to the police myself and give them that wig as well, which Kev could have used as a disguise when he was robbing those men.'

Hayes drew a deep breath and tried to rescue his tactless approach. 'Sorry, pet, but I worry about you. First you're swimming on your own, and then you're dabbling in deep waters with Kevin, who might well be involved in a murder. And this wig? What's that all about? Was that hidden at the boathouse too?'

'No! I pinched it from the studio and left it in my locker at the casino.'

'Then it's nothing to do with Kevin, is it? Anything else?' DeeDee, mollified by his conciliatory tone, admitted that she had hinted to Karl that it would be wise to keep his trap shut about the cannabis, seeing as he had already confided too much in a senior detective who was working under cover.

'You said what?' he exploded.

She repeated her warning to Karl, her voice diminishing to a whisper as she realized a volcano had erupted. 'Well, it's true, isn't it?' she said. 'You've been leading the rest of us up the garden path, pretending to be a poor bloody out-of-work convalescent, and all the time you're gathering sneaky information about your friends.'

'Hold it, DeeDee, I've got to go. We'll talk about all this on Wednesday when I get back. Just keep mum, do nothing and I'll sort it out.'

He cut the call and hurried to shower before rushing out to sit with Belinda at Charlie Lyons' bedside.

Twenty-Seven

Belinda was waiting for Hayes at the reception desk. Charlie's pit stop at the clinic was, she assured him, to be brief. 'In fact I'm hoping to take him home in a week.'

They moved to the lift that arrived at the top floor before Hayes had a chance to get more details on the patient's recovery. Belinda wore a white linen mini-dress which amply repaid the designer price, and which enhanced a juicy expanse of tanned thigh. Hayes decided Marty Lewis's harsh assessment of Charlie's ex had been well off the mark, even if their brief dalliance had cost him dear. Underneath the glossy veneer beat a heart of gold, and Belinda Belville, as she now wished to be known, must have been worth every penny.

She strode ahead and entered his room like a ship in full sail, Hayes hanging back, unsure of his welcome. She hugged the poor guy in a silk dressing gown seated by the window, who did indeed look a sad sack, although the only physical evidence of his brush with the Phantom Duo seemed to be a large dressing taped over a thinning pate. But, like Georgina Paget, the effects of the mugging seemed to have sucked the juice out of what Hayes guessed had been a lively character: sociable, fond of the gee-gees and up for a bit of a lark. Charlie's tan had taken on a yellowish tone, and his concentration was vague and unfocused.

But as Belinda introduced her companion, Charlie's view sharpened and he smiled, extending a hand in greeting and struggling to rise.

'Please don't get up,' Hayes insisted, 'I don't want to

disturb you, Mr Lyons, but Belinda thought you might be up to visitors.'

'You look tired, Charlie,' she put in, drawing up a chair and patting his hand.

'The heat gets me – I'll be glad to be back on the island. I miss the sea breezes.'

'All in good time, ducky. But Roger here arrived on your doorstep at home with good wishes from Bill and hoping to ask you about the mugging. You remember?'

'Of course I bloody remember. I'm not senile, dear girl,' he sharply retorted before turning back to Hayes and inviting him to pull up a chair. 'Belinda tells me you were attacked in just the same way by two hoodlums. Ghastly business. Gives me bad dreams, and before this happened I was out like a light as soon as my head hit the pillow. Now I'm lucky to get more'n a nap, though,' he chuckled, 'a shot of whisky'd do more good than these pills they dish out before lights out. You were stabbed, Bee tells me. Makes me count my blessings.'

'But you're recovering well I hear, hope to fly home soon.'

The bandaged head nodded. 'I was not too chuffed with the doc at the Marlborough, thought I'd better get a second opinion, and this dear little woman here fixed it up in a trice. Bossy cow under all that paint,' he said, his warm glance belying the teasing tone. 'You got roughed up by these villains in the Cut, Roger?'

'Er, no, in London, but the lady I was with suggested I convalesce on the island; Bill Caxton's sister, Mrs Paget, I expect you know her.'

He brightened. 'Our Georgie? Yes, of course. A grand gal, salt of the earth. Was she hurt?'

'I'm afraid so, but she's fine now.' Hayes felt it would depress Charlie to hear that 'our Georgie' was, he suspected, suffering from a form of post-traumatic stress, a sad result which he himself had entirely escaped. In truth, he had to admit, he had never felt better, thanks in no small part to the vivacious DeeDee.

'We mustn't stay long,' Belinda warned.

'OK if we go over your movements the night of the attack, Mr Lyons?'

'You had spent the early evening at the casino, Belinda thought? With friends?'

'Oh, Charlie, please. Right, fire away.'

'Well, yes, I'd been to the races at York, met a couple of chums and I'd had a lucky day. Flew back and, after a late-night snack at the casino I felt a little flat and decided to go on . . .' He faltered, his wary glance swivelling towards Belinda, who nodded encouragement.

'Yes, well, I'd been invited to a private party and I was waiting for a driver to pick me up in the Cut.'

'In strict confidence, Charlie, tell me about this party. A private invitation but you're not sure of the venue?'

He swallowed hard but continued. 'Bee says you are talking to *all* the victims, trying to get to the bottom of these Manx attacks. Why's that, Roger? What's your angle?'

'A purely personal crusade. I was mugged. Until now street robberies have not been of any real interest to me, but after being cut up I got really angry and when I moved to the island and found that vicious attacks were happening even there I just couldn't let it alone. People tend to shrug off this sort of thing, hardly realize the long-term anxiety which hangs on even if the injuries are slight. It's generally regarded as a fact of modern life, the result of poor policing or some such thing, and when I found I had waltzed into a *whole series* of muggings I was more than curious. Douglas is hardly a dangerous city location and a string of similar hits targeting a similar type of resident struck me as being quite unlike the random beating I was subjected to. I was due to come back to London for a check-up and Belinda thought it might help us both to talk about it.'

This seemed to satisfy his reluctant witness and, urged on by his lady love, Charlie Lyons decided to take Hayes at his word.

'I had been invited to this party late that evening.'

'By phone?'

'Text message with a password. Sounds very cloak-and-dagger, but the secrecy was all part of the fun, the actual parties were nothing special, just a bunch of friends having a naughty night out. The last-minute invite was a feature and the mystery of the venue spiked up the anticipation. The place was different every time. A driver took you to the house, generally an up-market holiday let at a guess, and even as a long-term resident it was difficult for me to pinpoint any location in the dark.'

He sipped from a glass of water Belinda passed over and then continued.

'The parties started after midnight and until one arrived it was unclear whether you would meet familiar faces or not. One rather hoped not! As it happened, I only met two people I knew, I think the bloke who set it up did his homework and tried to conjure up an interesting set, all sorts, people I wouldn't normally come across, some of them foreigners even. He knew his onions all right, the people there were a lively crowd. Living on an island one tends to move in a close social round, which can be a little tedious.'

'And how often did these parties occur?'

'Once every six or eight weeks, which was why I was keen not to miss out even after a tiring day at the races.'

'Was there a joining fee? A hefty subscription, perhaps?'

Charlie looked abashed but Belinda squeezed his hand and giggled, reducing Charlie's little indiscretions to no more than harmless fun.

'Well, we were all capable of spending over the odds now and again. The host required a substantial introductory sum which was augmented by five hundred quid each party plus a graduated tariff according to one's delights.'

'Girls were available? Professionals?'

'If they *were* hustlers they disguised it well, but, yes, I imagine that some of the ladies were non-membership – dancers and so on . . . But there were several who were older, rich widows, divorcees with comfortable alimonies, but no one I knew by name. It was a bit like a cruise encounter, a chance to let one's hair down in discreet surroundings. One guy I did know was Stephen Lockyer, a person to be avoided, a cocaine addict.'

'He was one of those attacked while hanging about in the Cut, I understand.'

'Lockyer moved back to the Caymans pronto after being mugged. A friend of Derek Fields, another victim, who may have introduced him to the party circuit. But Lockyer flew off before the police had a chance to interview him, couldn't face too many prying questions.'

'Mr Fields died from a heart attack following a mugging last year, didn't he?'

'Yes, poor devil, the stress hit him hard.'

'But no guests at the parties connected the muggings with the Spa? Or the casino?'

'No, why should we? Lockyer had dubious contacts and was a bit of an outsider, probably only got invited because he spent a bundle on extras.'

'Extras?'

'Drugs.'

'But wine flowed and the dancing was pretty hot, I imagine.'

'A pole dancer, group sex if you fancied it, a nasty little viewing room for voyeurs. Lap dancing, you mean? Nothing one couldn't find in clubs or suburban wife-swapping parties, Roger. Believe me, the real attraction was the secrecy, it gave a frisson to risqué entertainment within a group of strangers, people with excellent backgrounds who were all too anxious to play the game according to the rules.'

Charlie was beginning to fade, his voice growing hoarse and reduced almost to a whisper. Belinda looked anxious, shooting Hayes a silent warning. Hayes hurried to squeeze poor Charlie while he had the chance.

'To go back to your own encounter, Charlie. Normally you got a message where and when to meet your driver and when he arrived you gave a password and then got driven to a secret rendezvous. The driver took everyone home afterwards, no one arrived in their own transport, right? And the entertainment was tailored to the guest list. There were, I believe, gay parties including rent boys? The list of victims included a couple of names with special interests.'

Charlie bridled. 'Really? Well, it's news to me. None of that featured in anything *I* attended.'

'On the night in question you arrived at the Cut on cue and a man approached you and asked for the password. The driver?'

'I assumed so.'

'Someone you recognized from previous pick-ups?'

He shook his head, wincing a little. 'No, but there was something about the boy—'

'A teenager?'

'No, older, but wearing the scruffy gear all the kids wear these days, jeans and a ponytail under a baseball cap. Tall, skinny lad and didn't speak more than a couple of words but it was dark so you might be right, perhaps he was a driver who'd met me before. To be honest, I didn't take much notice once we'd got the password bit over with. Next thing I knew a second thug had crept up behind and bashed me over the head. There was a bit of a scuffle and the big one in the balaclava hit me again and I went down. But before I lit out I seem to remember one of them was a clumsy sort of clod, unsteady on his feet like he'd twisted his knee in the scrimmage.'

'Which one? The driver who approached you first?'

'No, the heavy bloke, I think, the one doing most of the damage, but don't quote me, it was just a fleeting fancy. When I woke up in the ambulance my wallet had gone, credit cards, the lot, so that was the end of my winnings.'

'Serves you right, Charlie,' Belinda chimed in. 'How many times have I warned you about flashing a fat wad in your money clip? But do you listen?'

Charlie paled at the recollection of his vicious encounter, a knotted vein throbbing at his temple. Belinda shot a glance at Hayes and pointed to her watch.

'I mustn't tire you, Charlie, but just one more question. The host at these parties — his name?'

'We all kept clear of names but later I spotted him. A real smoothie. Saw him at the Spa one day after I'd sprained an ankle on the tennis courts. It was that physio chappie, Baines. Mind you he was probably just the front man — organizing those private do's would take a brighter spark than young Baines. Struck me as a dimwit, surprised Bill Caxton employed him at the Spa, though, to be fair, he's bloody good with sports injuries.'

'But he must have realized you knew him?'

'No. I acted the old buffer and he swallowed it hook, line and sinker. That's the way with these young types, think anyone over fifty is mentally over the hill.'

Twenty-Eight

Hayes' check-up was scheduled for four o'clock, which left several hours to kill. After a desultory trawl through the bookshops and the purchase of some sheet music, he decided to ring Belinda on the chance that she would be free to lunch.

'Sounds lovely, Roger – where do you suggest?'

'You pick. Leonardo's? Or something swankier? I owe you.'

'My pleasure. Actually, I think it did Charlie good to get all that stuff off his chest. Was it any use to you? He wasn't terribly helpful in identifying the attacker, was he? "A skinny kid in a baseball cap" could apply to any one of thousands of roughs who come to the island for a holiday, run out of spending money and a silly old sod standing in a backstreet after dark's just asking for it.'

'Well, I hardly fit that description. I got turned over in a well-lit London square and it wasn't even midnight.'

'Mm. I suppose so. Anyway the hit must have been set up by someone in the loop. Someone who knew the procedure: the text message? The password?'

'That's the best chance we have of catching these guys. It narrows the line-up to those who knew about the parties and got hold of one of those likely to accept at the drop of a hat. I shall have to hustle Jeremy Baines, find out if there really was a party scheduled for that evening or whether poor old Charlie was the only invitee. It would be no problem lining up a victim on spec and inventing a password.'

'Do you think the police will find these guys?'

'Well, at present they're supposed to have their hands full with the one who died most recently, Francis Formby-Smith. Lockyer scarpered before they shook him down for details and Charlie's injuries were not too severe, so I'm guessing the crime team would have yet to have the chance to test his recollection of events, not helped, of course, by him being treated in London and virtually off limits for any sort of interrogation. Do you know any of the other victims well enough to put a word in for me? I'd like to ask a few questions before the trail goes completely cold.'

'As a matter of fact, I knew Francis, went out with him a few times,' she admitted. 'Young, only thirty-two according to the papers.'

'A likely partygoer on Baines' invitation list?'

'Possibly. A red-blooded type with no difficulty picking up girls. And rich, that always helps.'

'You liked him?'

Belinda shrugged. 'Wasn't really my type, too full of himself. He was involved in finance and got a lot of attention from the film companies that have set up on the island recently. But after the first couple of dates he suggested I might be up to some kinky games, Miss Whiplash stuff.' She laughed. 'Not my idea of a romantic evening. But he was fit, very fit, worked out at the Spa every morning before work, so I wasn't surprised to hear he'd put up a fight.'

They took a taxi to Knightsbridge and Hayes steered her to a fashionable eatery which put a sparkle in her eye. 'You're a bloody dark horse, Roger Hayes! I heard you lived in the backwoods before alighting on the Isle of Man. How come you know all the nice places to impress the girls? Not a gigolo, I hope?'

He grinned. 'Too old, and since the hoodies sliced me up I'm not pretty enough.'

'Sounds interesting.'

The lighting was low even at midday and the air-conditioning wafted a soft breeze between the sparsely occupied tables.

'It's quiet at this time of year,' he said with an apologetic smile. 'Normally this place is a magnet for minor celebs and the maître d' wouldn't give me a booking on the nod like this except I've brought a gorgeous bird along. Did you notice he gave us a table by the window? All thanks to you, Belinda – get Charlie to bring you back when he's given the all-clear, it would appeal to his eye for the ladies who lunch.'

'Smooth talk like that makes me wonder about you, sweetie. What's your line?'

'Between jobs at present – sort of security work, but it's very boring so let's talk about you. Tell me about this party-planning business you've got in mind.'

'Well, it's not the sort of lark Charlie got involved in, I promise you.' Belinda launched into an enthusiastic account of the services she hoped to offer, and Hayes listened attentively, impressed by her grasp of a chink in the market which would, he felt sure, be a winner.

Over coffee he pleaded a favour. 'If you're not too busy this afternoon, Belinda, I wonder if you could spare half an hour to help me choose a present for my girlfriend? She's learning to swim and I'd like to buy her a really nice swim-suit. Any ideas?'

They emerged into the sultry afternoon and she led him to a department store nearby. Shopping was, Hayes decided, one of Belinda's specialities and after they had decided on DeeDee's size, she swiftly whittled down the choice between an aqua bikini and a swimsuit in a sizzling jungle print.

'There you go,' she said as they hurried to a taxi rank. 'You'd better get a move on, Roger, or you'll be late for your hospital appointment.'

As he hailed a cab for her, he passed her a parcel. 'It's a couple of books for Charlie, a Dick Francis paperback he may have already read, and a coffee-table tome about Royal Ascot.'

'How sweet of you! Charlie will be tickled pink. Thanks for lunch, Roger, I'll give you a buzz when I get Charlie back home, shall I? You're staying on at Port St Agnes a little longer?'

'Probably another week or two. You've been a real gem, Belinda. Charlie would never have opened up to me without your encouragement. I'll ring you if there are any developments, OK?'

As it happened, Hayes' consultant was running late so he left a message on the desk and nipped down to the physiotherapy department to have a word with Gemma.

She was surprised to see her ex-patient looking so chirpy and led him through to her surgery and suggested running a swift check-up on his flexibility.

'Can't stop, I'm waiting to see Mr Harrison. Nice to see you again, Gemma, but I wanted to ask you about that colleague of yours, Jeremy Baines. You mentioned you knew him. Well, he seems to have settled for the end of the rainbow, got himself a cosy set-up specializing in sports injuries, and honestly Gemma, he looks pretty prosperous. Only thing is – and this is for your ears only – I've heard he's involved in organizing a sex-party ring on the island.'

'Wow. Well, that would account for some nice extra pocket money. You sure, Roger? Never struck me as being the type, though, now I come to think about it, he did have a bit of a reputation for harassment and, if we're speaking off the record, one of the girls in my year threw a wobbler and reported Jammy to the principal.'

'Rape?'

'Date rape, she claimed, after her drink had been spiked.'

'Serious stuff.'

'Yeah. But he denied it of course and the girl later withdrew the charge so nothing got as far as the police and she left soon after, decided to set up a massage parlour in Leeds.'

'Sounds expensive. Her parents put up the money?'

'No idea. Anyway, this was in her first year and the whole thing was glossed over.'

'Do you remember her name?'

'Danuta something. Let me think – this was way back, Roger, I'll have to dig deep.'

Hayes glanced at his watch, hoping the jolly consultant he remembered had not lost his cool at the disappearance of the copper sporting his neat stitchwork.

'Bronska!' she crowed.

Hayes came to with a start. 'You sure?'

'Absolutely. But keep it under your hat. Baines was officially innocent but, frankly, I believed Danuta.'

Twenty-Nine

Hayes tried to ring DeeDee from the airport but her phone was switched off again. He wondered if his abrupt response to her nosing about in his room and discovering his warrant card had seriously pissed her off.

This anxiety leapt into the stratosphere when he found a police vehicle parked outside Finch House — was it possible his identity had been reported to the local CID and he was about to be reprimanded for interfering in a murder investigation? Abandoning his car in the drive, he hurried inside, and rehearsed his alibi.

Roz intercepted him, her face grave.

'What's going on, Roz?'

'Bad news. DeeDee has had an accident.'

'What!'

'Drowned. The police are here talking to Phil, you'd better go in, they want to question you about swimming in the lake. I told that silly girl to be careful, but you know how crazy she could be . . .'

He stopped dead, his heart thumping, paralysed by guilt. It was all his fault, all those bloody swimming lessons . . . he should have guessed she was too impatient to wait for him to come back, determined to do it *her* way.

He went through to Phil's office, a converted butler's pantry on the ground floor next to the kitchen.

A uniformed sergeant was seated behind the desk arduously constructing his report. A young constable barred the way waiting for a nod from the big man in charge. Phil, ashen-faced, leaned against the wall, his eyes

144

alighting on Hayes with relief. 'Thank God you've come.'

The sergeant looked up, his flabby jowls reminding Hayes of Waller, an unblinking gaze focused on the interloper. Phil hastily introduced him.

'This is Mr Hayes, a special friend of DeeDee's. He can tell you all about her swimming lessons, Sergeant Fuller.'

The policeman removed his spectacles and waited. Hayes cleared his throat and launched into an explanation which, he had to admit, fell flatly into the silence. The sergeant was clearly unimpressed. It was an unnerving experience finding himself being questioned in this makeshift interview room and his voice faltered, the horror of the accident gradually seizing up his faculties to a stumbling recall of the sequence of events. It was not helped by his confusion about the discovery of the body.

'Are we inferring suicide?' the sergeant drily remarked.

Phil jumped into the breach. 'No! Of course not. Dee was a very bubbly kid, impetuous, full of confidence. As I told you before, Sergeant, she sang with the band at the tea dance at the Paradiso yesterday afternoon and was as happy as a lark and—'

'And never came back here afterwards? But you had a booking that night you said, Mr Bailey.'

'Well, yes, but she could have gone straight there, she knew the venue and had her dress from the tea dance. I wasn't worried at first. She was driving herself, said she had some shopping to do in Douglas and would see us later.'

'But she never returned?'

'No.'

'And you didn't wonder what had happened to her?' Hayes barked, impatient with the snail's pace of the investigation.

Phil chewed his thumb nail. 'Not really. DeeDee was what you could call a free spirit. Roz had occasion to tick her off before for turning up late for gigs and, once or twice, not at all. She was our vocalist, we just filled in, no sweat.'

'She went straight to the Spa?'

'Suppose so,' Phil murmured, 'but no one saw her there

and there's no check-in if you slip in off the side road which runs at the back of the lake. If you only want to use the cabin I rent for the season it's quicker to park by the boathouse and leg it from there. We all do it, it saves time.'

'Which was where her car was found,' the sergeant lugubriously noted, topping up the notes attached to his report form.

Hayes pushed forward. 'It is possible to enlighten me, Sergeant? I've only just arrived back from London, this has been a terrible shock and I'm not sure I've got the full picture. Who discovered the body?'

'One of Mr Caxton's gardeners, who was wading into the shallow end to help clear the surface of the lake. There was an excess of weed and rampant water lilies and a gang was working from two dinghies, raking out the worst and piling it on the jetty for disposal.'

'On Mr Caxton's orders,' the constable insisted. 'A terrible shock for the boys dredging up a body like that. One of the young lads is still in shock, Mr Caxton sent him home in a taxi.'

'What time was this exactly?' Hayes barked.

The sergeant looked up, frowning. 'You have a special interest, Mr Hayes?'

He decided it was time to show his hand and approached the desk, his anger barely under control.

'Look here, Sergeant, I need to speak with you privately, there are aspects of this accident which need clarification. Was Miss Miller's handbag in her car? She borrowed my keys and as soon as I can get into my flat upstairs I have information which seriously questions the accidental verdict which seems to be on the cards.'

'Suicide?'

'Certainly not. Now, let's get on with it, shall we? My keys?'

Thirty

'Keys?' The sergeant looked confused, and glancing down at his notes replied, 'No keys were found at the scene of the accident, only the car keys in the ignition.'

'You sure? Your men made a thorough search? At the boathouse? In the cabin?'

'Her towel and stuff were piled up in the boathouse,' the constable put in.

'Handbag?'

The sergeant shrugged. 'I shall have to check, sir.' He picked up the phone and, after a brief conversation, closed the file.

'Enquiries are being made, and now, Mr Bailey,' he said, turning to Phil, 'we must be on our way.'

'Hang about!' Hayes barked. 'I must speak to your chief, Fuller!'

His curt manner cut no ice with the sergeant, who made his way to the door, ignoring Hayes. Phil nipped off smartly, anxious to avoid any unpleasantness with the law.

Hayes barred the sergeant's exit. 'I need to get into my flat,' he repeated, 'and after that I must insist on speaking with your senior officer.'

Fuller drew himself up, backed by his young constable. 'Can't help you there, sir; but I'll pass on your message to Inspector Ross.' And with that he strode out, leaving Hayes impotently stranded in the passageway.

Hayes took a deep breath, crossed to Kevin's door and knocked loudly enough to alert the whole house, certain that

147

Kevin bloody Webber would be lying low with any police on the premises.

After a fresh attack on the doorbell a segment of the scrawny features of Caxton's caretaker appeared behind the half-open door.

'Oh, it's you, Mr Hayes . . . anything I can do for you?'

Hayes put his shoulder to the woodwork and barged in, his rage boiling over.

Kevin fell back, and Hayes slammed the door behind him. The curtains were closed, the room in semi-darkness.

'What's going on here, Webber?'

Kevin's eyes widened, feigning innocence. 'What? DeeDee's accident, you mean?'

'Don't piss about, shithead! What have you been up to?'

'I never touched her,' he squealed, flattening himself against the wall. 'Honest, Mr Hayes, I never even saw DeeDee all fucking day. Ask anyone. She was with the band and afterwards stayed on in Douglas so they say – it was nothing to do with me, on my mother's life!'

Hayes locked the door behind him and shoved his victim on to the bed. 'Right, *you* tell me. DeeDee left the others at the Paradiso and drove to the lake for a swim, OK?'

'How would I know? I was here all day painting the garage doors. You ask Mr Caxton – out in the boiling sun till the rain come down.'

'It rained?'

'Poured down. Thunder and lightning, the works.'

'What time was this?'

He shrugged. 'I dunno. Five, maybe half past. Come over black as night and I beat it back to the house.'

'And the others?'

'They'd got back from the Paradiso by then, and most of 'em was in their rooms for a bite to eat or have a kip most like. They went out again at seven as usual.'

'Everyone?'

'No idea. Some might've stayed on in town after the

afternoon session and gone straight on to the next gig. Don't always come back between shows.'

Hayes moved over to the chest of drawers and started rifling through the contents.

Kevin jumped up. 'Hey! Knock it off! What you after, mister?'

Hayes held up the Rolex.

'Craig's?'

He lunged forward but Hayes sidestepped, catching Kevin's foot and sending him sprawling. Hayes bent down and held the watch close to his face.

'Don't let's fart about, mate, I know all about your little racket. Insurance fraud. Drug dealing. Christ Almighty, I've got enough on you to have you banged up till hell freezes over.' He pocketed the watch and pulled Kevin to his feet, keeping a steel grip on the man's wrist.

'Now listen up, Webber. You're coming to DeeDee's room and opening up with your spare key. And afterwards you're going to give me the key to my flat – I've got something to show you which'll make your eyes water.'

'Yeah! And why would I do that?'

Hayes shrugged and let him go. 'Because I'm a police officer.' He gave him the direct eyeball treatment of a man with no need to lie and watched Kevin's belligerent stance crumble.

'OK?' Hayes murmured. 'We understand each other?'

'Who else knows about the Rolex?'

'DeeDee found out and Craig's boyfriend who works at the casino with her filled in the details. Craig is willing to cooperate, and if you play it straight, we can help each other. Got the message?'

Kevin's eyes narrowed. 'I don't know what you're playing at, but if you grass me up you'll find you've got another knife in your guts.'

The house was silent and the two men slipped through to DeeDee's flat like shadows.

'Did the sergeant try to search her room?'

'No way. I would have seen. You sure this is all right, her being dead an' all?'

'Just open up and don't touch anything. Keep this under your hat, right?'

The door swung open onto a scene of chaos: clothes strewn over the unmade bed, the wardrobe door hanging open and a litter of jars and cotton-wool scraps all over the dressing table.

'Hell – someone's been through here like a storm trooper!'

Kevin giggled. 'You never been in her room? It's always a tip like this. DeeDee was losing her keys all the time, I let her in so often I even offered to get a new set cut but Mr Caxton wouldn't have it. Very strict on security, Mr Caxton, no flat numbers on keys, spares always kept locked up. "Kevin," he says, "just tell the girls to be more careful."'

'So DeeDee never had an extra key?'

'Always found it eventually, though, looking round, it's a bleedin' miracle she found anythin' in this mess.'

Hayes swiftly searched the bedsit but found nothing. If someone had been through her things the interloper would have had no need to tidy up afterwards.

Kevin locked up and they retreated up the back stairs to Hayes' flat. The place was as he had left it, he could swear, but, pulling Kevin into the room, he claimed the spare key and shut the door.

'I'll keep this,' he said, pocketing the key.

'But Mr Caxton says—' Kevin protested.

'I'll square it with your boss, but frankly you're in deep shit, Webber, and I doubt whether Mr Caxton will be interested in retaining your services in the future.'

Kevin's face darkened. 'But you said—'

'I *said* if you cooperated. But I can't keep evidence like this out of the investigation,' he said, forcing the lock on the wardrobe door with his penknife. The flimsy wood splintered and the door swung open, revealing Hayes' neat row of hanging garments concealing a number of shopping bags and a sports holdall.

Kevin waited expectantly, wondering if there was time to

bolt while he had the chance. This Hayes bloke was a nutter, policeman or not.

With a cry of triumph Hayes emerged with a plastic carrier containing Kevin's biker jacket.

His skinny victim laughed out loud. 'Mine! So you was the bugger who pinched it!'

'Never set eyes on it before, but you recognize it? Swear it's yours?' he said, holding up the scuffed jacket from the neck tag.

'Where's it been, then? And how'd it get them oil stains?'

'Don't touch it!' Hayes snapped, dropping the jacket DeeDee had discovered back into the bag. 'It's evidence. And I doubt it's oil stains.'

'Well, I ain't pressing charges if I get it back – someone pinched it off my bike if that silly cow Roma didn't take it.'

'Why should she?'

'She borrowed my bike now and then to go into Douglas on one of her gigs.'

'And the jacket went too?'

'She said it was in the pannier – anyone here could have pinched it here or she must've left the bike in the street and someone fancied it. I don't lock the pannier. Can't believe anyone here would have snatched it, though, it's not their sort of gear. How did you get it?'

'DeeDee found it dumped at the Spa and locked it up here for safe keeping.'

'She knew you was a cop?'

'She found my warrant card. Here,' he said, rummaging in a drawer and producing the ID, a gesture which only stiffened Kevin's resolve to get out quick.

'Now we're alone, shall we go over this little scam of yours with Craig Durrant? If you play your cards right I can put in a good word for you but I shall have to produce this jacket to show the investigating officer. But can we do a deal, Webber? If you fill me in with the name of the big noise supplying you with class-A drugs, we could downplay the insurance fraud you and Craig cooked up, eh? Small beer compared with a murder enquiry. What do you say?'

Thirty-One

Hayes relocked his flat and drove to the Spa. He was ushered straight through to Bill Caxton's office.

The man looked older, his face drawn, the healthy tan now reduced to a yellowish pallor. He drew Hayes inside and phoned through to his PA that he was not to be disturbed.

'A drink, Roger? Whisky? Brandy? That poor kid was special to you, I hear. You must be in shock. When did you get the news?'

'Only a couple of hours ago. I've only just got back from London. I can't believe it, Bill. Drowned? In the lake?'

'Apparently. Crazy to be there so late in the afternoon. There was a storm, bloody dangerous to be out in the woods at all. You knew her well?'

Hayes accepted a tumbler of whisky, his mouth taut. 'Yeah. Something of a whirlwind romance. Did you ever meet DeeDee, Bill?'

'Once or twice at the casino. Great kid. After a request she played an old favourite of mine and whenever I sat in the piano bar on a Sunday night for a drink with friends she always remembered, and dropped into that number like I was a regular, which as it happened I wasn't. The casino never appealed to me but occasionally I'd be invited by my mates and it's good to size up the opposition. Food's excellent. You been there, Roger?'

'Only with DeeDee.' He paused and nervously passed a hand across his mouth. 'Look, Bill, I feel I owe you an apology. It was me who persuaded the girl to swim in the lake – it was my fault.' He went on to explain about the

152

swimming lessons. 'DeeDee got narked with me when she found out I was a policeman. I had kept it quiet from everyone at Finch House and it was only when we started a relationship that I wondered if I ought to come clean. It seemed dishonest to lie about it once I'd become friends with the other guys at the house, but you know how it is,' he said, opening his hands in despair, 'once you've laid down a false alibi it's hard to break. DeeDee found my warrant card in my room while I was away in London and she was the sort of girl to act impetuously, deliberately flout my rules about swimming alone and do the very thing I'd told her not to. She was younger than me, of course, and maybe I got a bit heavy, which is stupid when you're dealing with an independent woman who's been doing her own thing for years. So, there it is, Bill. I'm sorry. I feel I've brought one more disaster to your door just when we thought you'd seen the end of your troubles.'

'The muggings? You think they've ended?'

'I'm sure of it. When I was in London I had a long talk with Charlie Lyons and I reckon the attack on him was a final throw by the two thugs who've been terrorizing these men.'

'My members.'

'Mm. But that wasn't the whole story, Bill. OK, the victims were connected to the Spa but they were involved in something else, a sex-party ring which I'd stake my life folded after the last attack. It just got too hot.'

'Sex parties? Where did you get that idea? Some of my best friends were hit, and they were decent types. Why would they join in that sort of caper?'

Hayes laughed. 'Wealthy men, some of them past their prime? Think about it, Bill. Sex parties, exclusive champagne-style romps would be just the thing to tweak up a limp libido. And the more expensive, the more secret, the more fun.'

'How did you get on to it?'

'Charlie admitted as much with Belinda's promptings. She's a great girl, Bill, undervalued on this island in my opinion. She's been propping up poor old Charlie since he was beaten up and I think she can persuade him to help the police track down the link between the parties and the muggings. These men were targeted all right but not in order to ruin your business. Rest easy, your troubles are over, the Spa's not involved. There's just this drowning, which I'm far from certain was accidental.'

'The Miller girl wasn't involved in these sex parties?'

'No way. But she knew too much, poked her nose in too many ants' nests for comfort. I'm on my way to see the detective in charge, see what evidence he has to support the current thinking, which is accidental drowning.'

Bill Caxton stiffened. 'Christ, Roger, you're not inferring there's been a murder on my premises?'

Hayes drained his glass and rose to go, leaning across to pat Bill's shoulder. 'I can't let it go on the nod, chum. Sorry. I have to be sure, and I want to force the local man to check the forensics. Is there a criminal forensics laboratory on the island?'

'Search me. It's not exactly Hell's Kitchen, is it? Not till now anyway. I suppose Marty Lewis will splash this latest disaster all over the front pages, especially since I got that warning from the health and safety people about swimming in the lake.'

Hayes left Caxton to brood over the latest bombshell to hit the reputation of the Spa and dropped in to see the physio, Jeremy Baines.

The therapist was just seeing a patient out of the door, and raised an eyebrow as Hayes suggested a private talk. The surgery was exceptionally well appointed and Baines as smooth as any Harley Street quack.

'Business or pleasure?' he remarked, smiling, giving Hayes a megawatt flash of his perfect teeth. Hayes wondered if the Hollywood smile was as nature intended, Baines' gleaming gnashers quite the most attractive aspect of a podgy man with thinning hair who was already shaping up to an affluent middle age.

'Neither,' Hayes curtly responded, seating himself on Baines' leather sofa while the physio removed his white linen jacket and relaxed behind his desk with a cigarette.

'Smoking? I thought that sort of thing was banned here at the Spa?'

Baines blew a perfect smoke ring and regarded Hayes with amusement. 'I'm off duty. Fire ahead. I assume this is not a social call.'

Hayes toyed with the idea of firing off from all cylinders and blowing this self-satisfied tub of lard into a flat spin. But he decided to hold off, at least for the present.

'I've been getting to know some of your acquaintances, Baines. By the most fortunate of coincidences a colleague of yours has been treating me in London. She trained with you in Edinburgh. Gemma Dixey. Ring a bell?'

'Er, vaguely. It's a wide circle once one starts attending professional conferences. Pretty girl, I seem to remember. She mentioned me, you say?'

'Perfect recall, our Gemma. You clearly made an impression. She was, however, surprised to learn that you had settled for a practice on the Isle of Man.'

Baines laughed, a surprisingly falsetto chortle from such a large man. 'These city chicks think the big time only happens in London or California. This island is a gold mine, believe me. What did you say your business was, Roger?'

'I didn't. Actually, she recalled another colleague of yours, a girl who dropped out prematurely. Danuta Bronska.'

Baines smiled, not missing a beat. 'Sorry, old man, you've lost me now.'

'I don't think so, Jeremy. And while we are discussing mutual acquaintances, we also have another friend in common: Charlie Lyons. He has some interesting things to say about you.'

Thirty-Two

Jeremy Baines was clearly unfazed by the splash Danuta Bronska's name had made in the smooth waters of his professional space. Hayes wished now he had delayed this disclosure until after he had tracked down the girl at her massage parlour in Leeds. If, of course, Danuta was still pummelling away several years after her withdrawn rape accusation against Baines. Did this confident bastard seated behind his mahogany desk know more?

'Have you seen Danuta since college?'

'Look here, like I said, the name means nothing to me. Is that all?'

Hayes decided to hold his fire and switched to a new line of attack.

'OK. If Bronska doesn't register, how about Kevin Waller?'

Baines glowered. 'I have no reason to put up with an interrogation from you, Hayes, so I suggest you take yourself back to wherever you came from and leave us residents in peace.'

The phone shrilled and he picked up. 'Baines here. If you would please wait one moment I have a patient who is just leaving.' He laid the receiver aside and crossed the room, opened the door and waited for Hayes to take his leave.

He paused on the threshold. 'I'm not finished with you, Baines.'

The afternoon had gone badly and looked like deteriorating into an ineffectual punch-up with his uncooperative witnesses. It seemed there was no chance of presenting the local

156

investigation officer with any watertight evidence just yet, but DeeDee deserved more than a perfunctory wrapping-up on what was ostensibly a cut-and-dried case of accidental drowning.

The police station in Douglas was still busy with the minor disasters of the season: lost children, lost car keys and traffic flare-ups aggravated by the humid atmosphere but not yet escalating into road rage.

The account of the previous day's storm worried Hayes. Even taking into account DeeDee's determination to prove that she had beaten her water phobia, a lonesome splash in the lake in the midst of a storm was bizarre.

He recovered Kevin's jacket from the boot and presented himself at the front desk. Flashing his warrant card, he said, 'I would like to speak to the officer in charge of the Miller drowning incident. Inspector Ross?'

The duty sergeant scanned Hayes' ID with no apparent surprise, and after a brief phone conversation instructed one of the uniformed constables to show him through.

The name on the door identified Detective Inspector Brian Ross and Hayes marched in, in his element at last, the background hubbub of phones and slamming doors like music to his ears. He didn't think he would have missed it but maybe this lengthy sojourn on the island had confused his priorities.

Ross rose to shake hands; a young man, younger than Hayes, wearing casual clothes which Hayes decided senior officers could only get away with at the seaside.

'Chief Inspector,' Ross said, his handshake firm, the eye contact unwavering, 'you have information about Miss Miller's death, Sergeant Fuller informs me. You consider it suspicious? Please take a seat and tell me about yourself. Well off your beat, eh?'

'Convalescence.' Hayes briefly described the circumstances which had brought him to the island as a guest of Bill Caxton.

'Very generous. Were there no strings?'

Hayes paused before summarizing the anxieties of his

benefactor which had initially drawn him to take an interest in the muggings.

'And later you developed a special relationship with Delia Miller?'

'It was difficult to live at Finch House without becoming friendly with *all* the tenants but, yes, I did become fond of the girl. It was I who proposed swimming lessons in the lake.'

Ross frowned. 'Not a good idea – didn't you realize that the water was unsuitable for swimming? There *is* a notice to that effect, I saw it myself when I was called to the scene.'

Hayes looked uncomfortable. 'It was stupid, I agree, but the arrangement was that DeeDee would only go to the lake with me and swim under supervision because she was embarrassed to learn in the Spa pool, which is always busy.'

Ross smiled. 'Don't blame yourself, Mr Hayes, accidents happen. Is that all?' he said, glancing at his watch.

'Look here, Ross, can I put my cards on the table? I know it is unprofessional to interfere in an ongoing investigation but DeeDee and I were intrigued by this Phantom Duo spate of muggings and, quite by chance, she stumbled across some information which is important.'

Ross looked worried. 'Accidentally, you say? Miss Miller accidentally uncovered evidence pertaining to the murder enquiry?'

'Not specifically. But I have serious questions about the entire investigation and it may be that DeeDee's death is not unconnected.'

Ross's consternation hardened. 'If you will excuse me I must speak with the superintendent. The attacks on local men are being handled by Superintendent Broadhurst.'

He left the room and Hayes lifted the bag containing Kevin's biker jacket onto his knees. The shock of DeeDee's death had jolted him off balance and the effort of presenting the facts in a logical way seemed almost beyond him. Perhaps he had been away from work too long and had got too involved with an affair which was well out of his depth. And look where it had got him?

It was a lengthy wait before the two senior police officers, accompanied by Sergeant Fuller, returned to Ross's office and the room was suddenly crowded. The superintendent, a thin rasher of a man, easily six feet two and with the dour expression of a Calvinist minister, eyed Hayes with disfavour. Clearly, Hayes surmised, an off-duty detective on sick leave from the mainland was not a welcome sight as far as Broadhurst was concerned. Hayes wondered how his own boss would have reacted to such unwanted interference. Broadhurst's greeting was perfunctory and his manner cool.

The atmosphere in the room seemed to thicken and Ross's suggestion that they all repair to one of the interview rooms was not unexpected.

Hayes tucked his bulky carrier bag under his arm and followed the sergeant along a dark corridor, tailed by a disgruntled Broadhurst and his inoffensive sidekick, DI Ross.

Thirty-Three

The two senior men seated themselves at a table opposite Hayes, with Sergeant Fuller, the man Hayes had encountered at Finch House, standing sentry at the door.

Broadhurst pitched in first. 'Any objection to me taping this interview, Hayes?'

'Not at all. Fire away.'

'Name and address, please, sir,' Ross politely put in.

'Roger Hayes, Detective Chief Inspector, Thames Valley Police.'

'And your reason for being on the island?'

'Recuperation after a mugging. I was stabbed.'

'Ah, then I can understand your fascination with our own spate of attacks.' Broadhurst's voice had the hint of an accent; a long-abandoned link to Liverpool, perhaps? Hayes was on shifting sand when it came to accents and determinedly erased this passing fancy.

'Mr Caxton offered me self-catering accommodation in Finch House at Port St Agnes which suited my needs perfectly, and I settled in with a group of musicians working here for the season.'

'Bailey and the Blues,' Ross said, referring to his notes.

'The band Delia Miller sang with.'

'That's right. We became friends.'

Broadhurst frowned. 'A holiday romance, Mr Hayes?'

'You could say that, but our relationship quickly developed into one of trust. DeeDee discovered my file on the Douglas muggings and later found out that I was a police officer on sick leave. She became increasingly excited about

160

my findings and, despite my warnings, continued to make her own secret enquiries.'

'To what effect?'

'While I was away in London – I've been visiting friends and attending hospital for a medical check-up for the past few days – DeeDee overheard a heated argument in the yard at Finch House. The caretaker, a man called Kevin Webber, had an altercation with a tenant, a young woman called Roma. I don't know her surname. The crux of the row was the disappearance of his leather jacket, which the girl swore remained in the pannier of his motorbike.'

'She had borrowed it?'

'The bike. Presumably not the jacket.'

'But this item went missing?'

'Yes. I had a telephone call in London to say DeeDee had found the jacket stuffed in a locker in a disused boathouse by the lake. She locked it in my flat in my absence for safekeeping. Here it is.'

Hayes laid the jacket on the table and warned Broadhurst not to touch. 'See here,' he said, pointing to the stains, 'these could be bloodstains linking the jacket to the last attack, the mugging which put the final victim on your list, Charlie Lyons, in hospital with head injuries.'

Broadhurst leaned forward, positioning his bifocals for a closer look at this bombshell. 'What makes you think that?'

'Guesswork. We need to test these apparent bloodstains against a sample from Mr Lyons, who is willing to cooperate. There was also, according to DeeDee, something nasty in the pocket but I have handled this item as little as possible so the contents of the pockets are up to your forensic team. We need DNA tests, sir, and to persuade Mr Lyons to return to Douglas.'

'You know Mr Lyons?'

'We have talked about the attack, yes. He very importantly explained the real reason why he, and presumably the other victims, were in the Cut late at night.'

'He did?' Ross's voice almost squeaked with anticipation.

'Mr Lyons is willing to make a statement?' Ross eagerly put in.

'His ex-wife, Belinda Belville, has been encouraging him to come clean. I gather that he, presumably together with the other victims, have kept their mouths shut about their reason for loitering in the Cut and leaving themselves open to robbery.'

Broadhurst admitted that the witness statements had been less than satisfactory.

'These men were members of a sex-party ring, an exclusive gig open to rich residents on a strictly invitation-only basis. The membership fee was extortionate and the entertainment varied – some angled at gay evenings, others straightforward orgies.'

'You can prove this?'

'Mr Lyons has very bravely opened up and if you treat the other survivors with tact, you may well find they also will be willing to confess what they were really up to. I am certain the party circuit has closed down, the rumours were gathering momentum.'

'Can this man Lyons identify the attackers?'

'Not exactly. But he has described the way he was inveigled into play and that's where this biker jacket may link his evidence with his attack.'

'You suspect this Kevin Webber is one of the muggers?'

'Possibly.' Hayes took a deep breath and was about to continue when a voice behind him broke in. It was Sergeant Fuller.

'Excuse me, Superintendent, but I know Webber. He was one of my bad lads I had trouble with years ago. A right little tearaway, got nabbed in the end for GBH, put one of a rival gang in A&E with a broken collarbone.'

'Reformed character now, eh?'

Fuller grimaced. 'Well, as far as we know he's kept his nose clean and Mr Caxton's no fool, he wouldn't put a villain caretaking one of his holiday lets if he didn't trust him.'

'Well, take this evidence to my office, Fuller, and wait for me there.' Broadhurst shuffled the jacket back into Hayes' carrier and lit a cigarette, watching Hayes through a haze of smoke.

'Right, Hayes,' he said after several moments' reflection. 'What's your take on this Webber guy?'

'He's no angel, a minor drug-pusher at best, but he's on to a good thing with Bill Caxton and will turn somersaults to be cooperative if you treat him right.'

'Cooperative?' Ross snapped.

'Webber can put the finger on his supplier, who as it happens is the guy Charlie Lyons recognized as the front man at these sex parties.'

'Who is?'

'Jeremy Baines, the resident physiotherapist at the Spa Sports and Leisure complex.'

Ross let out a low whistle.

Broadhurst fiercely stubbed out his cigarette, his face reddening. 'Let's not get too excited about this. There's no obvious reason to bring in a respectable professional man for organizing private parties, and accusing him on drug running on the say-so of a runt like Kevin Webber won't wash, will it?'

'You've got Charlie Lyons backing you up. He can vouch for the fact that class-A drugs were available, on sale in fact, at these parties, and the guest list is definitely linked with the muggings. These victims were alerted to a party by text message at short notice. The routine was that the guest was told to wait at a certain location after midnight for a driver to arrive and, after spouting a password quoted on the text invitation, he was whisked to a secret location, different each time and at houses even Charlie Lyons, a long-standing resident, was unable to spot, then driven home at the end of the fun and games, sometimes not until dawn. The scam was to lure the mark to the appointed meet, knock him down and run off with the cash.'

'So the muggers had to know how to set it up?'

'And they had to have the contact numbers of the blokes on the party list.'

'But nobody said anything about parties,' Ross persisted. 'The victims all made various excuses about being in the backstreets so late but there was no suggestion of waiting for a driver. What about this organizer, Baines?'

Hayes grew exasperated. 'You've missed the bloody point. When the men were targeted there *was* no party. They got a false text message and password and assumed it was a kosher night out. Baines knew nothing about it and the victims kept mum to the police and quietly dropped off the list, possibly without warning Baines that his scam had been infiltrated by the Phantom Duo. It was not worth their while to get involved with the police once questions started crowding in about drugs, and most of these guys were respectable citizens far from keen to blow the trumpet and shine a floodlight on this crappy lark.'

Broadhurst thumped the table, his patience exhausted.

'You have lined up Mr Lyons, you say, but we're to play footsie with Webber. What about Baines? Does he know you're on to him?'

'Well, actually we did have words because I'd found out about an old scandal which Baines denies all knowledge of, but I think you should lay off Baines for the present and concentrate on pinpointing the mugger with scientific evidence from the jacket. Until you've got Charlie Lyons' blood test lined up with the stains on the jacket there's nothing to hang any future charges on. But if you can also score DNA evidence that would tie in with Charlie's description of the "driver" who met him in the Cut and kept his attention while his mate moved in behind with something like a truncheon you're well on the way to getting a watertight conviction.'

'Can he describe these thugs?'

'The so-called driver was, according to Charlie, a skinny kid wearing a leather jacket and baseball cap – oh, and the real bruiser in the balaclava was none too light on his feet, "clumsy clod" according to Charlie but he only caught a glimpse before he went down.'

'And that's *it*? Hardly worth organizing an identity parade, then,' Broadhurst muttered sourly.

'Ah, yes, the young lad had long hair bundled up under his cap and they both wore bovver boots to put the boot in, as your murder victim discovered when he put up a fight. Didn't the other victims describe their attackers?'

'I'll have to bring in Webber,' Broadhurst said with a heavy sigh. 'I hate pussyfooting with these petty drug-pushers, scum of the earth, but if you insist that this man's a valuable witness I'll play it softly at least until we've squeezed him dry.'

On that unhappy note Hayes left the station with a heavy heart, sadly aware that his promise to back up Kevin would probably get short shrift with the likes of Superintendent Broadhurst.

He spent the evening in Douglas, unwilling to face the grim faces of DeeDee's friends back at the house.

When he eventually turned in, sleep still evaded him, and after a restless tossing in the big bed DeeDee had been so fond of, decided to get up and make himself a cup of tea.

The memory of that first head-on collision with the girl flickered in his brain like a dream: the crash of wine bottles down the stairs: his initial flare-up: clearing up the broken glass into the fire bucket: her mischievous laughter . . . He sat at the kitchen table looking out at a clear sky filled with stars. Was it really all over?

Suddenly, it came to him. DeeDee must have hidden his key where he could easily find it if he returned from London while she was working, intending to phone him after her swim. Bingo! He rushed outside and sifted the sand in the fire bucket and brought up not only his door key but, attached to a blue ribbon, the key to his wardrobe where she had impulsively hidden the bloodstained jacket.

Thirty-Four

Next morning he phoned Belinda in London and warned her that matters had taken a disastrous turn. 'An officer from the Manx murder squad will be requesting a blood sample from Charlie.'

'Someone's already on his way,' she replied. 'He phoned Charlie at the clinic. He's agreed to see him this afternoon.'

'Superintendent Broadhurst?'

'No, Inspector Ross. Charlie seems OK about it, said the guy sounded reasonable. Is this the result of your connection with the local police, Roger?'

''Fraid so. The whole situation has taken on a new urgency, escalated by the death of my girlfriend, DeeDee.'

'The one we bought the swimsuit for?' she gasped.

'Accidentally drowned in the lake at the Spa, so current thinking goes. I'm not so sure. DeeDee was a feisty kid and took chances – I'll explain it all to you when you get back here. Is Charlie thinking about coming home soon?'

'Depends on the way things pan out with this Inspector Ross. He's insisting that Charlie's evidence is vital. Charlie won't be in any danger, will he, Roger?'

Hayes firmly reassured her but the security of their prime witness was certainly a worry. How discreet was Broadhurst's investigation likely to be? In all fairness, Hayes had to admit they were no nearer identifying the mugger and even if Charlie's blood sample tied up with the stains on the jacket, a DNA link would only come into play once a suspect was under arrest. Kevin's DNA would obviously exist in spades but could any evidence of the assailant be traced in the forensic lab?

A knock at his door forced Hayes to break off his conversation with Belinda and he hoped this visitor had not come bearing heavy-handed wads of sympathy. He felt raw with remorse, the accidental death of DeeDee something he found impossible to accept.

It was Karl Brecht, looking decidedly under par.

'Come in. Coffee? A beer?'

The bloke had, Hayes guessed, had as little sleep as he, his eyes heavy and his mouth grim. They sat at the kitchen table overlooking the courtyard. Several of the cars had gone, the minibus and Kevin's motorbike nowhere to be seen. Karl was wearing a Motörhead T-shirt and shorts, his thick hairy arms crossed over his chest.

'I feel terrible about DeeDee, man. And you look as if you could do with some company too.'

Hayes passed a can of lager to Kurt and silently nodded.

'She was a great girl,' Karl continued. 'Beautiful too. The rest of the band feel bad about it too, specially Phil. He's all broken up, nothing like this has ever happened to us before.'

'And I bet my name's mud, eh? Getting her to swim in that bloody lake.'

Karl sipped his beer, his bear-like form crouched over the table, his eyes downcast. 'Some people,' he began, 'like to point the finger, but we all loved DeeDee. It wasn't your fault, man.'

Hayes nervously slopped his beer onto the table, wishing this great-hearted slob would say his piece and leave him alone.

Karl took a video recording from his pocket and placed it on the table. 'There's something I've gotta show you, Rog. I even thought about keeping it to myself, but you'd better see it. I'm not proud of what I did, kidded myself it was artistic, see, but I'm just another peeper, a sick bastard, and you've every right to punch me on the jaw.'

Hayes looked up, totally at sea with all this, but Karl was on a guilt trip all of his own and it seemed that he'd been selected as the hanging judge. Karl went over to the TV and inserted the video.

The opening shot was of moorhens quarrelling by the lake, the sky overcast and the surface of the water choked up with lily pads. In the foreground the ruined boathouse and the jetty formed a theatrical framework for Karl's artistic endeavour, the zoom lens now focusing on a birdy sequence: two swans gliding between the overgrown vegetation.

Hayes grew impatient. 'Look, Karl, it's nice of you to call in but I've got to get into Douglas damn quick, the local fuzz are likely to mess up big time over DeeDee's accident.'

'Wait! It's just coming up. See?'

A sprite-like figure emerged from the boathouse, naked as Eve and impossible to recognize. Hayes wondered if Karl's idea of a cheer-up session was yet another showing of lesbian delights in the bushes. But suddenly he shot upright. Karl's zoom came into play and the delicate figure dipping her toe in the water was instantly recognizable.

'DeeDee,' he breathed. 'When was this, Karl?'

'Tuesday — between gigs. It was shaping up to a storm, the atmosphere was terribly oppressive. I decided to spend an hour by the lake in my makeshift hide to cool off, hoped to catch a shot of a barn owl that's been nesting in the boathouse.'

'Christ Almighty, Karl! You must have been the last to see her.'

The film started to wobble and the figure knee deep in the lake blurred, but the camera continued to focus on the girl who, after several minutes' hesitation, eventually splashed into deep water and struck out, sending the swans noisily flapping across the surface of the lake.

Hayes sat mesmerized, glued to the screen as if his life depended on it. The sky above the lake darkened and a fork of lightning briefly lit up the scene like a flash gun. The lone swimmer dog-paddled ruggedly towards the rowing boat tied up at the end of the jetty. She reached the boat and attempted to haul herself aboard but then the film cut out as a thunder clap heralded the first splashes of rain.

'I shut off and packed off back to the car before I got

soaked,' Karl apologetically murmured. 'Sorry, mate. Bad of me to film your girlfriend like that but, truly, it wasn't being dirty minded – DeeDee looked like some old oil painting by Claude, a woodland creature caught out in a storm.'

'You didn't wait to film any more?'

'*Nein*. Would you like to keep it?'

'Let's run it again.'

Hayes rewound the tape and they watched the short sequence again and again, Hayes becoming more excited at each run-though.

'Any chance of enhancing this, Karl? Blow up the detail?'

Karl shrugged. '*Ja*. Possible but how about if I enlarge individual frames of DeeDee? Is that what you want?'

'No. Look, that final sequence, the bit where she's trying to get into the boat – if you look close you can see the shape of a head poking out. It seems to me there was someone in the boat, lying down, sleeping maybe . . . And when DeeDee starts rocking the damn thing his head appears for a split second. See?' He stopped the video and waited while Karl took out his spectacles and peered at the spot Hayes pointed at on the blurred picture.

'You're imagining it, Rog,' he said at last.

'You saw no one else by the lake when you were there? Only DeeDee?'

'Her car and mine were the only ones parked in the back lane and no lights were on in the cabin despite the darkening afternoon so I guess the cabin must have been deserted when I ran back to get my gear in the car before the storm really broke. It was a thunderstorm, no one with any sense would stay out in all that rain.'

'You didn't think to stay to help her?'

Karl looked distraught. 'I was embarrassed. You knew DeeDee, she would have called me a dirty old man, a peeping tom, watching her like that. Don't think I haven't blamed myself since, my friend. I got hardly a wink of sleep last night.'

'But you weren't worried when she failed to turn up at the evening show with the band that night?'

'*Ach*, no. DeeDee gave Roz the runaround plenty of times. Worst timekeeper in the band and practically taunted Roz, all but dared her to sack her. It was only that she was an excellent vocalist and one of the few pretty faces on the stage – most of us are either too old or too ugly to attract any fans. DeeDee was special. She had star quality and the punters loved her for it. Roz just had to put up with her little ways.'

Karl stood up and formally shook hands, a gesture Hayes accepted with due solemnity. Privately, he suspected Karl had a hidden cache of girly pics tucked away, and filming DeeDee skinny dipping in the rain was too good an opportunity to miss. But who was he to hold grudges?

'I'm glad I didn't destroy the tape. We're still friends?' Karl anxiously poised the question but smiled as Hayes playfully punched his arm.

'Yeah, sure, mate. No grief, eh?'

'I was up most of the night wondering what to do,' he said. 'And when I did drop off I was shaken up by a frigging police car screaming to a halt under my window.'

'A dawn raid?' Hayes quipped.

'No, man. Poor bloody Kev was being bundled off. What do you think he's done?'

Hayes shrugged and held open the door. Karl turned to go, his huge feet squeezed into cracked patent dancing pumps, his creased jacket smelling pungently of deodorant. Hayes laughed and touched the big man's arm as he started to shuffle out. 'Your shoes look as if they're killing you, Karl – hope you're not in a dancing mood tonight.'

'*Ach nein*! It's my bloody bunion. Phil says we gotta fix up smart on stage and I ought've got these shoes stretched,' he said with a grin before lurching down the stairs like a dancing bear on hot coals.

After he had gone Hayes became lost in thought. Hadn't DeeDee said something about Karl having a torn ligament? Fixed up after physio sessions with Baines? He frowned. Surely not? Karl Brecht the limping 'heavy' Charlie Lyons had glimpsed before he passed out? The picture of a house in Chamonix edged into his mind; expensive for a third-rate double-bass player, surely?

But Karl would have got to know Baines really well in the course of the treatments, wouldn't he? Could this amiable fool have heard about the parties, wormed his way into Baines' confidence and, picking a likely accomplice like his supplier Kevin who was already on Baines' payroll as an occasional driver, hatched a scheme to relieve Baines' naive party guests of substantial amounts of cash? Brecht certainly had the weight to deck the unsuspecting victims . . .

His persistent friendly overtures suddenly took on a suspicious odour. And DeeDee had let slip to Brecht about Hayes' real identity: a detective chief inspector no less, someone to keep an eye on, share confidences with. Had he been so easily lulled into accepting Karl's assistance? Had taken the photographs and filming on trust? Hayes felt his blood run cold. Had he let himself be conned by such an unlikely killer?

Thirty-Five

Hayes drove into Douglas and beat a tattoo on Craig Durrant's door. He checked the time. Nearly noon. With luck the sour-faced loser would actually be out of bed. A curtain twitched and after a lengthy wait during which Hayes assaulted the doorbell, the scrape of boots in the uncarpeted hallway eventually heralded success.

Craig looked distinctly 'cold turkey', his eyes bloodshot, his thin cheeks grey with fatigue.

'Yeah? You back again, Hayes. What's it this time?'

Hayes pushed past, noting that the delay must have been caused by Craig's struggle to strap on his false leg and don his jeans. He felt a surge of pity for the guy, there didn't seem to be enough energy in the poor sap to pull himself out of the pit he had dug for himself. He followed Craig through to the kitchen, pleased to see that once he was togged up no one would guess about the disability. In fact, he hardly limped at all, possibly the result of being stone-cold sober for the first time since Kevin's cannabis supply fizzled out.

'How about a cup of tea, mate?' Hayes breezily suggested.

'Anything to eat? You look as if you haven't had a decent meal in weeks.'

Craig morosely filled the kettle, ignoring Hayes' unspoken observations of the lapsed housekeeping. The place looked much as before, unkempt and smelling vaguely mouldy, possibly the effect of the damp laundry hanging from an overhead drying rack.

The lad poured the boiling water over teabags and they took their mugs into the sitting room where, with the curtains

172

half drawn against another blistering day, the atmosphere was cooler.

Hayes regarded Craig with interest, and while they sipped their tea, quizzed him about the accident. Craig got into his stride, and grew enthusiastic with the retelling of his successful crusade against his employers.

No wonder he had been handsomely compensated, Hayes agreed, the construction company had clearly been indifferent to safety regulations. 'Well, Craig, when are you going to get down to the job centre?'

'Doing what?' he sharply retorted.

'You're no fool, Craig. And now you've begun to kick the habit – with no help from any bloody addiction centre either! – you could pick up something better than being dumped on by a ton of bricks.'

Craig's mouth dropped. 'You really think so?'

'Sure. I'll ask around, shall I? You'll have to get your act together, though, clean up, shave off that bum fluff on your chin – it makes you look a stupid kid straight out of school. Can you drive?'

'Automatics. But I ain't been behind a wheel since me motor was reclaimed.'

'But I bet you and Webber were a couple of speed-track kids, eh?'

'Kevin? Nah. He always preferred bikes, mad on the TT races our Kev.'

Hayes dived in at the deep end. 'Poor Kevin's been taken in for questioning about these muggings. Been cautioned so I hear.'

Craig slopped his tea, his eyes wide. 'The Phantom Duo stuff? Never!'

'Well, let's face it, you got a free ride on the back of all those attacks, didn't you, mate? And it was you who got Kevin involved in the first place.'

'But we never did nuffin', I swear it was just a scam to pay off Kev's supplier.'

'Who was?'

'How would I know? I just got this warning that if I didn't pay up the hard man was going to smash up my other leg. Kev said he was serious.'

Hayes shrugged. 'He was a good pal, then, Kev?'

'The best.'

Hayes drew out the Rolex from his pocket and dangled it at arm's length. 'Yours?'

Craig giggled. 'Yeah! Did Kevin ask you to bring it back? I ain't got the final cheque from my solicitor yet, them lawyers stick to payouts like glue.'

'No, he didn't exactly hand it over. I searched his room and found where he'd hidden it. He let me take charge of it till we'd had a talk, you and me. You see, there's something I forgot to mention when I was here last time.' He produced his warrant card. 'I'm a policeman. Not local, here on a private matter. I stumbled into this series of muggings by accident but now the police are getting their hooks into Kevin I think it's time you stood by your best mate, don't you?' Hayes passed over the Rolex, which Craig regarded with awe, lighting up like a girl eyeing a tray of engagement rings in the jeweller's window.

'You want me to give myself up? Tell them about our little game?'

'You owe it to him, Craig. *I'll* back you up, drive you to the nick now before they start dropping serious charges on poor Kev. You have to tell them that your mugging was an act. Kevin helped you jump on the bandwagon to claim the insurance money, that he was nothing to do with the other muggings. Right?'

Craig lowered his head, staring at the gleaming Rolex cupped in his hands. 'But they'll charge me with attempted fraud, won't they? They ain't got anything on Kev, it's just a bluff, they're desperate to pin them attacks on someone and Kev's been fitted up.'

'They've got his jacket and the chances are there's blood on it linking Kevin to this latest attack. It's solid evidence, Craig, no messing.'

'Blood? You're pissing me off, ain't ya? Kev's never killed anyone, the nearest he got to blood was knocking me about to make my story look good.'

'He's got a record for GBH.'

'Who says?'

'It's on file and you know what us rozzers are like when it comes to pinning down the nearest innocent bastard with a criminal conviction.' Hayes felt he was plumbing the depths with this bit but how else was he to plant any doubts in Broadhurst's investigation but to show that at least one alleged mugging by the Phantom Duo was all malarkey?

'If we set it up sensibly, Craig, the chances are they'll let you off lightly. You haven't even got all the money yet, your conscience got the better of you, and the insurance company may well take a generous view. But you will need a solicitor to go with you to the police, make a case for the desperation of your situation following threats from Kev's supplier. Emphasize the only reason you got into the cannabis was to dull the agony after the amputation, no need to go into the class-A stuff, keep it simple. If Kevin knows you're backing him up to get him off, he might be persuaded to name his drugs boss. If I know blokes like Superintendent Broadhurst, nabbing a big drug-dealer would sweeten his attitude to throwing the book at you and Kevin. Fraud's a nasty game, mate, and you were a fool to try it, but I can see the trap you were in and with a decent lawyer you and Kev will walk, I promise you.'

'You reckon?'

'Let's get it over with. This solicitor who's been handling your compensation claim. Any good?'

'Well, he *knows* me . . .' Craig admitted with a sly grin.

'Let's give it a go, eh? Local chap?'

Craig crossed to a roll-top desk in the corner and rummaged around until he unearthed a stack of paperwork. 'Here. Mr Snellgrove, 105 the Parade, Douglas.'

'Shall we see what he's got to say, then? I'd better go with you, just to keep you in line, OK? I'll wait while you smarten yourself up and then we'll have a bite to eat in town before we explain to Mr Snellgrove the way you and Kevin foolishly cooked up this crackpot scheme.'

'Can I keep the watch?'

'Wear it if you like. It might be your last chance. While you're in the bathroom I'll phone the solicitor and make an appointment.'

After a courage-boosting slap-up lunch at a pub on the promenade, Craig had convinced himself that by confessing his role in the insurance scam and eliminating his best pal from any link with the real muggers, Craig Durrant was playing a starring role at last. Real hero stuff.

Hayes was none too sure that his promise about Broadhurst's likely response was well founded but if this Snellgrove character put a decent gloss on it and played up poor Craig's pain, there would at least be a chance of bringing Baines into the frame and if Broadhurst's sworn disgust at drug-peddlers was true, tying up Baines with the sex-party organization would be a step nearer closing in on the two thugs who had used his party guest list as a way to roll over some of the wealthiest residents on the island.

Thirty-Six

The interview with the solicitor took up most of the afternoon, Hayes prompting Craig's confession which dwindled as his Dutch courage slowly evaporated.

Hayes and Snellgrove hit it off straight away, the middle-aged lawyer gently forcing the full story out of his reluctant client. Frank Snellgrove had been in the business long enough to have a nose for the half-truths bad lads like Durrant always tried on. His manner remained polite but the steely persistence of his questions gave Hayes hope that the wretched Craig would actually put enough doubt in Broadhurst's mind to let Kevin off the hook, if only temporarily. Hayes did admit that his own lack of any background knowledge was a big disadvantage and perhaps there was murky history behind Kev and Craig that wouldn't bear too much probing.

Fortunately, Snellgrove was persuaded to take on the business and he arranged an appointment with Detective Superintendent Broadhurst at eleven the next morning.

'Now you won't let me down, will you, Craig?' he said meaningfully. 'Inspector Hayes here has heard what you've got to say, and as a senior police officer, he will not take kindly to any backsliding. Understood?'

Hayes told Craig to wait in the car while he had a private word with Mr Snellgrove.

'I'll be responsible for your account, Mr Snellgrove. I have a personal interest in clarifying this series of muggings. Here's my card, I've written my current address in Port St Agnes on the back. You can reach me at any time. Would you like me to pick up Craig in the morning?'

'No, I think he's got the message. I'll drive him to the station myself, we don't want Mr Broadhurst to worry about your part in Craig's dose of conscience, do we? As a matter of interest Jim Broadhurst is an acquaintance of mine, a fellow Rotarian, so we can speak frankly to each other. He's no fool, Inspector Hayes, it would be a mistake to write him off on this Phantom Duo investigation. A murder on the island is not a familiar problem here and if my friend lacks your experience in such serious crimes, his local knowledge will certainly make up for it.'

Snellgrove smiled, showing Hayes the door with good grace in the circumstances. The man probably regarded acting for Craig Durrant an unsavoury professional burden, and Hayes perceived an understated admonition in his parting words.

After dropping Craig off at his house, Hayes felt in need of a drink, and made it to the casino piano bar in time for cocktail hour. The place was beginning to fill up with a surprising number of ladies of a certain age for whom a pot of tea just would not hit the spot. Tony was working the early shift, and a pianist quietly tinkled away in the background, fortunately leaving the vocals till later in the evening.

Hayes dropped onto a bar stool and ordered a vodka and tonic. Tony seemed jittery, too many ice cubes clinking in the tumbler like castanets. The atmosphere was tense and Hayes wondered if Tony had joined those who blamed him for introducing DeeDee to swimming in the lake.

After a thirsty slurp of the chilled cure-all, Hayes tried his luck. 'You must have heard about DeeDee's accident, Tony?'

He nodded, furiously scrubbing at the wet circles on the bar as if blood had pooled there. 'Yeah. Tragic waste if you ask me.'

Hayes nodded. 'Look, I admit it was wrong to encourage her like I did, but it was only a bit of fun to begin with, I had no idea she would try it on her own. I've been away. DeeDee phoned me in London, very excited about evidence she'd found at the boathouse. Did she mention it to you?'

'Haven't seen her since Sunday night.'

'She kept some clothes here, I believe. In a locker?'

'Yeah, we all have lockers so we can get changed before we go home.'

'Have the police emptied her locker?'

'No one's been here, as far as I know. Is someone sorting out her stuff to send to her family?'

Hayes shrugged. 'I don't know. You haven't heard anything, then?'

'What about?'

'Oh, never mind. I just wanted to cover all the avenues. Between you and me, Tony, I'm not happy about this accidental verdict everyone's so keen on.'

'Why?'

'Just a gut feeling. DeeDee was impulsive but not stupid enough to get out of her depth.'

'You reckon?' Tony said, his tone warming, the frenetic mopping up diminishing to a slow, rhythmic pass with the paper towel.

'There's something I have to tell you, Tony. You'll hear about it soon enough and I feel I ought to come clean since DeeDee . . ,' His voice faltered, the mere mention of her name clouding logical thought. 'Well,' he said, starting again. 'The thing is I'm a police officer, off duty and here on sick leave as it happens. I thought I'd like to stay incognito, and without wishing to deceive anyone, I've ended up looking a complete wanker. I found out about Craig's insurance scam and I've persuaded him to go to the police and admit it.'

'He's not implicating me in this, is he?' Tony burst out and, then suddenly concerned about the customers sitting nearby, lowered his voice. 'Craig's not saying I put him up to it, is he?'

'No way! He's taking a solicitor with him and he's going to admit the whole thing was struck up between him and Kevin Webber, a stunt to bring in cash to pay off his dealer. He was being threatened and poor old Craig was in no frame of mind to cope with a beating-up from the heavy mob.'

'But he'll be charged.'

'That's up to them but he's got a good lawyer and it's important we get Kevin out. You see, DeeDee found Kevin's bloodstained jacket at the boathouse and the investigation's shaping up to a prosecution. They're linking Webber with the real muggings and Craig's in a position to clear him.'

'Why's Webber so important? Why should Craig put his head on the block for that weasel? Webber's been supplying Craig with crack, Roger. Did you know that?'

'We're hoping to keep Craig's addiction limited to cannabis use.'

Tony laughed, causing one of the ladies to swivel round to stare at the two men having such a lively tête-à-tête over the bar counter. She raised her hand for a refill and Tony hurried over to take her order leaving Hayes to examine the clientele in the wall mirror behind the bar. The women seemed a mumsy sort on the whole, well dressed, nicely coiffed and apparently with all the time in the world for late-afternoon drinkies.

Tony served a couple more and then resumed his place behind the bar. 'What are you going to do about DeeDee?'

'I'm just snooping around, trying to make sense of it. It was shaping up for a thunderstorm when she decided to take this fatal dip.'

'Yeah, right. I remember. Sounded like a bloody avalanche. Came over dark as I was driving in to work, and as soon as we set up the heavens opened. People were dashing in here just to get out of the downpour.'

'Exactly.' Hayes finished his drink and slid off the bar stool. 'I'd better push off. Who's in charge of the staff-room lockers, Tony?'

'Mr Eldridge. He'll be in the office.'

'Right. Thanks, Tony. Here, buy yourself a drink, we've had our share of bad news.'

As he turned to go he chanced a weak sally about the customers and whispered, 'All these women, Tony? They here every night? You could set up a lucrative singles bar with this lot.'

Tony smiled. 'You'd be surprised. Plenty of old boilers meet here at this time like homing pigeons. Can't stay away. Addictive. They get tanked up then they move into the casino, start off throwing a few tenners at the roulette wheel, win a bit, and, before they know it, it's the only thing that matters. Most of 'em can afford to lose but I've seen chicks as young as that kid who lives at your place hooked, mortgaging their pay cheques every week, having to beg the management for time to settle up. Makes you weep.'

'Someone from my house?'

'Sure. More than one. DeeDee pointed them out to me, her boss was one.'

'Phil Bailey?'

'No, the real boss, his wife. And her friend, the pretty girl, she got in really deep so I heard. Tried to work off her debts moonlighting with an agency, some sort of escort girl I guess.'

Hayes absorbed this without a flicker of apparent interest and bid Tony au revoir.

He made his way to the office and found the house manager behind his desk studying time sheets. He wore a white tuxedo and a cyclamen bow tie, his smile as fleeting as a summer breeze.

'Mr Eldridge?'

He rose. 'May I help you, sir?'

Hayes produced his warrant card and Eldridge tersely invited him to state his business.

Hayes made short work of his confidential investigation on behalf of Mr Caxton.

'Bill Caxton asked you to make some quiet enquiries about the muggings? He was dissatisfied with the local police investigation? Can't say I blame him, several of our own regulars were targeted. People get jittery.'

'My effort was merely to reassure Mr Caxton that the muggings were not directed at Spa members in any conspiracy to weaken his business. As you say, some of your own clients were victims too and in fact it seems the link is not the Spa membership or the casino clientele but a secretive organization involving private sex parties.'

Eldridge stiffened, his commercial antennae alerted by this titillating disclosure, curious to know more.

Hayes refused to elaborate. 'The police have a suspect in for questioning but the investigation lacks hard evidence. One of your late employees, a girl called Delia Miller, died in what would appear to be a swimming accident.'

'Yes, I heard.'

'Miss Miller was in my confidence with regard to my investigation of the series of muggings and telephoned me in London shortly before she died to say she had left an item in her staff locker here which might be important. I don't think the police are treating her death as suspicious but I remain unconvinced. Would you object to opening the locker so that we could examine the package she left there for me?'

'She thought it was relevant?'

'Yes. I assume you keep duplicate keys? I am, of course, willing to sign a receipt for anything I remove from the premises.'

Eldridge looked worried but decided to play along with Hayes' game. 'This is official? I don't want to get on the wrong side of the local police, you realize.'

'No, of course not.'

Eldridge led the way to a staff room comfortably set out with sofas and a coffee machine. A door marked 'Ladies' led to a changing room and after Eldridge barked a warning hello he strode in, Hayes at his heels. The bank of steel lockers filled one wall, and Eldridge selected a key from a plastic sandwich box he had brought from his office and opened number seven, DeeDee's lucky number, Hayes remembered with a stab of recognition. The full-length locker contained two empty hangers and a spangled mini-dress which Hayes remembered DeeDee wearing on that first occasion when they had collided on the landing at Finch House. A pair of silver sandals was placed sedately side by side and a plastic raincoat was rolled up on the upper shelf together with a zipped make-up bag. Hayes felt cheated. What had DeeDee been playing at? Or had someone got into the locker ahead of them?

Eldridge insisted on turning out the entire contents, dropping the items onto a bench seat below a large wall mirror. Hayes hung back while Eldridge pawed through DeeDee's stuff, feeling slightly sick. Was she really dead? Was this pile of clothes the sad remains of such a vibrant personality? They returned everything to the locker after Hayes had checked the pockets of the screwed-up plastic mac before placing it on one of the hangers. He held onto the make-up bag and unzipped it. Like a jack in the box, the shiny wig she had stolen from Roz's rehearsal studio sprang out, the silky tresses as frisky as a little furry animal.

'Found what you were looking for?' Eldridge drily remarked, closing the locker with a clang. He peered into the inoffensive-looking make-up purse. 'All right, I take it?'

'No problem.'

Hayes hurried away and only when he was back in the car trusted himself to have a second look.

He unzipped the bag and the pungent scent hit him again like a dose of poison gas. Unmistakable. A musky perfume, civet-like. Aftershave?

Thirty-Seven

Hayes drove to the station but was turned away. 'The superintendent's gone home, sir, and Detective Inspector Ross is in London.'

'But I need to speak with DS Broadhurst urgently.'

'Sorry, sir, you'll have to come back tomorrow.'

Hayes fumed at the delay but declined to discuss his findings with one of the less senior members of the squad. It was all bloody infuriating — did none of these hick detectives realize that a murder investigation required round-the-clock policing? He bitterly imagined Broadhurst swanning off to his supper, leaving poor fucking Kevin sweating it out in one of the cells.

He retreated and fell in line with the holiday crowd beating a path to the theatre, which was putting on a seasonal romp entitled *Sailors Ahoy*. The prospect of returning to Finch House and facing the averted glances of his fellow lodgers seemed too much to contemplate and he decided to book in at a motel outside the town he had spotted on the way in. The place was filling up, tourists taking advantage of cheap rates for a minimum booking of three nights queuing at the reception desk.

The room he only just managed to secure before the 'Vacancies' sign was taken down suited his mood, an anonymous bolthole safe from the accusing stares of DeeDee's friends. Until the coroner decided on a verdict, the suspicion that Hayes was to blame would stay in their minds. It was easier, he supposed, for them to have a focus for blame. After all, DeeDee had been their pet, the only one brave enough to hold two fingers up to Roz, the one with the infectious laugh, the prettiest girl in the band.

Next morning he returned to the station and reluctantly agreed to accept an appointment with Broadhurst at four o'clock, apparently the earliest slot in the man's schedule. To fill in the day he drove to the Spa and spent an hour in the gym working off his frustration. The scars below his chest were no longer painfully taut, and after a punishing session under Lenny's beady eye, he showered and took off on the mountain bike for a bit of a spin. The lake drew him unmercifully but the boathouse had been roped off and men clearing the reeds and thickets of water-lily growth watched him approach. Hayes dumped the bike on the bank and strolled over.

'Out of bounds, sir,' one shouted, pointing to the disused boathouse. 'Loose floorboards. Dangerous. Mr Caxton's having it pulled down.'

'Right-oh. OK if I stretch out here in the sunshine? It's interesting watching you blokes clearing out all this jungle. Found anything? Alligators?'

The man laughed. 'Only about a million frogs.' He resumed attacking the mass of tangled stems, the ropes of weed coiled like snakes as he threw them onto the jetty.

After an hour of this, Hayes cycled the full circuit of the Spa estate, checking the access road behind the lake where DeeDee had parked her car. The road was empty, her little blue Toyota presumably driven away to the police compound.

He left the bike in the shed and strolled back to the gym to change into his street clothes. The face in the mirror in the gents stared back at him like a stranger, the newly tanned features stony.

After lunch the afternoon yawned ahead, the hours ticking away with monotonous slowness. He tried phoning Belinda but no joy. It was as if the whole world stood on tiptoe waiting for something to happen.

His appointment with Broadhurst eventually came around and he was shown into the office. Broadhurst was in no mood for him and, before formally addressing him, rang through for his sergeant to be in attendance. Hayes seated himself across from the desk, reining in his impatience. There was no point in riling Broadhurst. He was the man standing outside this investigation, and if he was to expect any cooperation it would be necessary to proceed with tact.

Finally, after closing the files in front of him, Broadhurst settled, his manner frosty. 'You have information pertinent to my investigation, I understand.'

'Yes, sir. An important piece of evidence. May we use your video machine?'

'What for?'

'I have a tape filmed by a colleague of Miss Miller's, shot shortly before she died.'

Broadhurst accepted the video and signalled to the sergeant to do the necessary. While it was being set up Hayes ventured a critical observation.

'It was never mentioned that the body was naked.'

'Ah, well, it hardly seemed relevant. The girl was not sexually assaulted, the pathologist assures me. Who did you say shot this film?'

The recording came into play, the birdy scene clearly trying Broadhurst's patience.

'Karl Brecht. He's the double bass in Bailey's band.'

Suddenly the dreamlike sequence of DeeDee's final dip came up and Broadhurst stared intently at the screen until it broke up. 'Not much there, Hayes. What's your point?'

He moved across and grabbed the handset from the sergeant, rewinding the film to the point where DeeDee was attempting to climb into the boat. It rocked wildly and the film seemed to lose focus. Hayes stopped the reel. 'See! There! Someone's head. Someone was lying in the boat.'

Broadhurst adjusted his specs and peered at the spot Hayes indicated. After a moment he leaned back. 'Too blurred, Hayes. It could be anything.'

'But worth blowing up. We could get a detailed enlargement. You have the facilities here?'

Broadhurst nodded. 'Bit of a long shot, Hayes.'

'But if someone saw her that afternoon why haven't they come forward?'

The question hung in the air like a sword, Hayes' urgency infecting Broadhurst with a glimmer of suspicion. 'Anything else while you're here? Don't say I haven't been patient with you, Hayes. I gather you were instrumental in forcing Craig Durrant to come clean.'

'Well, that's one alleged mugging that you can scrub off your list, sir. Did Inspector Ross get the blood sample from Charlie Lyons?'

'It's on its way. Mr Lyons is flying home tomorrow. He wants to make a full statement about these sex parties. We shall have to put Webber and Durrant on an identity parade when he gets here.'

'He's well enough to participate?'

'His doctor is agreeable.'

'Then I suggest he's given protection. Mr Lyons is our key witness.'

'*Our* witness! You seem to forget who's in charge here, Hayes. If you interfere any more I shall have to register a complaint.'

Hayes pushed on regardless. 'Has Webber been released?'

'Temporarily. Mr Caxton gave his assurance that Webber would be available. Did you know he worked at the Spa?'

'Apart from caretaking at Finch House?'

'Mr Caxton employs him part time in the summer to help with the swimming-pool maintenance. Your protégé – if I may call him that – is no stranger to the Spa estate and could easily have disposed of the leather jacket in the boathouse himself.'

'You're not convinced he had nothing to do with the other muggings, are you, sir?'

'Webber has a history of violence and that pal of his, Durrant, fits the description of Lyons' attackers which is on record: long hair and skinny. You may have a personal reason to meddle in the Delia Miller investigation but as far as these so-called Phantom Duo muggings go, my enquiries are — let's make no mistake about this, Chief Inspector — none of your business. May I keep this video recording?'

Hayes nodded.

'But there's something I should mention. It has recently occurred to me that the man who has provided us with all this interesting footage may be more involved than as a mere onlooker. The tape breaks off at a vital moment, presumably just before Miss Miller drowned. A discreet investigation might uncover certain inconsistencies and I'm interested in Brecht's ability to purchase property in Chamonix.'

'An alpine retreat?' Broadhurst sourly retorted.

'For the winter months, he told me, rents it out in the summer when he's working here. But we have agreed that two men were working this scam, haven't we? The outline of another bloke in the boat on the lake could have been an accomplice, eh? Brecht must have followed DeeDee from the gig and if he is the mystery second man remember Charlie Lyons' comment about his attacker being clumsy on his feet? Brecht suffered a ligament injury and was treated by the Spa physio, Baines, and he could have heard about the parties Baines fronted from either Kevin Webber, who supplies him with cannabis, or from small talk at the gay bar he goes to, one of the victims being Porlock, who was a good friend of his.'

'This is all conjecture, Hayes. I prefer to work on facts.'

'Just a thought.'

Broadhurst's lips stretched to a thin smile. 'Now, if you'll excuse me, Chief Inspector, I have work to do.'

Thirty-Eight

Hayes thought about staying another night at the motel but decided that Sunday afternoon was as good a time as any to literally face the music at Finch House. At least Karl bore him no grudges and, as five days had passed since DeeDee's accident, perhaps feelings had softened towards the stupid guy who had urged her to swim in the lake in the first place.

The inquest was scheduled for Thursday, by which time he hoped to have found some support for his theory about her death. Linking DeeDee's death with her overenthusiastic nosing around in the mystery of the muggings was a long shot. How careful had she been? How discreet about his police connection? How much had leaked out at the house regarding his own undercover enquiries? The place was a hotbed of gossip. But how else would they amuse themselves, clamped together all summer like a travelling circus?

The sun continued to burn and the near-empty courtyard confirmed his guess that the residents would be making the most of their free day. Karl's motorbike was parked together with Kevin's, which posed the question, should he dig them out and catch up with the news?

He locked the car and was making his way towards the back stairs as Kevin emerged from his pad. The bloke looked shattered, and as soon as he spotted Hayes he turned tail and attempted to bolt back inside.

Hayes grabbed his arm. 'Hey, Kev! Good to see you back. Fancy a beer in my room?'

'You're bad news, Mr Hayes. If it wasn't for Mr Caxton I'd still be banged up.'

He tried to break away but Hayes held on. 'No, don't be like that. I thought we had a deal? I need to know how much got spilled to Broadhurst. You may not believe me, Kev, but I'm on your side. I'm the one who's been trying to get you off the muggings charge. If I hadn't leaned on that wet nelly, Craig, Broadhurst could have charged you both, do you know that? And with a murder case on his hands, he's not going to break his heart if the evidence points to you, believe me. Your jacket's his key piece of evidence and Broadhurst has only got your say-so that it disappeared from your bike pannier. Now, calm down, mate, and let's talk about this.' He let him go.

Kevin hesitated, unsure which side Hayes was really on, but decided taking a chance on this lying bastard of a copper was, on balance, worth a bet. 'OK. Come in and I'll tell you what I know.'

Kevin's bedsit was a crappy set-up made worse by most of the floor space taken up with spare parts from the bike. He dumped the assorted metalwork in a cardboard box and shoved it under the table, closing the door behind Hayes, who looked around for somewhere to sit. Kevin cleared a pile of girly magazines from the sofa and after dragging a chair from the kitchen alcove, lit a cigarette and waited for Hayes to set the ball rolling. Truth was he was sick of all these bloody questions but fear took the upper hand and he decided that with only Mr Caxton on his side he needed all the help he could get.

'Right. First off, Kev, how much did you spill to Broadhurst about the drug-peddling?'

'Just a bit of weed now and then.'

Hayes laughed. 'And he believed you?'

'Well, I said I *was* asked for a few tabs of Viagra sometimes . . .'

'And who supplied you? Did you mention Baines?' Kevin's clenched fist punched the air. 'D'ya take me for a fucking moron?'

'You're scared of Baines?'

'You bet I am. And who d'ya think'd believe me if I said that pot-bellied git was running the game?'

'But you can't be his only runner.'

'How would I know? I just make a bit extra getting stuff for my mates and Baines fixes the supply.'

'How?'

'You think he'd tell *me*? No, Baines keeps his hands clean, leaves the face-to-face stuff to fools like me.'

'Well, I've got good news for you, chum. A very respectable witness is flying back here today and he's willing to put Baines' fat arse on the griddle.'

Kevin stubbed out his fag and squinted at Hayes, weighing up the strength of Hayes' information.

'Craig told you?'

'Don't piss me about, Kevin. No one would trust Craig with stuff like that.' Hayes decided it was time to try a flyer. 'Have you picked up guests for this party merry-go-round? Has Baines sent you to drive punters to the venue, told you the password you had to ask for?'

Kevin shrugged. 'Once or twice, when his regulars couldn't make it.'

'Regulars? You knew them?'

His face broke into a sly grin. 'You'd be surprised, gob-smacked if I told you that.'

Hayes let it go, unwilling to stretch this tenuous trust too far. 'OK. But where were the venues? Houses you'd know again?'

'Might've. Different every gig, so I heard. Like I said, I only did it a couple of times and the only gaff I spotted was a big place out in the wilds called West Winds, a holiday villa place, different people every other week, easy enough to rent it for a weekend and Baines had a load of people to set it up and clear up after. These were smart do's, Hayes, you've no idea: brilliant food, unlimited booze, coke by the shovel and fancy tarts flown in from the mainland. No wonder it cost a bomb.'

'Did you stay and take the guests home afterwards?'

'Only back to the car park in Douglas. Some blokes didn't want anyone to find out where they lived.'

'Did you ever see the guest list?'

'No. I was only the driver, and that only twice, the paperwork was very hush-hush. God knows how Baines laundered the cash. Do you think he had a deal with the casino?'

Hayes shrugged. 'You stayed backstage always? What about the caterers? Anyone you know?'

'I asked about that but it was all flown in by helicopter and Baines' own people handled the service.'

'When this new witness convinces Broadhurst that the parties are the key to the muggings, would you be willing to give a full statement? Tell them what you've told me? It's your best shot, Kevin. Until Broadhurst puts the finger on the real killers you're top suspect. It's your jacket, and the bloodstains will put you in the frame. You and Craig will have to go on a line-up before this guy, he's the only one able to give a decent description of the attackers.'

Hayes rose and cheerfully punched him on the shoulder. 'Don't look so glum, Kevin. With me and Mr Caxton on your side you're practically in the clear. Just keep your nerve and don't for a moment consider doing a runner or you might as well confess to the whole "Duo" scam. Stay clear of Craig, he's about as reliable as a jellyfish. Keep your head down and do as I say. OK?'

He left his reluctant informant with a lot to think about and took the back stairs two at a time.

His room smelt musty, the windows sealed against the fading afternoon. After a shower and a swift assessment of the state of play, he knocked at Karl's door. The burly bass player gave him an effusive welcome, clasping Hayes in a bear hug as if he'd been off on an Arctic exploration instead of two days in the next town.

'Hey, man! Where've you bin? I thought you'd split for good.'

'Yeah? You don't get rid of me that easily. How about if I take you for a slap-up meal somewhere? I owe you, Karl, that video you gave me is likely to be a breakthrough. The police are going to jazz up the detail. I'm hoping we'll be able to give the coroner something to think about. I've got stuff to tell you. Let's go.'

Playing along with his role as best buddy was a bitter pill to swallow and not something he was proud of. But he doubted Broadhurst would follow up his suggestion to investigate Karl Brecht, and as an off-duty copper, his own ability to dig into the man's financial status was ticklish. In the event his apparently innocent curiosity proved fruitless. Karl's smooth avoidance of any details was impossible to penetrate.

Thirty-Nine

After a night out with Karl, Monday morning shafted into his bedroom like a laser beam. Hayes checked his watch. Ten thirty! Christ, he was getting too old for partying. He padded into the bathroom and stood under a cold shower until his head cleared then put up a pot of seriously strong coffee and slumped at the kitchen table totting up the cars in the courtyard.

Finch House had seemingly died overnight, the silence in the building only intermittently broken by the distant sound of a vacuum cleaner downstairs. He wondered if it was too early to phone Belinda to assure himself that Charlie Lyons *had* flown back to the island to give his evidence about the parties. Charlie was a game bird. It couldn't have been easy for him to admit to being a regular participant in what the media would inevitably dub 'orgies'. On the other hand, some would applaud the testosterone of a man in his sixties cavorting with a gaggle of professional young 'escorts'. Or maybe sexy go-go girls were the end of the rainbow to rich older men?

He decided it was too soon to present himself on Broadhurst's patch but playing second fiddle was an almost impossible performance to keep up, the local crime squad regarding the interference of an off-duty officer from the south with deep suspicion.

Perhaps it was time to go back to square one, consolidate his findings so far. He retrieved the file and reassembled it in order, DeeDee's scamper through the news clippings and notes leaving his meticulous paperwork in total disarray.

With hindsight he realized that allowing DeeDee to get involved was a stupid move, but the girl had breezed through his professional defences like a whirlwind and, blown over by her charisma, he had been putty in her hands. The dread that ticked away like a metronome at the back of his mind would not let him go: DeeDee's involvement had put her in mortal danger.

He polished off the coffee and started to work through the file.

Caxton's fear about the muggings had started the previous summer with the attack on Derek Fields, aged sixty-six, who was found by a passer-by suffering from minor injuries in Petty's Yard, a pick-up spot for hookers only a short distance from the Cut. He had left his car on the main street and insisted on driving himself straight home, refusing any assistance. His wife reported the mugging the next day when he suddenly died from a heart attack. 'He didn't want any fuss,' she had told the reporter. The incident caused a minor stir for a few days, such attacks being new to the island, and the passing sex trade in the Cut and the warren of dark lanes surrounding it temporarily cooled.

When similar muggings occurred the following season the general public latched onto the local rag's assumption that a rogue element dubbed the 'Phantom Duo' had moved into this quiet tax haven and was making rich pickings from its quarry.

Hayes skimmed through the current year's list and wondered if that first hit on Fields was, in fact, the work of the same thugs. The trouble was Derek Fields was dead and his widow presumably had no knowledge of her late husband's involvement in any sex parties, even if it was true. How could she? The poor woman claimed to be unsure why he had been loitering in Petty's Yard that night, although in Hayes' book a late-night rendezvous in a known pick-up venue was unlikely to be a first-time encounter.

He sighed, setting aside the flimsy evidence on the first so-called victim of the Duo.

The editor of the local paper, Marty Lewis, had smelt a circulation surge in the offing when further muggings hit the headlines and the name tagged to the attackers had gripped local imagination, setting off an insatiable thirst for more media coverage.

But why, Hayes wondered, had the subsequent victims put themselves in the Cut in similar circumstances as the unfortunate Mr Fields? Was Baines' entertainment too frisky to miss? *Had* the Duo acquired a guest list and used it independently of any real parties?

This scenario appealed to Hayes and as he scanned the list of victims it was obviously impossible that Baines would risk putting his guests in danger by cooperating with any muggers. Baines had hit on a lucrative game, which was probably legal apart from Charlie Lyons' assertion that drugs were on tap. No, the parties were kosher; the muggers had hit on a clever simulation which tempted the victims to meet as usual. It crossed his mind that there must be other pick-up points. If each guest was driven to a mystery destination there must be several drivers, each with a meeting place.

Hayes cursed the meagre information Kevin Webber, the only driver he had managed to track down, had produced. Kevin was keeping names back for sure. That skinny toe-rag knew at least one of the other drivers. What was he playing at? Craig with his drug habit would have been an unreliable participant even if he could actually drive the car but Hayes was willing to bet that Kevin was a local lad who knew all the likely villains Baines could confidently call up.

He scanned his list of victims, considering whether any of them would be emboldened by Charlie's public admission to add their own faggots to the fire. Pete de Verne, seventy-one years old, a pal of Derek Fields and, according to Marty Lewis's private observation, 'scared witless' at any possibility of publicity, and unlikely to cough. Hayes crossed him off, the old guy would have been devastated by the latest fatal attack and, in Hayes' experience, increasingly fearful of public embarrassment once the sex-party link was out in the open.

Terry Porlock, the hairdresser, was the most likely one to brave it out once Charlie Lyons' evidence came into play. Porlock had lost a bundle of cash and with a thriving clientele was not open to suffer commercially by admitting his participation in Baines' organized raves. He might even agree to view an identity parade . . .

Craig Durrant could also come off the list, his flagrant use of the Phantom Duo scare only masking an insurance scam. Similarly, Lockyer, openly gay by all accounts, had skipped the country and would be unavailable to join any chorus denouncing Baines or adding any description of his attackers.

The man who had fought back and died, Francis Formby-Smith, was the youngest genuine victim. Only thirty-two years old, and according to Belinda an S&M enthusiast. That totalled two gays, one coke addict and a couple of elderly hopefuls.

Hayes sighed. This was going nowhere. Until Charlie came up trumps the investigation was at a standstill.

A noisy assault on the front-door bell reverberated through the house. Hayes went down to the next landing, where Karl was standing at his open door.

'It's a police car, Rog. D'ya think they've come back for Kev?'

Voices sifted up the stairwell and Hayes recognized Phil's breezy tones. He leaned over the banisters and caught a glimpse of Sergeant Fuller and his sidekick being led into Phil's office.

Karl shrugged off Hayes' suggestion that they took a closer look. 'I'm sorting my bird shots, man. The tourist office has offered to print some in their new brochure. Can't stop. See you later? We could take a stroll down from the cliff to the fish-and-chip shop.'

Hayes was left standing on the landing and felt that just lately he seemed to be in everyone's way. Or perhaps Karl had smelt a rat?

After boosting his ego with a shot of vodka and tonic he wandered down to Phil's den to catch the latest. The posse had departed, leaving an air of gloom which hung over the entire house. Phil was sorting through a pile of sheet music with Teddy Arnold. The atmosphere was tense and Hayes had the impression that he had burst in on a bit of a barney over the Blues' repertoire.

'Am I interrupting?'

Phil smiled like the trooper he was, professionally upbeat as always. 'No, join us, lad, we're all but through. We would have finished by now but the police had some routine questions about our movements between gigs on Tuesday.'

'The day DeeDee died?'

'Yes. The sergeant needed to check where we all were that afternoon. Didn't take long. I was here with Roz having a sandwich before we took to the road for our evening engagement. DeeDee stayed in town.'

'As did Karl,' Hayes put in.

'Yeah,' Teddy said with a grin. 'Birdwatching, so he says. I made up a poker game here with the Driscolls and Jimmy, which satisfied Sergeant Plod that none of us were unaccounted for, apart from you of course.'

'I was in London.'

'Lucky blighter,' Teddy snapped. 'This place gives me the willies. I'll be glad when the season ends and we can pack off home. You staying all summer, Rog?'

'No, I'm off in a week or so. Just anxious to see DeeDee's given a fair hearing.'

'The inquest is this week,' Phil muttered. 'Her folks are coming down to see about the funeral. You'll be here, won't you, Roger?'

'Yes, sure. A local service?'

'No idea.'

Hayes backed off, sensing the conversation was likely to turn nasty. 'Cheers, Phil, I'll be away to the Spa, Bill Caxton wants to have a word. See you, Teddy.'

Forty

Broadhurst refused to see Hayes until Wednesday and Charlie Lyons had been spirited by Belinda to a secret address while the investigation continued.

Hayes reassured Bill Caxton that the case was nearing completion and he had nothing to worry about, a hopelessly optimistic view considering that the Spa's sports physiotherapist was likely to be shown as, at the very least, a promoter of the island's exclusive porn circle. But heaping more anxiety on the guy when the extent of Broadhurst's prosecution was still unknown seemed premature.

Hayes kept clear of Douglas and spent the time tramping the inland tracks with a backpack. The hill walking improved his stamina and the enforced period of quiet reflection calmed his mind. This spell of sick leave had been a crossroads in more ways than one, a time to get off the treadmill and plan ahead. The decision about the career move his boss had put to him remained unclear but at least he would return to work fitter than he had been in years.

Broadhurst agreed to a meeting at four o'clock and greeted Hayes with more favour than he had anticipated; and, surprisingly, it turned out to be one-to-one. Supposedly, the official investigation had gone well although Hayes doubted that the drowning accident had featured at the foreground of the superintendent's mind.

He set off briskly with a terse enquiry about the enhancement of Karl's video.

'Ah, yes, the poor girl's last swim.' Broadhurst stepped over to the machine and set it off. The shots came up in stronger focus, the lighting of that stormy afternoon brightened to firm up the outlines. Sections of Karl's film had been separately enlarged, DeeDee's body clear against the background of the jetty. Hayes eagerly leaned forward as the sequence shifted to the moment when she grabbed the side of the boat. The spherical shape rising above the rowlocks was now almost in focus and was revealed as indeed a person's head.

Broadhurst stopped the film. 'You were right, Chief Inspector, someone *was* lying at the bottom of the boat, but, as you can see, the head is silhouetted against the bright water, the features are almost blank.'

'But the shape's there all right, a man or boy most certainly, eh? And why hasn't he come forward? Any ideas about identification, sir? Have the gardeners been given a viewing? If one of the labourers was having a quiet kip in working hours he'd be reluctant to admit being there when a naked lady tried to get in the boat with him.'

'DI Ross has double-checked. All Caxton's men have been accounted for.'

'A stranger, then.'

'Access from the back road's open to trespassers. But, frankly, Hayes, I think this inconclusive shot is irrelevant. The pathologist can't give an exact time when the girl died, this footage could have taken place an hour before she took her final dip.'

'But then it started to rain really hard. Thunder and lightning, the works. DeeDee wouldn't have hung about in conditions like that.'

Broadhurst opened his hands in perplexity. 'No, I agree. But there's nothing to say she didn't take cover and continue later. From what I hear from Mrs Bailey, Miss Miller was a determined girl, intent on proving herself in the water, possibly before your return from London the following day. Mrs Bailey says she warned her on a previous occasion, pointed out the danger sign by the lake, but Delia Miller was always intent on doing things her way.'

Hayes drew back. 'You're saying the report to the coroner will recommend an accidental verdict?'

'Yes, I am. This theory of yours that her death's connected to her dabbling in the muggings investigation just doesn't hold up, Hayes. There's no witness to say what happened, the post-mortem came up with no injuries. She drowned, Hayes, simple as that. Those lily pads are like bloody ropes, easy for even an experienced swimmer to get caught up in. I'm glad to see that Mr Caxton's getting the lake weeded out and a new fence securing the boundary.'

Broadhurst switched off the video and settled back behind the desk. 'Anything else while you're here?'

'Well, there's quite a lot to catch up on, sir,' Hayes retorted with asperity. 'Charlie Lyons, for a start. I was the one who put you on to him, if you remember.'

'Ah, yes, the sex parties. We're still working on that. The legal situation is fluid. We only have Mr Lyons' assertion that drugs were available and as an older man with a head injury his memory could be challenged in court. As soon as we have a second witness we can bring in Mr Baines with some authority.'

'Have you tried talking to Terry Porlock, the hairdresser?'

'You think he would back up Mr Lyons' story?'

'With certain assurances, I'd bet on it.'

Broadhurst made a note in his file. 'But you haven't spoken with him about Mr Lyons' evidence.'

'No.'

'Good. I need to know where I stand. May I have your assurance that you have not pursued this vendetta of yours with the other victims?'

'Apart from Craig Durrant? Well, I did meet Porlock socially and he seemed a man with less sensitivity about possible embarrassment regarding the sex club. But no, he didn't mention being a guest at Baines' circus, but I rather think he was, the MO is too similar to ignore.'

'We don't even know that Baines was the top dog, do we? He was the compère, if that's what you'd call it, but with so much capital involved I can't see a physiotherapist being anything more than a front man. Renting the venues, ordering expensive catering to be flown in, booking staff, possibly hiring cuties would be no mean outlay.'

'Have you access to his bank account?'

'Certainly not.'

'But you do believe Mr Lyons?'

Broadhurst grudgingly admitted, 'Well, it seems to ring true. The man is a resident of long standing, a few vague areas of his statement could be attributed to his head injury but his doctor assures me that the fracture was a minor crack to the back of the skull and should not cause any appreciable mental confusion.'

Hayes felt that the meeting was going nowhere fast and desperately flung out, 'But the jacket? The bloodstains? Did the lab compare Charlie Lyons' sample?'

'Now, that's an interesting point, Hayes. The bloodstains are definitely from Lyons, so the jacket was used by the mugger. That puts Kevin Webber in the frame and I shall be bringing him in tomorrow.'

'Did Charlie identify him on the line-up?'

'No, but it all fits, don't you agree? We got Durrant up on the look-see too but Mr Lyons couldn't give much of a description of the second bloke, though as he went down he distinctly remembers the so-called driver's biker's boots. Good enough, I'd say. All we need is to pin the boots back to Webber or Craig Durrant and they're both in the can.'

'You can't be serious!'

Broadhurst's face darkened. 'You have other ideas, Chief Inspector?'

'What about the pockets? DeeDee said there was something in the pocket.'

'That's correct. A bloodstained handkerchief which ties up with Mr Lyons' head wound. Oh, and a snotty sample as yet unidentified.'

'But not Webber's? Or Durant's?'

'Not yet identified,' he patiently repeated. 'But there was

one other thing since you ask. The lab found some hairs caught up in the collar.'

Hayes shot up. 'Human hairs? Then we might be able to test the DNA?'

Broadhurst laughed. 'No. Nylon, some sort of fancy neckwear maybe, bikers wear scarves even in a heat wave, don't they?'

'Not fur tippets, sir!' Hayes suddenly had an eureka moment. 'Hang on. I think I've got the answer. Can you wait a few minutes while I get something from the glove compartment in my car?'

Broadhurst glanced at the wall clock. 'I haven't got all bloody day, Hayes. This had better be good.'

He hurried out to the car park and returned with the wig. He placed it on the desk and the superintendent viewed this latest unwelcome input into the case with deep suspicion. 'What's this?'

'DeeDee found it in the rehearsal studio the band use in Petty's Yard. Don't you see? If the lab confirm a match with the nylon hairs from the jacket, this would mean that the mugger wore this wig and didn't have long hair like Durrant at all.'

'Yes, but if even if this does tie up, it could mean Webber wore it himself. I'm still bringing them in,' he added defiantly.

Hayes lowered his tone. 'But how would Webber get hold of it?'

'In the band's rehearsal room, you say? Well, we'll just have to ask him, won't we?'

Forty-One

By the time he got back to the house Phil was hurrying his musicians into a minibus for their evening gig. Hayes pulled Roz aside. 'Any idea where Roma might be?'

'Relaxing on the roof terrace. Roma's feeling a bit low just now, her hay fever's bothering her. Can I help?'

'No thanks, Roz. You off with the others?'

'I've got some catching up to do in Phil's office, he's let the accounts slide lately and I'm trying to sort out the tax.'

'Phil's a lucky man. Any chance of you helping with my self-assessment, Roz?'

'Really?'

'No, not really. Just testing.'

Hayes waved goodbye as the bus rolled out of the courtyard and left Roz to make tracks for the office.

He took the stairs at a pace his trainer would have been proud of, passed his own door and continued up to the attic. He'd never explored this part of the house and was impressed to see dozens of cases of wine and beer stacked neatly against the wall in one of the rooms which he guessed to be originally servants' quarters with their low ceilings and tiny dormer windows. This storage area was surprisingly cool and the faded, peeling wallpaper gave a spooky insight into the lives of the scullery maids and skivvies who must have slept here under the eaves.

The adjoining room was stacked with a pair of iron bedsteads and an assortment of broken chairs and old leather suitcases still bearing luggage labels for exotic locations. A door stood open giving access to the roof space where Roma had tucked herself away for a quiet snooze. It wasn't really a terrace, just a square of Astroturf set about with a few garden chairs and a sunbed. The sun was slipping low on the horizon and the terrace was now half shaded, but the view of the sea was stupendous.

Hayes knocked on the door jamb, unsure whether the girl was asleep or just relaxing with her iPod. She heard nothing and it was not until he stood by her that she opened her eyes with a start and sat bolt upright. She whipped off her stereo and gazed at him as if she had seen a ghost.

'Hey, Roma, sorry. Did I startle you? I knocked but you couldn't hear. Roz said you were up here. Nice place. Is it a house secret?'

'Well, I'm the only one who seems to use it. I prefer it to the garden.'

She wore cotton shorts and a strapless top but her skin was remarkably white, and her slender figure looked almost fragile. She shaded her eyes and invited him to draw up a chair.

'I've got a personal stereo like yours,' he said. 'They're great, aren't they? Problem is what was once an occasional diversion gradually takes over if you're like me. Then it becomes an obsession. You can walk through crowds sealed in your own private cocoon, oblivious to everyone around you, isolation clamped to your ears shutting out the world.'

She relaxed and for the next ten minutes they talked music. Roma's favourite tracks were esoteric compositions for the harp which Hayes had never heard of, even on Radio Three. 'I expect Roz went off with the band,' she said. 'She keeps a sharp eye on them, thinks Phil lets them run rings round him – which they do.'

'She's working on the accounts in the office downstairs. I particularly wanted to find you. We have to talk, Roma.'

Her wide eyes opened like seashells, and Hayes considered how to phrase it. With so little proof he would have to wing it, kid her there was more evidence and hope she was too confused to back off.

'Yes?'

'It's about the muggings. The police have evidence linking the wig to the attacks.'

'The wig?'

'Yes, the wig DeeDee found at the studio. I recognized your scent, Roma. It's a unique perfume. Unforgettable.'

'Yes, isn't it?' she happily agreed. 'I get it from a friend in the business, a perfumer in Grasse who was experimenting and there was no market for number sixty-two, too sharp, too green, so he keeps a small supply just for me.'

'You admit wearing the wig?'

'Oh, often.' She smoothed the neat cap of her hair, which lay over her skull like birds' feathers. 'Just for fun. Roz found it at the studio, left behind by one of her clients and forgotten I expect. It's not an expensive one, not real hair.'

'You wear it for performances?'

She laughed. 'Not likely! As I said, occasionally for laughs. Roz hates it, says it makes me look like a rent boy in drag.'

'I'll be straight with you, Roma. Fibres from the wig have been found on the leather jacket which was hidden in the boathouse. DeeDee discovered it and you saw her take it. You knew it was dangerous.'

'It wasn't my jacket!'

'You stole it from Kevin's bike and used it when you acted out this scam to rob Baines' house-party guests. You were employed to drive his clients to the secret venues, weren't you, Roma? He employed you, gave you the passwords and you hit on the bright idea of mugging these guys, rich has-beens who were too old or too scared to resist. Except the one who died, the youngest target. It's now a murder hunt, my girl, and you're in it up to your neck. The evidence points to you and someone's going to sing like a canary. Karl? Kevin? Why did you do it? For drugs money? For kicks?'

She had visibly paled, her fair skin now white as marble. She struggled to rise but Hayes leaned across, pinning her thin arms, forcing her back.

'You're mad!'

'Who was your partner, Roma? Who was the guy who came up behind and brought them down?'

'Who told you I was on Baines' payroll?'

'I say you were. And tomorrow the ringmaster if that's what he is will be brought in. Baines is going to give up a complete list of the people he employed – he's only been running private parties, he's nothing to lose. After your attacks the clients are getting jittery, I dare say the game is up as far as Baines is concerned and doing a deal over the names and secret addresses will probably see him home and dry. The dates of the muggings will not tie in with his parties and he will be able to prove it: no venue booked, no catering staff, no nothing. Yours was a brilliant idea, Roma, but how did you get hold of the telephone numbers of his little circle?'

She struggled to get free but Hayes held on. 'The wig locks you in and once they set up DNA tests who knows what they'll find? DeeDee unearthing that leather jacket was vital. Did you intend to dispose of it safely later when you had the chance? You're cooked, Roma, my love, but if you tell me the real story, tell me who your partner was, it seems to me you were the fall guy in this racket, never strong enough to land any blows let alone kick a fit young man like Formby-Smith to death.'

'Let go! You're hurting my arm.'

'Listen, Roma, the game's up. There's video footage of you at the lake when DeeDee died and you're the only one here who has not accounted for her movements that afternoon. How did you avoid the sergeant's check on the others? I bet he was told to question the band and Phil forgot to give your name, never counting you as part of the Blues. You were in the rowing boat, you drowned her.'

'It was an accident. She tried to climb in and woke me up, and before I realized it, the boat was tipping over. We struggled and eventually I pulled her in. We argued about the jacket. She knew I had worked for Baines, driving people from the Cut, though later Jeremy let me hostess for him.'

'Who told her?'

'Kevin. She wheedled it out of him somehow, you know what she was like with men. She promised never to tell but it was stupid of him to say anything. DeeDee got really nasty that afternoon, threatened to tell you everything as soon as you got back from London. I stood up in the boat to climb back onto the jetty but she grabbed my leg and we both fell into the water. She couldn't swim at all really . . .'

'You let her drown?'

'What could I do? She got caught up in the lilies and as she struggled they just pulled her down.'

'You didn't try to help her?'

'I can't swim.'

'Christ Almighty, Roma, why didn't you come out with it straight away? The inquest's tomorrow, you'll have to tell the coroner what happened.' He let her go, too shocked to continue.

She scrambled to her feet, her eyes wild. 'Are you crazy? Once I admit to all that the police will make Kevin tell them about me using his motorbike, sometimes borrowing his jacket.'

'They know that. It's the wig, stupid. The wig ties you into five attacks including a murder, not counting the man who was mugged last summer. Was that what gave you the idea?' He tried to cool it, sensing that the confrontation was getting out of hand, goading the girl too far wouldn't help. 'Look, Roma, your only chance is to make a clean breast of it, say who put you up to it. Was it Baines?'

'No, of course not.'

'Kevin?'

'I wouldn't trust Kevin to keep his mouth shut.'

'Are you afraid of your partner in this? We can protect you, Roma. Do yourself a favour, let me take you to the station and get this whole sorry mess cleared up. Don't be scared, I won't let this guy get to you.'

She laughed, a brittle sound like a cracked bell. 'Get to me? You don't know what you're talking about!' She slowly walked to the parapet and stared out at the glowing sunset.

Hayes let her go, knowing that the silly kid would, given enough space, hand over the real mugger. Roma was a frail personality, a weak vessel for such terrible secrets.

And then, without a moment's hesitation, she threw herself off the ledge and plummeted to the ground, all of fifty feet below.

Her scream shrilled in the evening air, bringing Roz racing outside to kneel by the broken body. She looked up at Hayes silhouetted between the jagged pinnacles of the gothic roofscape. Then she started to wail, a low ululation of deep sorrow. Kevin came running from the garage.

Hayes suddenly knew he had totally misjudged Roma Sewell and his chances of identifying her accomplice were gone for ever.

Forty-Two

Hayes phoned the emergency services, and the police and an ambulance were on the spot within fifteen minutes, arriving to witness the distraught trio grouped around the body that lay like a smashed doll on the drive.

Roz continued screaming at Hayes, her misery now transformed into bitter hatred.

'You pushed her, you bastard! You threw her off the roof, I saw you.'

Kevin attempted to break in but the woman was a virago, and it took all Hayes' strength to fend her off. He made no attempt to deny her accusations and not until the squad car drew to a shuddering halt on the tarmac did he try to shake her off. A second police car piled in behind and the simultaneous arrival of the ambulance crowded the front entrance with vehicles.

The officers erupted onto the forecourt like a posse, headed by Sergeant Fuller. He pulled Hayes to one side. 'DI Ross is on his way, sir. Nothing like this has ever happened here before. You knew this young lady?'

'Shall we go inside, Sergeant? We're blocking the paramedics' efforts. Has the police surgeon been alerted?'

Before he could answer Roz had thrust herself forward, her eyes wild. 'He did it! Forced Roma off the parapet. That man's a fiend, planned it when he knew everyone was going to be off the premises. It's a miracle I was here to see it.'

'You saw the victim being pushed off the roof?'

Kevin swiftly intervened. 'I saw it. I was in and out of the garage, working on Karl's bike, I saw it all.'

The sergeant felt himself ambushed, ringed about by hostile witnesses, wishing that the inspector would put his skates on. 'We'll go inside,' he insisted.

The three were reluctantly frog-marched into the big drawing room on the first floor, Roz now weeping uncontrollably, Kevin looking shell-shocked like a man who had narrowly escaped a head-on car smash. Hayes was almost composed, his racing thoughts swirling to only one conclusion.

They were corralled at one end of the room, and the sergeant instructed one of his constables to close the windows, shutting out the distressing sounds of the ambulance men's dispute with the police efforts to keep them away from the body. Not that there was anything more to be done, the girl was clearly dead, her fragile limbs sprawled in an untidy heap, pools of blood seeping into the cracked tarmac.

A WPC was dispatched to the kitchen to brew up some strong tea, and the small party disposed themselves about the room. Roz lay face down on a sofa, her arms cradling her head, her stumpy legs stiffly extended. Hayes couldn't shake off the comparison with Roma's near anorexic limbs spreadeagled on the ground.

The shock of her extraordinary suicide was hard to rationalize; one moment the girl was cheerfully describing her personalized perfume and the next she had hurled herself off the roof. Had her admitted preference for being alone up there slowly fostered a latent death wish? DeeDee's drowning must have played on her mind. Did she become filled with a feeling of hopelessness perched among the gargoyles and stone pinnacles? But then, what did anyone know about the kid? Surely, no normal person would have participated in a series of vicious muggings? Hayes persisted in the view that Roma was also a victim, the weak partner in a folie-à-deux.

The WPC returned with mugs of tea, heavily sugared as Hayes had anticipated. Roz refused to accept it, turning her head away, her vituperation finally silenced. Kevin and Hayes drew closer together but Fuller insisted they did not confer.

'We must wait for DI Ross,' he said firmly. 'First impressions are important.'

Hayes retreated to the dais and sat on the piano stool while Kevin lit a cigarette and nervously paced up and down.

At last the waiting ended and Ross hurried to join them. He looked around the former salon with flickering interest. Finch House was certainly an appropriate setting for such dramatic events. Sergeant Fuller drew him aside and reported Roz's accusations.

The inspector chose to bring Hayes over for his version of events, leaving Roz and Kevin to wait expectantly out of earshot. Then he called them together. 'In view of the seriousness of the accusations we shall have to conduct our interviews at the station. Would you all follow me, please?'

The three were taken to Douglas in separate cars, Hayes riding in the back of Ross's vehicle, the brooding silence during the short journey leaving a sour note. Did Roz seriously imagine he would push Roma to her death? It was madness, especially as the crazed creature had still been working in the office as far as he knew. At least Kevin backed him up, though whether anyone would believe the word of a man on the verge of being charged with six muggings was a moot point.

Hayes was led to a basement room and left to stew for twenty-five minutes while, he guessed, DI Ross tried to plot his interview technique. Questioning another senior police officer on an alleged murder charge was tricky.

He looked around the airless bunker and idly wondered whether it had been planned as a safe cell for dangerous suspects. Eventually Ross and a detective constable arrived and, after the usual cautions, set the recording equipment running. They quickly got through the necessary preamble and Ross nervously set off at a gallop.

'I have spoken with Webber and he confirms that he saw you trying to save the girl as she climbed onto the parapet.'

'That's absolutely right. But she moved so quickly I was taken entirely by surprise. By the time I jumped to the edge she had gone over. How did Mrs Bailey see it?'

'Actually, we haven't finished with the lady just yet. The superintendent wants to interview her himself, but from Webber's account she wasn't even outside when the incident happened. He says Mrs Bailey ran out through the front door just after the victim's screams were heard. Webber swears he was first on the scene so we shall have to await her reconsidered statement. I am worried about her fury, though. Obviously the woman was hysterical, and may have jumped to conclusions seeing you looking down from the roof, but why such venom? I thought the people in the band were supposed to be one big happy family?'

'I thought so too but there's one important aspect of the relationship between Roz Bailey and the dead girl which you can confirm with at least one of the group, Karl Brecht. He has pictures proving a lesbian association.'

'Blimey!' Ross burst out. 'Did this guy spend all his time snapping girls?'

'A spin-off from his birdwatching, allegedly, but there are probably, when you make discreet enquiries, others who knew about it. I'm pretty sure her husband was in the dark but the deep affection between these two women explains a lot.'

'What were you doing on the roof with Roma Sewell?'

'Well, that was the reason she jumped. I think perhaps we had better wait for Superintendent Broadhurst to get here before I tell you what happened. Do you think we could find another interview room? This place is like a dungeon.'

Forty-Three

It was a further hour before Hayes was escorted upstairs to Broadhurst's room. His fears evaporated; Kevin Webber must have convinced them that he was in the clear.

The boss presided over their thin party like a magistrate, his ascetic features stern. Ross hovered in the background together with Sergeant Fuller but Hayes was ushered to a seat opposite the superintendent and a tray of coffee and sandwiches indicated that this meeting was likely to be prolonged. Broadhurst poured the coffee and passed a cup to Hayes, Ross and Fuller apparently out of the loop on this.

'Right, let's get one thing straight, Chief Inspector. Were you on the roof by arrangement with the young lady or had you, as Mrs Bailey insists, planned to take her by surprise while the rest of the occupants were working?'

'There was no plan. I had no idea Roma would be sunning herself on the roof, I only knew that it was imperative to confront her with the question of the wig.'

'The wig?'

'Yes. I left it with you, remember. Didn't you notice the odd scent? The fibres on the bloodstained jacket presumably match those from the wig and the perfume she wore was so distinctive I knew it had to be Roma Sewell who had worn it during the mugging attacks.'

'Hold on there! You said nothing before about any perfume.'

'It only hit me later. I thought it was aftershave or a man's deodorant, it was like no women's scent, too sharp, almost acidic, no wonder it wouldn't sell. She told me it was a spin-

214

off from a perfumer's batch, something she bought from this specialist in Grasse, a friend of hers apparently.'

'OK, we can check that out, but why would such an observation put her in a suicidal state?'

'I told Roma the fibres were important. She knew the jacket was bloodstained and dared not return it. I suspect it was temporarily hidden in the boathouse but Roma saw DeeDee take it away with her. She was worried but not unduly at that point, assuming that if DeeDee got overly curious Kevin would be implicated. There was nothing as far as she knew to connect her to it, so she thought.'

'We are still conducting tests. There is an unidentified sample from the handkerchief that doesn't fit Webber's DNA, which was already on file from previous arrests.'

'If you test Sewell's DNA I think that will answer your question.'

Broadhurst leaned back, regarding Hayes with an unflinching gaze. 'It is not my style to share information with an outsider but in view of your close involvement, Chief Inspector Hayes, I have no alternative. The suicide-victim's room has been searched and a credit card belonging to Charlie Lyons was found. Also, a pair of hiking boots was stowed in the boot of her car, not exactly the biker's boots our witness mentioned that one of the muggers wore but near enough to require a further identification by Mr Lyons.'

Hayes slapped his knee in glee. 'Well, that's it, sir, it backs up what I said: Roma Sewell was the lure, dressed up to look like a long-haired adolescent, posing as Baines' driver. She admitted she had been employed before by Baines to collect his guests and convey them to the designated party venues. She knew the form, the text messages, the password check, the location of the regular pick-up points.'

Broadhurst pursed his lips. 'This is all hearsay, Hayes. Will Baines confirm it?'

'Like a shot. He's not yet in trouble for organizing private parties and employing staff to make it happen. He promoted Roma to hostessing later and how she disguised herself when acting as a chauffeur wouldn't concern him. As a harpist in popular demand at social functions and teatime entertainments in hotels, she wouldn't have wanted any of the so-called guests to recognize her as a minicab driver, would she? Her physique was boyish, it wouldn't take much to change her appearance sufficiently and I doubt whether the men took much notice of the driver anyway.'

'But there must have been others?'

'You were in a unique position to get friendly with these people, Hayes. Lucky, I'd call it, not much detective work there,' he added with a touch of pique. 'Well, where do we go from here?'

'I haven't finished yet, sir. When I approached Roma on the roof I wanted to persuade her to give herself up, confess to the attacks and give me the name of the other mugger. I got entirely the wrong impression of the girl. I thought she was the weak element, dragged in on these robberies by a stronger personality. But I couldn't have been more wrong. Sewell was the mastermind, her sidekick was pulled into this vicious series of attacks by infatuation.'

'Webber!'

'No, not Kevin. The one she died for was her lesbian lover, Roz Bailey. Even when she knew there was no way out she would not give her away.'

'Mrs Bailey? You think so? Her husband's downstairs now. He wants to take her home.'

'For God's sake don't allow her off the premises, sir!'

'She won't go with him, as it happens. Refuses point blank, wants to fly back to their home in Manchester, which seems perfectly reasonable, Finch House being the scene of such a gory death.'

'But she can't leave tonight, there're no late flights.'

'Webber was one, he can tell you more about Baines' operation and he knew Roma was on the payroll. He was overheard taunting her about moonlighting, threatening to blow the gaff to Roz Bailey. It was Webber who tipped off DeeDee.'

'Says she prefers to stay at her studio here in Douglas overnight.'

'That's it! She needs to tidy up the evidence. You'll have to find an excuse to keep her here while you get an urgent search warrant for her place in Petty's Yard. There won't be anything at Finch House, too dangerous, but I'd stake my pension she's up to something. Roz was capable of laundering all that stolen money. She's the obvious third party in this. There's a safe at the studio and probably clothing that she may not have had the chance to dispose of yet. Petty's Yard was hers alone, long before she married Bailey, and it's the perfect place for hiding evidence.'

Ross shuffled his feet in the background, the audacity of this interloper snatching the initiative from his boss taking his breath away. Sergeant Fuller looked stolidly on, giving nothing away.

Broadhurst rose, his face like thunder. 'Well, Chief Inspector, we'd better get to it, there's a night's work ahead of us.'

Forty-Four

Broadhurst insisted Hayes accompany him downstairs to the room where Phil Bailey was waiting, waiting to drive his wife away if only to her rehearsal studio in Petty's Yard.

He stumbled to his feet, his perma-tanned cheeks creased with anxiety, and grabbed Hayes by the arm. 'Roger! What the hell's going on?'

Broadhurst smoothly intervened. 'Sorry for the delay, Mr Bailey, but we are still coordinating your wife's statement with Webber's version. It all takes time. While you're waiting may I suggest we adjourn to Petty's Yard? You do have keys?'

'Y-yes. But can't we wait for Roz?'

'There are items of property belonging to the dead girl which are likely to be at the studio. If you are agreeable we could go there now and pick them up. It would save disturbing Mrs Bailey later.'

'Yes, right. But it won't take long, will it?'

'Half an hour at the most. Shall we use my car? You don't mind if Mr Hayes tags along? And a couple of my constables? The more hands to the pump the quicker we'll be back here, OK?'

Broadhurst's smooth delivery left Hayes in awe, the bloke even smiled, his normally severe expression dissolving into polite concern. Poor Phil Bailey didn't stand a chance against this guy's quick thinking, it seemed.

Hayes sat in the front with the driver, Broadhurst conducting a one-sided conversation with Phil, who sat slumped in the back with him, his Blues Band sparkly jacket glimmering in the passing headlights of the late night traffic. The streets were still crowded with holidaymakers and it was not until they turned into the Cut that the main flow peeled off towards the promenade. A squad car pulled in behind them and Broadhurst waited for Phil to alight, then led him to the shuttered premises.

The place was well secured, presumably the amplifying equipment and computer being of potential interest to burglars. Phil took a heavy bunch of keys from his back pocket and activated the various mortise and Yale locks, then hurried inside to switch off the alarm.

When the lights blazed down on the empty studio it took on the appearance of an abandoned film set, the small stage strongly top lit, a row of seats pulled back to leave floor space where Roz's clients could strut their stuff.

Broadhurst nodded to Hayes to get Bailey off the scene while he and his men took the place apart and said, 'I'll have your keys if you please, Mr Bailey.'

'Hey, Phil, you look as if you could do with a drink,' Hayes said, 'let's see if there's anything in the kitchen to perk you up. You've had a nasty shock.'

Phil allowed himself to be propelled into the tiny kitchen annexe and Hayes firmly closed the door on the clatter of policemen's boots invading the theatrical set-up.

'Nothing for me, Rog, I'm driving. Got to get back to the house after I've seen Roz is OK. I need to check on the band. I left them at the Paradiso when I got the emergency call from Roz. She was hysterical, I've never seen her like it, she's always the one in control, I'm the panic merchant.'

'The band all right without you out front?'

'Yeah, they're a fantastic bunch of guys. Karl took charge, and the music's pretty standard.'

Hayes boiled the kettle and made tea, topping up each mug with a shot of whisky from a miniature he found in the cutlery drawer, someone's perk pocketed from a flight.

Phil sat at the counter, increasingly agitated by the sounds of upheaval in the studio. 'What are they looking for, Rog?'

'Stuff belonging to Roma. Look, you'd better hear the worst, man. Roma was involved in these Phantom Duo muggings. The superintendent has evidence linking her to at least one attack.'

'No, never! Roma was such a frail little thing, Roz felt sorry for her, took her under her wing last season, got her regular gigs, set her back on her feet.'

'What d'you mean?'

'Oh, the poor girl had been ill, a breakdown, she told Roz. But Roz recognized her potential, gave her a fresh start here, and mucking in with the band up at the house gave her a sense of belonging. You've got it all wrong, Roger, Roma couldn't hurt a fly.'

'We all got it wrong, Phil. That piece of work was a siren, an evil seducer. We all thought she was what she seemed to be but there are rumours you'd better be warned about.'

'Rumours?'

'About Roz and Roma. Did you never suspect Roz was physically attracted to this girl?'

'You mean like lesbians?'

'There are shots of them together, Karl caught them on film by the lake together. I'm sorry, Phil, but, as a friend, I think you should be ready for some nasty stuff emerging once Roma's background is investigated. Had you no idea?'

Phil dropped his head into his hands. He looked like a man on the rack. 'She is my star,' he mumbled. 'Kept us all on the road. Without Roz I'd have given up the band years ago. Bookings were drying up, the regulars like Karl and the Driscolls were hanging in, but the writing was on the wall, believe me. The band was all but washed up when Roz suggested we got married. Shocked me rigid. A lovely woman like Roz, clever, with a flourishing agency business of her own. Why me?' He raised his head, his confusion begging for a response.

Luckily for Hayes, at that moment Broadhurst breezed in. 'We need to open the safe, Mr Bailey. You have the combination?'

Phil jumped to his feet. 'Why? That safe belongs to Roz, it's nothing to do with Roma.'

'I can get a warrant,' Broadhurst pointed out, the conciliatory manner now evaporated.

Phil led them through to Roz's office, where the filing cabinet and the drawers of her desk hung open, the contents spread out on a side table. He gasped. 'You can't do this! Roz's files are private. She'll sue you!'

'I don't think so, sir,' Broadhurst wryly remarked. He waited patiently for Phil to pull himself together, then delivered the KO punch. 'I'm afraid your wife will be spending the night in the cells. We have found her heavy boots and a balaclava, plus a bloodstained denim jacket which we suspect links her with Roma Sewell's scam. Now, let's waste no more time, Mr Bailey. Open the safe.'

The two officers stood back while Phil bent down to spin the combination, Hayes holding himself rigidly to attention. The chips were down.

Phil straightened and the door of the small steel safe swung open. Broadhurst pushed forward, remembering, just in time, to put on protective gloves before pulling out bundles of banknotes and, with a flourish that deserved a trumpet fanfare, a small black truncheon.

'I think you should take Mr Bailey home, Hayes. We shall not be interviewing his wife until the morning and he may decide to send a solicitor to attend. You will join us?'

This last was spoken with a thin smile and Hayes knew the superintendent's reluctant decision to include him was almost too bitter to swallow.

Forty-Five

Hayes spent a restless night worrying about the inquest. Should he alert the coroner to Roma's admission that she had witnessed the drowning? He was far from convinced that his initial suspicion that DeeDee was murdered could be ruled out on the mere say-so of a bitch like Roma Sewell. But with both girls dead and the coroner's hearing scheduled for this morning, there was no time to convince Broadhurst that the inquest should be postponed pending further police enquiries.

In fact he was certain that the superintendent had already crossed the drowning off his list of outstanding cases, and persuading the man to put his team on to a less than hopeful investigation was highly unlikely to be greeted with enthusiasm. And who could blame him? Karl's video had cut out at the point when Roma hauled DeeDee into the boat, if that was what really happened. Or did she hold the poor kid under the water by her hair, Roma's frail appearance being as deceptive as her nature? Webber looked a skinny specimen but there was no doubting the strength of his sinewy muscles.

The conundrum went round and round in his head, his professional conscience balking at a temptation to let Roma's involvement go unreported.

But there were the parents to consider. He had heard that they were due to arrive on the island in time to obtain the coroner's permission to bury their daughter. Would delaying his decision be worth the heartache? In their situation Hayes felt sure an accidental verdict would be preferable to a

222

protracted police investigation of a possible murder now that the guilty party was already dead.

As a pearly dawn gradually put the room in focus, Hayes decided to let it go. In his heart he knew DeeDee deserved better but, working as an off-duty copper with no clout on the island, he needed to keep on Broadhurst's side if only as a humble observer.

Karl opened the door, his bleary eyes all too indicative that he had just woken up. The musicians were normally late risers and the previous night's drama would have fuelled one hell of a confab into the small hours. He wore a towelling dressing gown, chest hairs spilling out of the gaping robe like jungle undergrowth.

'Hey, man, come in. Phil got back late and was all shot to pieces. He says Roz is being held on suspicion of murder. That can't be right, can it?'

Hayes edged in, picking his way between piles of folders dotted about the floor. Karl kicked a few aside to make a pathway. 'Excuse the mess, I'm still trying to catalogue my bird shots to pick something for this tourist brochure I told you about.'

They settled at the kitchen table and Karl brewed a pot of coffee so bitter Hayes reckoned it could tar a road. But the steaming mug was just what was needed and he started speaking.

'I'm just on my way back to the station. After Roma's suicide the enquiries into the muggings really took off. It looks as if Roma was the brain behind the operation and Roz laundered the money. One bloke died and there's enough evidence to charge her, I'm afraid. I'm only telling you this in confidence, Karl, because poor Phil's going to need a lot of support from an old pal like yourself.'

'There's proof, you say? Proof that Roma and Roz were this Phantom Duo the papers have been going on about?'

''Fraid so. Roma thought that by killing herself Roz would escape, but there is too much evidence and, frankly, I can't see Roz getting away without a life sentence. There's still a question about a possible third party involved.' The suspicion hung in the air like a bad smell but Karl remained incredulous.

'No! But why would she do it? Roz was rich, she didn't need the money.'

'For kicks? Drugs? Who knows? Once a crazy game like that succeeds and the chances of being caught are so remote as to be unbelievable, the risk seems negligible. Who would have guessed that a pair of women could carry out a series of vicious muggings? It probably started as a dare, scaring silly old sods into handing over wads of cash because they'd been caught in the backstreets in dubious circumstances. The game only got out of hand when they kicked the poor sap who put up a fight. What worries me is that the murder didn't stop them going out for one more hit after that. Were they so fired up that they thought they were invincible, or was it just greed?'

'Roz was keen on raking in the last penny, but she was an astute businesswoman, Rog, that was why she was so successful.'

Hayes rose. 'I've gotta go, Karl, but I've spelt it out so the rest of the gang here don't go haywire with rumours that only add to Phil's troubles. I'll get back to you. Will he cancel the band's bookings for the rest of the season? Disband the whole crew? I can't see him carrying on once Roz is brought to trial. This Phantom Duo shit has run and run, there's never been anything like it on the island before, public opinion will come down on Phil like a ton of bricks. People won't believe he knew nothing about it.'

Karl walked with him to the car. 'Will you be back, Rog?'

'Yeah, later, but don't wait up. I may decide to stay at a motel in town, keep my head down for a bit.'

Hayes drove off at speed, wondering if Broadhurst had a plan to break down Roz's defences. He couldn't picture Broadhurst as any sort of psychological profiler but it would be a mistake to underestimate the man. And what about Roz? Was she clever enough to try to talk her way out of it: blame

Roma, tell how she was forced to launder the money, hoping that the prosecution would take a lenient view if she cooperated?

And what about Jeremy Baines' part in all this? His sex ring was the key to the whole set-up, playing innocent host would not wash if, after the publicity following Charlie Lyons' evidence, one or two of the Baines' party guests were brave enough to confirm that drugs were on sale at the parties. On second thoughts, Hayes admitted that was a very long shot. Why would respectable people admit to buying cocaine or E's and lay themselves open not only to ridicule but prosecution? Even Kevin would be stupid to admit complicity in any drug dealing.

He mulled over all possible scenarios on the way into Douglas and arrived in time to hear the coroner's verdict. Accidental death. He sighed. It was what he had expected but the unanswerable question still remained: had DeeDee really got into difficulties trapped in the waterweeds, or had Roma spun him a plausible story? He determined to put it out of mind and waited to observe DeeDee's parents leave and push their way past a group of curious onlookers, the sort who cluster on the steps of crown courts, scenting tragedy like smoke alarms. The parents were swiftly shoved into a waiting limousine by a man Hayes guessed to be an undertaker's representative if his bleak expression born of years of professional condolence was any guide.

The police station was a short walk away and Hayes buttoned his raincoat, a soft drizzle misting the air as if in sympathy. He strode ahead and entered the station at a trot shortly after eleven.

Sergeant Fuller accosted him as he crossed the threshold. 'The superintendent's in his office, sir. Wants to see you right away.'

He hurried through. Broadhurst's door stood open and he looked up with a rare smile, dismissed the woman who had been taking dictation and rounded the desk.

'Ah, Hayes. Glad you're here but you've missed the action, I'm afraid.'

'I wanted to hear the coroner's verdict.'

'As we expected?'

'Yes.'

'Good. Now let's get back to Mrs Bailey. She's admitted wielding the truncheon and putting the boot into Formby-Smith. Coughed the lot, but her solicitor is angling for a reduced charge, manslaughter, which won't go down well with my superiors.' He punched Hayes arm in a gesture which was almost chummy. 'So, as soon as you've signed a statement about the Sewell suicide, we can pass the paperwork to the legal department. Brilliant result! I appreciate your input, Chief Inspector. An interesting collaboration, something new to me, but all's well that ends well, eh?'

Hayes stood dumbfounded. 'Roz Bailey confessed to everything? Her partnership with Roma, the whole box of tricks?'

'We stepped in early. She'd had a bad night in the cells, seemed totally defeated, a broken woman. Refused to see that husband of hers, poor devil was in tears. The charge sheet is being processed as we speak.'

Hayes slumped into a chair, his mind reeling. 'I don't understand. She didn't make a deal?'

Broadhurst frowned. 'What are you talking about? Your lot may negotiate with suspects where you come from, but here we do things by the book. The lady was cautioned, her solicitor was present and she decided to plead guilty.'

'All done and dusted, then,' Hayes bitterly retorted.

'Before you were up and running, lad. We're no sluggards on this island, you'd have to smarten up your ideas if you were posted here though I wouldn't say no if you asked for a transfer. You could do worse, it's a smashing place even in the summer when we're clogged up with incomers.'

'Thanks.' Hayes could hardly contain his rage but knew a measure of control was imperative. 'Superintendent. May I make a suggestion? I know Roz on a social level, I've been accepted in the Blues' circle as a friend. I'm curious about motive. Did she say why she agreed to be cashier?'

'I'd have thought that was bloody obvious, Hayes. For the money, of course.'

'There's more to it than that. On an informal basis, would you allow me to speak with her?'

Broadhurst let out a loud guffaw. 'You planning to retrain as a prison chaplain, mate?'

'It would help underline the case. Roz will talk to me, I'm sure.'

'Well, she doesn't want to talk to that husband of hers!'

The silence grew as Broadhurst thumbed through his notes, the tension rising.

'OK. As a special favour mind and only if her solicitor agrees. Come back after lunch when I've checked with my chief. This interference of yours, Hayes, stirs up all sorts of precedents. If I let you talk to the accused, it will have to be recorded. I'll see what I can do. Say two o'clock?'

Forty-Six

Hayes spent the rest of the morning with Bill Caxton, going over the latest developments. He made no mention of the part Baines had played in all this, best to leave Broadhurst to handle the case in his own time.

Caxton was obviously relieved and suggested they had a celebratory lunch in the restaurant.

'It was good of you to call in on Georgie while you were in London. She's had a bad time since the mugging, it's knocked the stuffing out of her. When the season's calmed down I'm taking her to Switzerland for a little holiday. You've coped with the attack better, Roger, but then, in your line of business, street violence is all too familiar I imagine. You look well, chum, working out in the gym has paid off. Kicked the cigarette habit yet?'

'I wouldn't bank on it once I get back to work.'

'When are you leaving?'

'Soon. I'm very grateful to you, Bill, setting me up in Finch House was a great idea. They're a decent bunch, though God knows how Phil Bailey will carry on after this. Maybe the band will re-form, get a make-over once Phil makes up his mind what to do. He's all broken up and Roz refuses to see him, which makes everything worse. I'm hoping to visit her myself this afternoon, she probably needs some moral support.'

After lunch Hayes walked back to the station. Broadhurst was out with DI Ross – consulting with the brass hats, presumably. Luckily Sergeant Fuller had been instructed to allow Hayes a short visit with the accused, and led him through to a pleasant interview room bathed in afternoon sunlight.

'I must stay with you, Chief Inspector, the superintendent doesn't want you alone with Bailey.'

'She's not dangerous, you know.'

'No, but sir prefers any conversation to be recorded and has asked me to sit in.'

The door opened and Roz came in. She looked strained, her dark hair dragged back into a ponytail, her face devoid of make-up: a shadow of the woman Hayes had been familiar with. She sat down at the table and lit a cigarette.

'Thank you for agreeing to see me, Roz. Is there anything you need?'

'Nothing.'

'I'm here as a friend. I gather you don't want to see Phil at present. I can understand that.'

'Can you?' she snapped. 'I doubt it.'

'I knew about your special relationship with Roma, her death must be traumatic for you. I didn't push her off the roof, you know. You were confused. Have you thought about it since?'

She drew deeply on the cigarette and regarded him from hooded eyes. 'Why are you here, Roger?'

'Your confession. You didn't put up any sort of defence, Roz, didn't give any explanation. How did Roma persuade you to join her in this terrible scheme? I'm asking you now as a friend but your lawyer will need to ask you about motives for your defence. How on earth did a sensible, mature woman like yourself get dragged into it?'

Her look softened. 'I loved her. Simple as that. You can't understand that, can you? I hardly understood it myself. But being with Roma changed my life. I felt young. I was happy for the very first time, it was if the world had suddenly burst into bloom. It wasn't just sex, she was the light of my existence.'

'But why? Why agree to her plan? You didn't need the money, Roz, and the excitement of this criminal adventure must have struck you as manic even before Formby-Smith got kicked to death. Did Roma need you to filter the money through your business accounts? I presume some income comes in cash payments?'

She laughed, leaning back in her chair, transfixed by a paroxysm of sheer amusement. 'The money? Everyone thinks it was about the money. I never took any money. The money was Roma's.'

'What about all that cash in your safe at the studio?'

She sobered. 'It was just passing through. Roma had nowhere to hide it until she needed it.'

'Needed it? What for? Drugs? Was she a user?'

'No! Roma never touched medication of any sort after she left hospital.'

'What was wrong with her? Schizophrenia? Hearing voices?'

'Nothing like that. Some sort of depressive illness, she said. She wouldn't talk about it. I brought her here to the island last season and got her bookings at various hotels. I'd seen her perform at a wedding Phil and I attended in Manchester and admired her talent. We fell in love later.'

'You've had relationships with women before?'

'No. It was a complete revelation, as if I'd been living in the dark all my life and suddenly it was perpetual summer.'

'And you fostered her career, got her regular spots here on the island. When did the idea of staging the muggings take hold?'

'We read about this old guy being robbed last summer and Roma worked out that we could put on a similar scam because she knew how to set it up. She'd worked as a driver on Baines' party lark and it seemed worth a try. Roma would get them to one of the usual pick-up places with a text message. It was easy as falling off a log.'

'So you didn't mug the old man who was hit last year?'

'No, but it was the trigger. Roma was a clever girl, Roger, not a stupid airhead like DeeDee.'

Hayes flinched but let it go. 'Yeah, I can see that but, Roz, why did you agree to be cast as the attacker? Or was there a third person in this?'

'A man, you mean?' She wiped the perspiration from her lip with a trembling finger. 'No way. We were a team, there was no necessity to drag in any man!'

She paused and Hayes let the silence hang in the air like a web, not daring to break the thread.

'We didn't plan to hurt anyone. We thought they'd pay up, no questions, but once we'd had to get rough it didn't seem to matter any more, we had nothing to lose. Roma looked the part as the male driver and I had the weight and power to lay them out if necessary.' She gave a twisted grin.

'Those men were fucking porno addicts, deserved everything they got.'

'Roma told you about what went on at the parties? She was hostessing, you know, not just a driver. Didn't you get jealous knowing she was working alongside the hookers Baines brought in to sex things up? Was she one of the three-in-a-bed cuties or did she put on a lezzie show to titillate the old men?'

Roz leapt to her feet, her eyes blazing. 'How dare you!'

'Calm down, Roz, it was just my nasty macho imagination. Sit down, have another cigarette, it's important you give me your side of the story. Roma assumed it wouldn't come to this. I think she killed herself to protect you, Roz, but now you've confessed we might as well be honest with each other. Roma was the strong-minded one, wasn't she? Why did she need the money?'

Roz slumped in her seat, her mouth slack. 'For the casino. Roma didn't drink, do drugs, stuff like that, but when she got here she discovered roulette. It was like a terrible compulsion, she couldn't stop. She used to spend hours there when the rest of us were working in the evenings. Tarted herself up, sometimes tried to disguise herself with that stupid wig which we'd bought for the other business. Ask those croupiers, they all know her, watched her throw hundreds of quid down the drain. Gambling's worse than drink or even sex, believe me. Even someone as bright as my own darling couldn't break away. Sometimes she won but mostly she lost and one night she got into a terrible state, lost two thousand in one evening, said the casino was going to ban her – or worse – if she didn't pay up.'

'They let her run a tab?'

'Not at first but to start with she had money from a legacy plus cash from work with Baines and fees from the harp-playing. But when her money ran out she got desperate. I offered to pay it off but she said no, she could handle it. And that's when she suggested mugging those silly old men she'd been picking up to drive to Baines' parties. She broke into his surgery at the Spa one night after he'd gone home and rifled his computer for the list of the names of people who were in on the party circuit. Roma was brilliant at IT, could have made a wicked hacker, she once said to me.'

'And you agreed to be part of her vicious game?'

'You don't know how it feels to be in love, do you, Roger? Roma threatened to run away, leave the island and disappear in France. She had friends there who would look after her, she said. I couldn't bear to lose her and at first it didn't seem so terrible, those guys were going to spend their money at the parties anyhow. They could afford it.'

Sergeant Fuller broke in. 'Time's up, DI Hayes. The super-intendent puts a limit on visitors.'

Hayes rose and gripped her hand. 'May I come to see you again?'

She shook her head and allowed Fuller to escort her back to the cells without another word.

Forty-Seven

He did not wait for Broadhurst to come back from his meeting. What was the point? The superintendent had an open-and-shut case as far as he was concerned, a long-standing series of attacks was cleared up and one of the muggers had made a full confession. The lesbian angle would be shunted to one side he felt sure, the passion Roz Bailey felt for her young protégé hardly a mitigating circumstance in her defence. Her lawyer would have to persuade her to admit that it was Roma who so desperately needed the money.

Hayes felt defeated. It would have been wiser if he had refused to come to the island at Caxton's invitation, and it was even less intelligent to get embroiled in a police investigation which was none of his business and which might have resulted in DeeDee's death.

He drove over to Marty Lewis's newspaper office. The place was humming with activity, the breaking news of the arrest of a woman who had confessed to being a partner in the Phantom Duo story nothing short of dynamite.

Marty obligingly invited Hayes into the editorial department, where he was holding a staff briefing. It was clear to Hayes that his own appearance was inconvenient but, never one to miss an opportunity, Marty drew him aside.

'Great news, Roger. What was your part in all this?'

'I can't talk about the case, Marty, you'll have to wait for an official press conference. I just called in to say goodbye. I've decided to cut short my stay on the island.'

Marty looked puzzled. 'I thought you liked it here.'

'Yes, sure. Everyone's made me very welcome, but it's

time I got back to work. When all this has blown over perhaps we could meet up during your next trip to London? I'd like that.'

'Absolutely. Leave your card with my PA. I'll definitely be in touch.' His eyes drifted back to the hacks seated round the conference table and Hayes guessed that any passing friendship with Marty was ephemeral. He doubted whether any of his new friends would stay posted. Had he made such a fleeting impression?

Before letting Marty off the hook he begged a favour. 'One small thing, Marty. The girl who was drowned in the lake, Delia Miller, the vocalist with the Blues. Any idea when the funeral is to be?'

'As a matter of fact one of my girls has been following the story, filling in the human angle. The parents are taking the body back to Scotland for a private interment.'

'Right . . . thanks.'

Hayes shook hands and Marty slapped him on the shoulder with a smile. 'Well, cheerio, Roger, it's been a pleasure.'

Hayes drove back to Finch House wondering what sort of welcome, if any, would greet him after being blamed for encouraging DeeDee to swim in the lake and then accused of throwing Roma off the roof. Presumably the full story would come out in due course and in absentia his name eventually cleared.

What was less certain was the reaction to his dabbling in the Phantom Duo investigation, which would receive massive publicity here if not attract too much attention on the mainland. He hoped Broadhurst's hubris would prevent him from giving any credit to an off-duty copper in closing the case, though his own superiors might well wonder what sort of officer they were planning to shunt to a job in the security arm of the force.

Hayes still hadn't decided whether to accept the promotion. A transfer away from Detective Superintendent Waller was tempting and a fresh start in London would be an interesting step up, but did he really want a desk job? A medical would be required and he felt confident that it would present no problem, but his mind was still confused by the recent dramatic events in which he had found himself: one alleged accidental death, one suicide and the confession of the most unlikely killer in criminal history.

Finch House was very quiet, only Kevin on hand, it would seem. He parked on the back courtyard and strolled over.

'Hi, Kev. You out on bail?'

'Mr Caxton's looking after me.' He shrugged. 'You know how these things go, Broadhurst needs me to back up Mr Lyons about the parties so I reckon I'll get away with minor charges. What d'ya think?'

'Sure to. It looks pretty deserted round here. Everyone out?'

'Tea dance at the Paradiso.'

'Business as usual, then. What about Phil?'

'He's gone to ground. Staying with friends the other side of the island, so I heard. Karl's holding things together till the end of the season. The show's gotta go on, so they say.'

'Good. I'm packing up, Kevin, say cheerio to the gang for me, will you? I shall have to come back for Roma's inquest at some time but I'm hoping to fly home in the morning.'

'You will put in a good word for me, won't you, Mr Hayes, you being a DCI an' all.'

'With Broadhurst? Course I will, mate. I'll say goodbye then, see you around.'

'Yeah. Cheers.'

Hayes turned away and made for the back stairs. Packing up took less than twenty minutes and he took a last look round with affection. It hadn't been all bad. He was left with a lingering heartache when he thought about DeeDee but it was time to move on. He phoned a motel and was able to book in for the night, the approaching TT races filling the holiday accommodation with a fresh crowd of motorbike fanatics. He'd be sorry to miss it.

He called in at the station for a word with Broadhurst and caught him on the run.

'Just off to see my chief, Hayes. Can't stop. Anything I can do for you?'

'I'll leave my card with Sergeant Fuller, shall I? You listened to the tape, I suppose, Roz Bailey's take on the Duo attacks.'

'She won't get much public sympathy peddling the lesbian angle, Hayes, but she's not backing off from the confession so we're still on track.'

'What about Baines?'

'Yes, well, we've hit a snag there. The slippery bugger's scarpered. Mr Lyons' information somehow got out, God knows how, and Ross stupidly let slip that, as a matter of procedure, the tax people would have to be informed about undeclared income from the party planning.'

Hayes laughed. 'Forget about the drugs, hit him with a tax investigation! Terrific. It would have been a clever move if it hadn't set him off like a greyhound out of the slips. Where's he gone? Do you know?'

'Caught a flight to Manchester last night and after that could have gone anywhere. Spain most likely, the favourite bolthole for low-life con-men like Baines.'

'Banked his ill-gotten gains off shore, presumably.'

Broadhurst glanced at his watch then held out his hand with a smile. 'I'll not say goodbye, Hayes, you'll be back in due course. Likely to change your address, are you? Talk of a move to London, I hear.'

'I'll let you know, sir.'

Hayes watched Broadhurst hurry to his waiting car and admitted that at least one man on the island had left him with a cheery farewell.